高职高专创新大学英语系列教材

Creative College English Series

重庆大学出版社

高职高专创新大学英语系列教材 编委会
Creative College English Series

总主审 石 坚 邓 海

总主编 敖 凡 柳吉良 高 红

编写单位（按笔划排序）

乐山职业技术学院	四川大学
四川工商职业技术学院	四川工程职业技术学院
四川天一学院	四川司警职院
四川电力职业技术学院	四川建筑职业技术学院
四川信息职业技术学院	四川省干部函授学院
四川航天职业技术学院	四川烹饪高等专科学校
四川职业技术学院	四川警安职业学院
成都大学	成都艺术职业学院
成都市纺织高等专科学校	成都电子机械高等专科学校
成都农业科技职业学院	成都航空职业技术学院
西华大学	泸州职业技术学院
绵阳职业技术学院	

Creative College
English Series

创新 大学英语 1

【教师用书】

主　编　　高　红　　常淑丽　　王朝晖

编　者　　高　红　　常淑丽　　王朝晖

　　　　　向群英　　曾　剑　　李桂林

　　　　　陈宏霞　　黄　静

内 容 提 要

《创新大学英语1教师用书》是《高职高专创新大学英语系列教材》教师参考书的第一册。《创新大学英语教师用书》除了提供基本的练习答案和课文翻译以外，既有课文的相关背景知识介绍、长难句分析、词汇和语法点讲解，又有语法和构词法方面的专题知识、阅读技巧分析、写作词汇拓展和实用文写作常识简介，内容相当丰富，老师可以根据学生的实际需要对症下药，灵活选取讲解内容，同时教师用书还配有教学课件光盘，方便老师备课和组织课堂活动。

图书在版编目(CIP)数据

创新大学英语教师用书.1/高红等主编.—重庆:重庆大学出版社,2008.7
(创新高职高专大学英语系列教材)
ISBN 978-7-5624-4525-8

Ⅰ.创…　Ⅱ.高…　Ⅲ.英语—高等学校:技术学校—教学参考资料　Ⅳ.H31

中国版本图书馆CIP数据核字(2008)第102081号

高职高专创新大学英语系列教材

创新大学英语1 教师用书

主　编　高　红　常淑丽　王朝晖
责任编辑:韩　鹏　向　璐　　版式设计:牟　妮
责任校对:任卓惠　　　　　　责任印制:赵　晟

*

重庆大学出版社出版发行
出版人:张鸽盛
社址:重庆市沙坪坝正街174号重庆大学(A区)内
邮编:400030
电话:(023)65102378　65105781
传真:(023)65103686　65105565
网址:http://www.cqup.com.cn
邮箱:fxk@cqup.com.cn(市场营销部)
全国新华书店经销
重庆东南印务有限责任公司印刷

*

开本:787×1092　1/16　印张:12.25　字数:283千
2008年7月第1版　　2008年7月第1次印刷
印数:1—1 000
ISBN 978-7-5624-4525-8　定价:29.00元(含教学光盘)

总　序

　　目前,国内高职高专院校的大学英语教学改革不断走向深入,"以应用为目的,实用为主,够用为度"的指导原则已经深入人心。在这一背景下,出现了不少各具特色的大学英语教材,它们都不同程度地、从不同的角度反映了新形势下高职高专院校大学英语教学的需要。但是由于创新型国家的建设与和谐社会的构建不断对高职高专实用创新型人才的培养提出更高的要求,由于高职高专院校大学英语教学改革不断深入,也由于高职高专生源的地域差异和学生毕业后所就业的行业差异较大,更好地反映和引导改革中种种新的尝试和新探索的新教材的开发仍然十分必要。

　　基于这一考虑,重庆大学出版社组织四川省相关领域的专家和20多所院校的一线教师,在广泛调研的基础上,编写了这套《高职高专创新大学英语系列教材》。参与教材编写的既有教育部在该地区重点高校的骨干教师,也有长期在高职高专教学一线的骨干教师。

　　本教材以教育部《高职高专教育英语课程教学基本要求》为依据,以四川省和其他西部省市的高职高专教育以及大学英语教育的实际为出发点,以"打好基础,注重培养实际使用语言的技能,特别是使用英语处理日常和涉外业务活动的能力"为原则,以"实用为主,够用为度"为编写指导思想,使本套教材具有以下特点:

　　(1)着眼于培养技术、生产、管理和服务等领域的高等应用性专门人才的实际需求,强调学生基础知识的扎实掌握和基本能力的充分训练,注重培养学生的语言应用能力,特别是实用口语和实用写作等方面的交际能力。

　　(2)将学生的应用性交际能力的培养融汇在基本技能的雕琢中,充分体现"双基"教学的需要;让学生充分扎实地掌握大纲所规定的知识和能力,强调学以致用和学用结合。

(3)以高频词汇贯穿听说读写译的基本技能训练之中,不一味追求教材梯度,强调通过高频词汇的反复综合训练,提升学生的语感,培养其实际语言交际能力。

(4)学习材料短小精炼,练习形式丰富多样,着眼于对词汇的积极运用能力的培养,通过对传统练习模式的突破来带动教学理念的改变。

(5)在体例编排上充分考虑学生的自主学习能力的提高,促进学生的自我发展。

(6)在练习设计和教材体系上注重课内外学习的有机结合,充分利用学生课外的时间,既方便教师对学生的课外学习进行有效的管理和监控,又服务于丰富第二课堂和提高学生文化素质的需要。

(7)有完善的立体开发体系,这种立体开发既体现于载体形式的丰富性,也体现在不同载体形式在内容上的互补性,而不是相同内容的简单重复,从而使教材的立体开发和课内外学习的配合相得益彰。

《高职高专创新大学英语系列教材》由主教材《创新大学英语》、《创新大学英语教师用书》和《创新大学英语综合训练》各 4 册组成,并配有相应的多媒体学习课件和电子教案。

《创新大学英语》每册含 8 个单元,每个单元有 2 篇简短生动的阅读课文,在每个单元内,为了实现 input 对于 output 的引导,练习板块按照 Reading, Speaking, Listening 和 Writing 的顺序安排,既体现了对同一交际主题的反复强化,又使得学生的语言输出"水到渠成","顺理成章"。在单元之间的关系上,每个单元分别覆盖不同的交际主题,强化不同的语法知识,培养不同文体的应用文写作能力。多条线索之间既相互平行,又通过共同训练的高频词汇、共同强调的实际能力以及交际内容与交际形式的有机联系而充分融合在一起,共同服务于提高学生实用交际能力这一目标。同时本书还配有多媒体学习光盘,可供学生自学或复习时使用。

《创新大学英语综合训练》中每一单元由 Micro-skills Practice 和 Comprehensive Skills and Practice 两部分组成,前者包括 Vocabulary 和 Sentence Pattern 两个板块,后者包括 Listening, Speaking, Reading for Skill, Translation 和 Writing 等板块。《综合训练》在练习的词汇、强化的语法点与训练的交际形式上与学生用书保持一致,但在训练的量、练习的形式以及阅读技巧的培养上又有所拓展,教师可根据需要灵活选择布置给学生练习,这既体现了课内学习和课外学习的有机结合,又扩大了本系列教材的适用面。

　　《创新大学英语教师用书》除了提供基本的练习答案和课文翻译以外,既有课文的相关背景知识介绍、长难句分析、词汇和语法点讲解,又有语法和构词法方面的专题知识、阅读技巧分析、写作词汇拓展和实用文写作常识简介,内容极为丰富,教师可以根据学生的实际需要对症下药,灵活选取讲解内容。同时《教师用书》还配有教学课件光盘,方便老师备课和组织课堂教学活动。

　　由于本系列教材有上述种种新颖之处,因此在推出之后将为四川省和西部其他省区公共英语教学改革做出独特的贡献,在提高学生实用英语交际能力的同时,也为高职高专大学教材的编写和大学英语的教学开展了一定的创新尝试。

　　因为本系列教材在许多方面都进行了新的尝试,在实际编写过程中可能会出现一些疏漏和不当之处,请各位老师、专家和读者批评指正并将相关意见和建议及时反馈给我们,以促进本教材的进一步完善。

总主编

2008 年 5 月

编写说明

本书为《高职高专创新大学英语系列教材》第一册的教学参考书。全书共 8 个单元,旨在为教师提供教学建议、补充材料、练习参考答案、课文参考译文及听力脚本。

具体来讲,本书主要提供了如下几个方面的内容:

1. 相关背景知识。

2. 热身问题:目的在于激活学生已知的相关知识,并将课文学习与学生的现实生活联系起来,激发学生的学习兴趣。

3. 难句分析:该部分对课文中的难句予以解释,并对一些重难点进行适当扩展。

4. 课文 A 词汇学习:该部分对课文 A 词汇表中搭配力较强的二级词汇和全部三级词汇进行了例释,并列举出相关词条最常见的派生词。

5. 单词、短语辨析:词语、短语辨析一直是外语学习中的重难点。本教材针对学生易犯错误,作出了详细的讲解。

6. 语法聚焦:该部分对各单元语法项的重难点进行了例释,旨在为学生用书的语法部分提供相应的支撑。

7. 构词方法:该部分总结归纳了学生用书中相应单元出现的 3 - 4 种前缀、后缀形式,目的在于唤起学生对英语构词方法的重视,帮助学生熟悉英语的构词方法及词缀给英语单词带来的词性和意义上的变化。这些词缀在学生练习册中都配有相应的练习。

8. 写作语言点睛:恰当的选词和丰富的句型是一篇好的作文的最基本的要素。该部分针对学生用书的写作任务,提供了丰富的词汇和句型,旨在帮助老师在写作教学中有更多的选择。

9. 阅读技巧:该部分根据《大纲》所要求的八种阅读技巧分列在八个单元中,逐一进行阐释,并在配套的练习册中配以相应的练习,以期学以致用。

10. 课文 B 词汇学习:同课文 A 一样,该部分对课文 B 中搭配能力较强的二级词汇和全部三级词汇进行了例释,并列举出了相应单词最常见的派生词。

11. 练习参考答案。

12. 课文 A、课文 B 参考译文。

13. 听力脚本。

《高职高专创新大学英语系列教材》总主编为敖凡、柳吉良和高红。教师用书第一册主编为高红、常淑丽和王朝晖。参加编写的人员有高红、常淑丽、王朝晖、向群英、曾剑、李桂林、陈宏霞、黄静,分别负责第一至第八单元的编写。石坚、邓海审定,在此一并表示感谢。

编 者
2008 年 7 月

Contents

Unit One   Learning English ·· (1)

　Text A   American Small Talk ······························· (1)

　　　　　Background Knowledge of the Text ············· (1)

　　　　　Warming-up Questions ······························ (1)

　　　　　Sentence Analysis ································· (2)

　　　　　Word Study ··· (3)

　　　　　Phrases and Expressions ······················· (9)

　　　　　Differentiations and Analysis of Words and Expressions

　　　　　··· (10)

　　　　　Word Building ······································· (12)

　　　　　Grammar Focus ····································· (13)

　　　　　Language Tips for Writing ······················ (17)

　Text B   Successful English Learning ················· (18)

　　　　　Reading Strategies (1): Reading for the Main Ideas

　　　　　··· (18)

　　　　　Word Study ··· (19)

　Key to Exercises ··· (22)

　Translation of the Texts ··································· (23)

　Scripts for Listening ·· (24)

Unit Two   Higher Education ······························ (26)

　Text A   College Life: A Worthy Experience ········· (26)

　　　　　Background Knowledge of the Text ············· (26)

　　　　　Warming-up Questions ······························ (26)

　　　　　Sentence Analysis ································· (27)

　　　　　Word Study ··· (31)

　　　　　Phrases and Expressions ······················· (35)

　　　　　Differentiations and Analysis of Words and Expressions

　　　　　··· (36)

　　　　　Word Building ······································· (38)

　　　　　　　　　Grammar Focus ……………………………… (38)

　　　　　　　　　Language Tips for Writing ………………… (41)

　　　　Text B　Mother Goes to College ………………… (41)

　　　　　　　　　Reading Strategies (2)：Reading for Specific Details

　　　　　　　　　………………………………………………… (41)

　　　　　　　　　Word Study ………………………………… (42)

　　　　Key to Exercises ……………………………………… (45)

　　　　Translation of the Texts …………………………… (47)

　　　　Scripts for Listening ………………………………… (48)

Unit Three　Being Mature ………………………………… (49)

　　　　Text A　Am I Normal? ……………………………… (49)

　　　　　　　　　Background Knowledge of the Text ……… (49)

　　　　　　　　　Warming-up Questions ……………………… (49)

　　　　　　　　　Sentence Analysis ………………………… (50)

　　　　　　　　　Word Study ………………………………… (51)

　　　　　　　　　Phrases and Expressions ………………… (55)

　　　　　　　　　Differentiations and Analysis of Words and Expressions

　　　　　　　　　………………………………………………… (56)

　　　　　　　　　Word Building ……………………………… (57)

　　　　　　　　　Grammar Focus ……………………………… (57)

　　　　　　　　　Language Tips for Writing ………………… (61)

　　　　Text B　How to Be a Young Adult ………………… (62)

　　　　　　　　　Reading Strategies (3)：Skimming ……… (62)

　　　　　　　　　Word Study ………………………………… (63)

　　　　Key to Exercises ……………………………………… (66)

　　　　Translation of the Texts …………………………… (68)

　　　　Scripts for Listening ………………………………… (69)

Unit Four　Ways to Success ……………………………… (70)

　　　　Text A　The Way to Success …………………… (70)

　　　　　　　　　Background Knowledge of the Text ……… (70)

　　　　　　　　　Warming-up Questions ……………………… (70)

　　　　　　　　　Sentence Analysis ………………………… (71)

Word Study ·· (73)

Phrases and Expressions ···················· (76)

Differentiations and Analysis of Words and Expressions

·· (77)

Word Building ······························· (79)

Grammar Focus ······························· (80)

Language Tips for Writing ···················· (86)

Text B　The Role of Luck in Success ···················· (87)

Reading Strategies (4): Reading for Inference

·· (87)

Word Study ·· (87)

Key to Exercises ······························· (89)

Translation of the Texts ···················· (90)

Scripts for Listening ···················· (91)

Unit Five　Friendship ·· (94)

Text A　The Elements of Friendship ···················· (94)

Background Knowledge of the Text ···················· (94)

Warming-up Questions ···················· (95)

Sentence Analysis ···················· (95)

Word Study ·· (96)

Phrases and Expressions ···················· (99)

Differentiations and Analysis of Words and Expressions

·· (100)

Word Building ······························· (101)

Grammar Focus ······························· (102)

Language Tips for Writing ···················· (107)

Text B　How to Mend a Broken Friendship ···················· (108)

Reading Strategies (5): Identify Topic Sentences ··· (108)

Word Study ······························· (109)

Key to Exercises ······························· (111)

Translation of the Texts ···················· (112)

Scripts for Listening ···················· (113)

Unit Six　Sports ································ (115)

Text A　Revival of the Olympic Games ········ (115)

Background Knowledge of the Text ········ (115)

Warming-up Questions ·················· (116)

Sentence Analysis ···················· (116)

Word Study ························· (117)

Phrases and Expressions ·············· (121)

Differentiations and Analysis of Words and Expressions

································ (122)

Word Building ····················· (124)

Grammar Focus ···················· (124)

Language Tips for Writing ············· (127)

Text B　A Woman at the Wheel ············ (128)

Reading Strategies (6): Reading for Detecting the Author's

Purpose ························· (128)

Word Study ························· (129)

Phrases and Expressions ·············· (130)

Key to Exercises ····················· (131)

Translation of the Texts ················· (132)

Scripts for Listening ·················· (133)

Unit Seven　Leisure Time ················ (134)

Text A　The Problem of Leisure ··········· (134)

Background Knowledge of the Text ········ (134)

Warming-up Questions ·················· (135)

Sentence Analysis ···················· (135)

Word Study ························· (137)

Phrases and Expressions ·············· (142)

Differentiations and Analysis of Words and Expressions

································ (144)

Word Building ····················· (145)

Grammar Focus ···················· (146)

Language Tips for Writing ············· (152)

Text B　How Do the British Spend Their Leisure Time?

································ (154)

Reading Strategies (7): Reading for Drawing

a Conclusion ·· (154)

Word Study ·· (155)

Key to Exercises ··· (158)

Translation of the Texts ·· (159)

Scripts for Listening ··· (160)

Unit Eight **Internet** ······································· (162)

Text A The Internet ·· (162)

Background Knowledge of the Text ················ (162)

Warming-up Questions ····························· (162)

Sentence Analysis ································· (162)

Word Study ··· (164)

Phrases and Expressions ························· (167)

Differentiations and Analysis of Words and Expressions

··· (167)

Word Building ····································· (168)

Grammar Focus ·································· (169)

Language Tips for Writing ······················· (171)

Text B The History of the Internet ····················· (171)

Reading Strategies (8): Scanning for Wanted Information

··· (171)

Word Study ··· (172)

Phrases and Expressions ························· (175)

Key to Exercises ··· (176)

Translation of the Texts ·· (177)

Scripts for Listening ··· (178)

Unit One Learning English

Text A American Small Talk

The culture in which each of us lives influences and shapes our feelings, attitudes, and responses to our experiences and interactions with others. Because of our culture, each of us has knowledge, beliefs, values, views, and behaviors that we share with others who have the same cultural heritage. These past experiences, handed down from generation to generation, influence our values of what is attractive and what is ugly, what is acceptable behavior and what is not, and what is right and what is wrong. Our culture also teaches us how to interpret the world. From our culture we learn such things as how close to stand to strangers, when to speak and when to be silent, how to greet friends and strangers, and how to display anger appropriately. Because each culture has a unique way of approaching these situations, we find great diversity in cultural behaviors throughout the world.

Learning about cultural diversity provides students with knowledge and skills for more effective communication in intercultural situations. The first step in being a good intercultural communicator is to know your own culture and to know yourself — in other words, to reflect thoughtfully on how you perceive things and how you act on those perceptions. Second, the more we know about the different cultural beliefs, values, and attitudes of our global neighbors, the better prepared we will be to recognize and to understand the differences in their cultural behaviors. The knowledge of cultural differences and self-knowledge of how we usually respond to those differences can make us aware of hidden prejudices and stereotypes which are barriers to tolerance, understanding, and good communication.

1. Whenever we run into somebody, we will greet each other. But have you ever noticed any differences in greeting different people such as your parents, neighbours, teachers, colleagues, classmates or superiors? List one or two ways you use in greeting different people.
2. Even if in the same culture, there exist some differences in greeting each other. In different

cultures, greeting varies even more. Can you give some examples to show these differences?

Sentence Analysis

1. The topics of these conversations are very general and often situational — people start talking about anything in their common physical environment, such as the weather, the room in which they are standing, the food that they are eating, etc.

   句中破折号之后的部分进一步解释破折号之前的内容。这是英语破折号的重要用法之一。破折号的这一用法比冒号更有强调作用,但没有冒号正式。破折号在英语中还可用于:

   1) 概括前面列举的若干项,如:Jane, Susan, and I — we all could not believe our ears when we heard the news. 珍妮、苏珊和我——我们听到这消息时都不敢相信我们的耳朵。

   2) 在对话中,用来表示犹豫或迟疑,如:I — I think I should at least have a try. 我——我认为我们至少应该试一下。

   3) 用来表示意义的转折,如:This is the most important point — Are you listening to me? 这是最重要的一点——你在听我讲吗?

   4) 引出需强调或说明的成分,如:John — her boyfriend — bought the roses for her. 约翰——她的男朋友——给她买的玫瑰花。

   此外,在 in which they are standing 中,in which 相当于 where。

2. Asking someone about his/her occupation is also very common, especially for Americans, who place a high value on working.

   place a high value on sth. :十分看重……,例如:

   People in America place a high value on punctuality. 在美国人们非常看重守时。

   类似的说法还有 place great emphasis/importance on sth. :

   Nowadays, many people in China place great importance on learning English. 现在许多中国人都很重视英语学习。

3. Last, in a country like the United States where people move so often, places of origin are often discussed as well.

   此句中 where 作为关系副词引导的从句在结构上是定语从句,但在意义上却隐含着原因,以说明后半部分的句子。故此句翻译为:最后,在美国这个国家, 由于人们搬迁过于频繁,故而询问对方是哪儿的人也是很常见的。

4. Two other subjects will immediately make Americans uncomfortable: age and money.

   此句中,冒号后面的部分进一步说明冒号前所指的两个另外的话题的具体内容。正如句1所讲,当冒号用于列出表示列举、解释或说明性的词语时,其意义比破折号正式。

   冒号在英语中还可用于:

   1) 引出较长的正式用语或大段引语,如:The daily newspaper contains four sections: news,

sports, entertainment, and classified ads. 每天的报纸包括四个部分：新闻、体育、娱乐和分类广告。

2）用于信件或演说词的称呼语之后（英国英语中多用逗号），如：Dear Madam：/Ladies and Gentlemen：

3）分隔书名的标题与副标题，如：*Relevance：Communication and Cognition*《关联性：交际与认知》。

4）表示时间或比率，例如：10:10 a.m.   上午十点十分

The new swim record is 3:38:17.   最新的游泳记录是 3 分 38 秒 17。

Your chances of winning the lottery are 1,117,693:1.   博彩获奖的机率是 1 117 693 分之一。

5. Regarding financial matters, income and the price of possessions are also personal matters and should not be used to start a conversation with an American.

此句中，regarding 为介词，意为：关于，至于。相当于：with regard to, as regards。

6. Being aware of these acceptable and unacceptable topics may help people from other cultures feel more comfortable around Americans they are meeting for the first time.

句中 help 一词可以跟带 to 的不定式，也可以跟不带 to 的不定式。这里 feel 前不带 to，在句中作宾语 people from other cultures 的宾语补足语。

Word Study

1. topic   *n.*   话题，题目，主题

例：The topic for today is "Environment & Urbanization". 今天的话题是"环境与城市化"。

This is the topic sentence of the paragraph. 这是这段话的主题句。

2. general

a. 1）一般的，普通的

例：This is the general principle we should follow in dealing with such matters.

这是处理此类问题时应该遵守的总的原则。

general knowledge 一般知识，常识

general education 普通教育

general public 普通百姓，公众

2）总的，普遍的，全体的

例：Just tell me the general idea of the story. 你只需告诉我这个故事的梗概。

The general opinion is that the film is a great success.

人们普遍认为这部电影非常成功。

the general belief 普遍的信念

United Nations Secretary General 联合国秘书长

n. 将军。例：General Michael 密歇尔将军

3. common　*a.*

1）常见的，普通的

例：It has become more and more common for women to hold important positions in the government. 妇女在政府部门身居要职已越来越普通了。

Li is one of the most common names in China. "李"是中国最常见的姓氏之一。

2）共同的

例：They share a common interest in classical music. 他们在古典音乐方面趣味相投。

in common 共用的，共有的

4. physical　*a.*

1）客观存在的，现实的

例：Besides studying in the classroom, we should provide more opportunities for children to examine the physical environment around them.

除了课堂学习之外，我们还应该为孩子们提供更多的机会，来考察他们周围的自然环境。

2）身体的，肉体的

例：People over thirty should have a physical examination each year.

30 岁以上的人每年都应该进行一次体检。

Physical Education = PE 体育课

3）物理学的

例：physical chemistry 物理化学

4）自然的，按自然规律的

例：He strongly believes that there must be a physical explanation for these strange phenomena. 他坚信这些奇怪的现象一定可以根据自然规律作出解释。

5. environment　*n.*　环境，自然环境

例：We should try our best to create a pleasant learning environment for ourselves.

我们应该尽可能为自己创造一个愉快的学习环境。

Last year, they did a survey on the public environment awareness.

去年他们就公众环境意识作了一个调查。

World Environment Day（June 5th each year）世界环境日

environment-friendly products 环保产品

6. weather　*n.*　天气（指某地一时的天气，如：寒暖、晴雨和干湿的变化情况）

例：In early spring, the weather is very changeable. 在早春，天气变化无常。

Cf. climate 气候（指某地的平均气候或经常性的气候）

The climate in Chengdu is mild. 成都气候温和。

7. stand　*v.*

1）站，站立

例：Don't just stand there. Come and help me. 别光站在那儿，过来帮帮我。

2）坐落，被放置

例：Our library stands next to Classroom Building One. 我们的图书馆位于第一教学楼旁。

3）容忍，经受，抵御

例：I can no longer stand his bad temper. 我再也不能忍受他的坏脾气了。

　　stand by 袖手旁观；站在……一边；遵守；做好准备

　　stand for 代表，象征

　　stand out 突出，显眼

　　stand up（使）站起；耐用；站得住脚

　　stand up to 勇敢地面对；经得起

8. culture *n.*

1）文化，文明

例：In globalization, people should learn to respect different cultures.

　　在全球化时代，人们应该学会尊重不同的文化。

　　Chinese/American culture 中国/美国文化

　　traditional culture 传统文化

　　popular culture 大众文化

2）教养，修养

例：Smith is a man of culture and taste. 史密斯是一个有教养有品味的人。

9. period *n.*

1）一段时间，时期，时代

例：These measures are to reduce traffic at peak periods.

　　采取这些措施的目的是缓解高峰期的交通状况。

　　Which period of history are you most interested in? 你对哪一段历史最感兴趣？

2）学时，课时

例：Each week we have four periods of English. 我们每周有 4 节英语课。

3）句号，句点

例：Use a period at the end of a statement or request. 陈述句或祈使句末尾要用一个句号。

10. occupation *n.*

1）职业，工作

例：Please state your name, age and occupation on the form.

　　请在表格上注明你的姓名、年龄和职业。

　　Cf. job, work 和 occupation 都可以指谋生的职业。但 job 是可数名词，work 为不可

　　数名词，occupation 是可数名词，但用于较正式的文体。

2）占据，占领

例：The money was used during Japanese occupation. 这种钱在日本占领时期使用过。

11. value

n. 1) 重要性,有用

例:You'll find this map to be of great value in helping you to get around Beijing.

你会发现这张地图对你在北京活动大有用处。

Generally speaking, Americans place a high value on individualism.

通常美国人非常重视个性。

2) 价值

例:In the past few months, gold rose/went up/increased a lot in value.

在过去的几个月黄金增值不少。

to go down/fall/drop in value 贬值

3) (常 *pl.*) 价值观念,标准

例:Each nation has its own cultural values. 每个民族都拥有自己的文化观念。

cultural/social/moral values 文化/社会/道德观念

v. 1) 重视,尊重,珍视

例:If you value your health, then do some exercise each day.

如果你重视健康,那么每天都要锻炼锻炼。

I really value her as my best friend. 我真的把她当作最好的朋友。

2) 评价,估价

例:He value this vase at over $20,000. 他估计这个花瓶值 2 万多美元。

This house is valued at over ￥80,000. 这座房子估价为 8 万多人民币。

12. taste

n. 1) 爱好,趣味

例:Our travel agency offers trips to all tastes.

我们旅行社提供适合游客各种喜好的旅游项目。

Such books are not to my taste. 这种书不对我的口味。

2) 味道,滋味

例:This soup has very little taste. 这汤没什么味道。

v. 1) 品尝

例:Taste it and see if there is enough salt in it. 你尝尝看咸味是否够了。

2) (of) 有……味道

例:The apple tastes sour. 这苹果有酸味。

The candy tastes of grapes. 这糖有葡萄的味道。

The drink tastes like lemon. 这种饮料的味道像柠檬。

13. origin   *n.*

1) 起源,来源,起因

例:This particular custom has its origins in China. 这种特有的风俗源于中国。

2)出身,血统

例:One of my friends, Albert, is of German origin. 我的一个朋友艾伯特祖籍是德国。

14. inappropriate *a.*   不合适的,不恰当的

例:It's inappropriate to go into the classroom in shorts. 穿短裤去教室不合适。

15. consider *v.*

1)认为,把……看作

例:Mary considered herself (to be) very lucky. 玛丽认为自己非常幸运。

He considers himself as / to be an expert in computer. 他自认为是电脑专家。

2)考虑,细想

例:We are considering what to do next. 我们正在考虑下一步做什么。

Please take time to consider the problem. 请仔细考虑一下这个问题。

3)关心,考虑到

例:He has done a wonderful job if you consider his age.

考虑到他的年纪,他已经做得非常棒了。

16. personal *a.*

1)个人的,私人的

例:This is just my personal opinion. 这只是我的个人看法。

personal details (= one's name, age, etc.) 个人基本资料

personal belongings/possessions 私人财产/财物

2)亲自的

例:The mayor made a personal appearance at the event. 市长亲临现场。

3)针对个人的,有关私人的

例:You'd better try your best to avoid making any personal remarks on this matter.

就此问题,你最好尽量避免发表针对个人的言论。

17. subject

n. 1)话题,主题

例:Today we are going to have a discussion on the subject of air pollution.

今天我们将就空气污染问题进行谈论。

2)学科,科目

例:Maths is my daughter's favorite subject. 数学是我女儿最喜欢的科目。

3)主语

例:The subject of this sentence is "I". 这句话的主语是"I"。

a. (to) 易遭……的,受……支配的

例:This area is subject to earthquakes. 这个地区容易发生地震。

China's oil prices are subject to international market prices.

中国的油价受国际市场油价的影响。

This project is subject to your approval. 这个项目需要得到你的同意。

As an overseas student, you are subject to the law of the country you stay in. 作为一名留学生,你要受到所在国家的法律的约束。

v. (to) 使遭受,使服从

例:Ancient Rome subjected most of Europe to its rule. 古罗马将欧洲大多数地区置于其统治之下。

Beggars on the street are often subjected to abuse. 街头的乞丐常常受到辱骂。

His conduct subjected him to public ridicule. 他的行为使他成为公众的笑柄。

18. keep　*n.*

1)保留,保存

例:You can keep it as long as you like. 你可以想保留多久就保留多久。

2)(from)阻止,防止

例:We thought it best to keep the bad news from her mother.

我们认为最好不要让她妈妈知道这个坏消息。

3)履行,遵循

例:I hope you'll keep your promise/word. 希望你能遵守诺言。

4)(使)保持,使继续

例:I'm sorry to keep you waiting. 对不起,让你久等了。

Do you know how to keep fit and healthy? 你知道怎样保持健康吗?

keep back 留下

keep in mind 记住

keep off 让开,不接近

keep on 继续进行,反复地做

keep on (doing sth.) 继续(做某事)

keep out of 置身于……之外,避免

keep out 使不入内;留在外面

keep to 坚持,维持,继续

keep up with 跟上,不落后于

19. financial　*a.*　　财政的,金融的

例:Wall Street is the financial centre of America. 华尔街是美国的金融中心。

financial crisis 金融危机

20. income　*n.*　　收入,收益,所得

例:Half of our income goes to paying for housing loans.

我们一半的收入用在付房屋贷款上。

people on high/low incomes 高/低收入的人

income tax (个人)所得税

Phrases and Expressions

1. one another 相互,彼此

例:As classmates, you should help one another. 作为同学,你们应该相互帮助。

The children followed one another into the room. 孩子们一个接一个地进入房间。

2. to begin with 从……开始,以……为起点

例:He began his lecture with a story he experienced in South Africa. 他以他在南非亲身经历的一个故事开始了他的讲座。

Knowledge begins with practice. 知识来自实践。

to begin with:首先;起初

To begin with, this house is too far away from down town, and besides it's a bit too small. 首先这房子离城太远,再者也太小了点。

3. talk about 谈论

例:Today we are going to talk about greeting in different cultures. 今天我们将谈谈不同的文化中人们如何打招呼。

4. be aware of 觉察到

例:In globalization, people should be well aware of the cultural differences in different countries.

在全球化的时代背景下,人们应该清楚地知道在不同国家间存在着文化差异。

Be aware of those who fish in troubled water. 当心那些浑水摸鱼的人。

5. lead to 导致,通向

例:His carelessness led to his failure in the exam.

他的粗心大意导致了他在考试中的失败。

6. carry on 继续做,坚持

例:Let's carry on (with) the work even though we may run into still greater difficulties.

我们继续做这项工作吧,即使会遇到更大的困难也要坚持下去。

Rising costs make it hard to carry on the business.

成本上升给生意经营带来了困难。

Margaret decided to carry on learning Chinese until she was able to communicate with Chinese people freely.

玛格丽特决定继续学习中文,直到她能与中国人自由交流。

Don't worry about money. Just carry on. 别担心钱,只管进行下去。

Differentiations and Analysis of Words and Expressions

1. but, however

从意义上看,but 同 however 都起转折作用,但 but 的转折意味较 however 强。从词性上看,but 为并列连词,而 however 是个副词。从词序上看,but 总是位于它所引出的分句之首,而 however 却可位于分句之首、之中或之尾,但是译成汉语时一定要把它放在分句之首。从标点符号来看,当 but 用来连接两个分句或两个较长的短语时, but 前面一般要加逗号;而用 however 时,要用逗号将其与句子其他成分分开。例如:

1) It was sunny but still very cold. 当时虽然出着太阳,但仍然很冷。

2) My name's Robert, but most of my friends call me Bob for short.

我是罗伯特,但大多数朋友都称我鲍勃。

3) I'd like to go with you; however, my hands are full.

我很想和你一块儿去,可是我忙不过来。

4) He was feeling bad. He went to class, however, and tried to concentrate.

他感觉不舒服。但是他仍然去上课,并且努力集中精神。

5) We have not yet succeeded; we shall try again, however.

我们还没有取得成功,不过我们还要再试一下。

2. specially, especially

especially 是副词,意为"尤其"、"特别",通常用来对前面所述的事件进行进一步的说明或补充。例如:

1) It's especially cold today. 今天天气特别冷。

2) He likes all subjects, especially Chinese. 他喜欢所有的学科,尤其是中文。

specially 也是副词,意为"专门地"、"特地",表示"不是为了别的,而只是为了……",强调唯一目的。例如:

1) John came here specially to ask for your advice. 约翰特意到这儿来听取你的意见。

2) He returned to her hometown specially to see her sick grandfather.

他回到家乡专门看望生病的爷爷。

3. for example, such as, like

for example 作"例如"讲时,一般只以同类事物或人中的"一个"为例,作插入语,用逗号隔开,可置于句首、句中或句末。例如:

1) For example, water is liquid. 例如,水是液体。

2) Water, for example, is liquid. 例如,水是液体。

3) Water is liquid, for example. 例如,水是液体。

such as 也作为"例如"讲,用来列举同类人或事物中的几个例子。但一般来讲,使用

such as 来举例子,只能举出其中的一部分,不能全部举出,并且不与 and so on 连用。若需列出所有例子,应改用 namely(意为"即")。例如:

1) We have planted lots of flowers, such as roses, orchid and sunflowers.

我们种了许多花,如玫瑰、兰花和向日葵。

2) Cities such as Chongqing and Chengdu are densely populated.

像成都、重庆这样的城市人口都非常密集。

在现代英语中,like 也常用来表示举例,其意义与 such as 非常接近,尤其在口语和非正式文体中常常可以互换。例如:Boys like Jack and Morris are very friendly. 像杰克和莫里斯这样的男孩都很友好。

4. as well, too, also

also 和 too 都用于肯定句,是"也"的意思。also 通常用于正式场合,一般用于句中,其位置通常在行为动词之前、助动词之后。too 通常用于句末且用逗号与前面的词隔开。too 可以紧接在主语后面,这样说比较正式。as well 意为"同样地"、"和前者一样地",通常置于句末。例如:

1) My father is a teacher. My mother is also a teacher.

我父亲是老师。我母亲也是老师。

2) He can not only speak Chinese, but many Chinese dialects as well.

他不仅能说汉语,而且还能说许多汉语方言。

3) Last summer my sister went to Lijiang. My daughter and I went there, too.

去年,我姐姐去了丽江。我女儿和我也去了。

4) I, too, know where she is. 我也知道她在什么地方。

应该注意的是:as well 和 too 可以指主语,也可以指句子的其他成分,视情况而定。如:Mary teaches English as well. 这句话可能有三个不同的意思:

1) Other people teach English, and Mary does as well.

2) Mary teaches other things, and English as well.

3) Mary does other things, and teaches English as well.

在具体情况下,意思一般是清楚的。在英语口语中,意思还可以通过重读表现出来(表示第一个意思,重读 Mary;表示第二个意思,重读 English;表示第三个意思,重读 teaches。)

Also 有时在同一个句子也可以有不同的理解。如:I also washed the car. 这句话可能有三个不同的意思:

1) Besides washing the car, I have done something else.

2) Besides washing the car, I have done something else to the car.

3) Besides washing the car, I have washed something else.

Word Building

　　词汇学习一直是外语学习中的一个难点。而熟悉英语的构词方法无疑是扩大词汇量的一个重要途径。英语词汇的构成方法很多,如词缀法、转类法、合成法、拼缀法、逆成法、缩略法等。但其中最常用的是词缀法、转类法和合成法。

　　词缀法是借助词根和词缀构成新词的方法。英语词缀分成前缀和后缀。通常,前缀只改变词义,但不改变词性。而后缀则不仅改变词义也改变词性。例如:当我们在 acceptable 前面加上否定前缀 un- 时,其词义发生变化,但词性不变;当我们在 teach 后加上后缀-er 时,则该词由动词变为名词,且意义也发生了变化。

　　转类法的特点是无需改变词形就把词从一种词性转化为另外一种词性。这种转类主要体现在如下几种形式:

1. 名词转化成动词,如:a target → to target
2. 动词转化成名词,如:to look → a look
3. 形容词转化成名词,如:black(黑色的)→ black(黑人)

　　合成法是把两个或两个以上的词以一定的组合方式排列,组成为一个新词的方法。由此方法构成的词称为合成词。合成词在书写时有的中间有连字号"-"相接,有的则没有。现代英语中的不少新词都是借助原有的词组合而成的。常见的合成词有:

1. 复合名词,如:blackhole 黑洞, housewife 家庭妇女
2. 复合形容词,如:kind-hearted 好心的,well-known 众所周知的
3. 复合动词,如:mass-produce 成批生产,baby-sit 照看小孩

在本课中出现较多的前缀、后缀有:

1. 否定前缀:in- , un- , non-

　　　否定前缀 in- , un- , non- 均带有"不"、"没"的意思。其中 non- 通常表示否定,in- 和 un-表示相反的性质。例如:

　　　native→nonnative　　　　　alcoholic drinks→nonalcoholic drinks

　　　appropriate→inappropriate　　sensitive(敏感的)→insensitive

　　　acceptable→unacceptable　　　comfortable→uncomfortable

2. 形容词后缀:-al

　　　形容词词缀-al 常常置于名词后,构成形容词。表示"与……有关的"。例如:

　　　person→personal　　　　　origin→original

　　　situation→situational　　　occasion→occasional

　　　profession→professional　　physics→physical

3. 形容词后缀:-able

　　　形容词后缀-able 常常置于动词或名词之后,构成形容词,表示"可被……的"、"具有

……性质的"、"处于……状态的"。例如：

comfort→comfortable　　accept→acceptable

break→breakable(易碎的)　knowledge→knowledgeable(有知识的、博学的)

4. 副词/形容词后缀：-ly

后缀-ly 常置于形容词或名词之后,构成副词或形容词。当用于副词时,表示"以……方式"、"从……角度"。当用于形容词时,表示"像……一样的"、"有……特性的"。另外,当用于形容词或副词时,均可表示"每隔……时间"。例如：

especial→especially（*ad.*）　immediate→immediately（*ad.*）

obvious→obviously（*ad.*）　simple→simply（*ad.*）

hour→hourly（*a. & ad.*）　month→monthly（*a. & ad.*）

friend→friendly（*a.* 友善的）　mother→motherly（*a.* 慈母般的）

Grammar Focus

1. 名词的数

1) 名词的定义及分类

名词是表示人、事物和抽象概念的词语。名词可以分为专有名词(proper nouns)和普通名词（common nouns）。专有名词是某个/某些人、地方、机构等专有的名称,如：England,China 等。普通名词是一类人或东西或是一个抽象概念的名称,如：chair, information 等。

普通名词一般分为四类：个体名词(individual nouns)：表示某类人或东西中的个体,如 book；集体名词(collective nouns)：表示若干个体组成的集合体,如 family；物质名词(material nouns)：表示无法分为个体的实物,如 water；抽象名词(abstract nouns)：表示动作、状态、品质、感情等抽象概念,如 anger。

2) 名词数的概念

名词的数有两层意思：意义上的数和形式上的数。

所谓意义上的数,是指名词所指对象在数量上是单数还是复数。例如：a man 指"一个人",是单数；men 指多个人,是复数。再如：a cow 指"一头牛",是单数；cattle 指"一群牛",即多头牛,是复数。

所谓形式上的数,是指名词在形式上是单数的形式还是复数的形式。例如：man 是单数的形式,men 是复数的形式。再如：从形式上说 cow 和 cattle 都是单数形式。又如 water 与 waters,一个是单数,一个是复数。

意义上的数与形式上的数是有关系的两个对象,但它们又是两个不同性质的对象,不可混淆。

3) 名词数的构成

根据是否能用数目来计算,名词可分为可数名词（countable nouns）和不可数名词

(uncountable nouns)。可数名词的复数形式的构成规律如下:

(1)一般名词词尾加-s(在清辅音后读/s/,浊辅音后读/z/),如:talks, conversations, starters。

(2)以字母-s, -sh, -ch, -x, 结尾的词尾加-es(读作/iz/),如:boxes, buses, watches, brushes。

(3)以字母-f (或-fe) 结尾的名词变成复数时,一般将 f 或 fe 变为-ves(读作/vz/),如:leaf—leaves, life—lives, knife—knives, shelf—shelves, half—halves(例外的有:roof—roofs,belief—beliefs,chief—chiefs,cliff—cliffs,gulf—gulfs,proof—proofs)。

(4)以字母-o 结尾的名词,有些加-s,如:pianos, photos, zoos, bamboos, kangaroos, radios;有些加-es,如:tomatoes, heroes, potatoes, mangoes, volcanoes, cargoes, echoes, mosquitoes。

(5)以辅音加-y 结尾的名词,将 y 变成 i,再加-es(读作/z/),如:baby—babies, city—cities。

(6)有些词的复数构成不规则:

①内部元音字母发生变化:foot—feet, tooth—teeth, goose—geese, mouse—mice, man—men, woman—women, analysis—analyses, basis—bases。

②词尾的变化:ox—oxen, child—children, datum—data, medium—media/mediums。

③单复数相同的:deer—deer, fish—fish, sheep—sheep, means—means, species—species; works—works。

(7)专有名词:

①单复数同形:Chinese—Chinese, Japanese—Japanese, Swiss—Swiss。

②词尾加-s:German—Germans, Russian—Russians, Roman—Romans, American—Americans, Australian—Australians, Indian—Indians。

③变 man 为 men:Frenchman—Frenchmen, Englishman—Englishmen。

(8)复合名词一般把主体词变成复数:daughter-in-law—daughters-in-law, a passer-by—passers-by(过路人)。

如没有主体名词,则在词尾加-s:a grown-up—grown-ups。分开写者,通常在第二部分加复数词尾:a boy student—boy students。但一部分为 man, woman 时,两部分皆变复数。如:a man teacher—men teachers。

4)名词数的用法

(1)有些集合名词在形式上是单数,但它却代表着复数的意义。如:people,police, cattle 等。例如:

Some American people are very humorous. 一些美国人非常幽默。

The police are searching for a short man with a pair of glasses. 警察正在搜索一个戴眼镜的小个子。

但是不要把 people (=human beings,人) 与 a people(= a nation 一个民族)混淆。另

外,当表示一个警察时,要用 a policeman。

(2)有些集体名词虽然其形式上是单数,但根据其在具体的语言环境中的意义,视其所代表的是整体还是集体中的各个个体,其谓语动词应作相应的变化。前者可看作单数,而后者则应与复数动词搭配。例如:

Her family is large. 她家人很多。(强调整体)

Her family are all doctors. 她家的人都是医生。(强调家庭里的各个成员)

类似用法的名词还有:audience,army,union,class,team,government 等。但应注意:

当这些词语前面有 a(n),each,every,this 或 that 的时候,就不常和复数的动词连用。例如:

The team are full of enthusiasm. 队员们情绪高昂。

A team which is full of enthusiasm is more likely to win. 情绪高昂的球队获胜的可能性更大。(这里不能用 who 代替 which。)

(3)有些名词形式上是复数,意义上却是单数,谓语要用复数。可在它们的前面用单位词表示数量意义,如 a pair of 等,此时后面的动词就要根据单位词的形式使用单数或复数动词。比如由两部分构成的物体的名词:scissors,glasses,trousers,gloves,shoes,shorts,stockings。例如:

The shoes are nice. 这鞋不错。

This pair of shoes is nice. 这双鞋不错。

Both of these two pairs of shoes are nice. 两双鞋都不错。

(4)有些名词以-s 结尾,但意义上是单数,谓语动词用单数。如:news,maths,works,physics,electronics,politics,the United States,the United Nations。例如:

The news today is very important. 今天的新闻很重要。

The United Nations is playing a more and more important role in today's world. 联合国在今天的国际舞台上扮演着越来越重要的角色。

(5)有些名词单复数同形,在使用时,谓语动词的单复数要根据上下文来定。如:species, means,crossroads,series,sheep 等。如:

At the end of this road, there is a crossroads. 在这条路的尽头,有一个交叉路口。

There are two crossroads before you turn right. 走过两个交叉路口,然后向右转。

(6)英语中有很多的名词既可以作可数名词,也可以作不可数名词,但是往往词义不同。例如:

Tomato is a fruit. 番茄是种水果。(某种具体的水果)

Apples, bananas, peaches, pineapples and grapes are all fruit. 苹果、香蕉、桃、菠萝和葡萄都是水果。(水果的总称)

一些常见的例子还包括:communication(通讯)— communications(通讯系统,通讯工具);cloth(布)— clothes(衣服);content(内容)— contents(目录);necessity(需要)— necessities(必需品);ruin(毁灭)— ruins(废墟,遗迹);wood(木材)— woods(树林),

experience(经验) — an experience(经历);joy（欢乐） — a joy（令人快慰的人或事），等等。

（7）有些专有名词变成复数后意义有所不同。如：Mr. Green（格林先生） — the Greens（格林一家人）。例如：

Mr. Green is one of my best friends. 格林先生是我最好的朋友之一。

The Greens are very nice. 格林一家非常好。

（8）在区分可数名词和不可数名词时，不可以完全依照汉语的思维。例如，在汉语中，"家具"这个词显然是可数的，但是在英语中，"家具"这个词 furniture 是不可数的，不能说 a furniture，some furnitures。类似的容易用错的词还有：information，advice，equipment，luggage，baggage，sugar 等。

（9）用名词作定语，一般用单数，但也有例外。如：students reading-room（学生阅览室），sports meet（运动会），talks table（谈判桌）。但数词 + 名词作定语时，这个名词一般保留单数形式，如：a five-year plan，two-dozen eggs。

2. 名词的所有格

名词的格在句中表示该名词与其他词的关系。在英语中，名词有三种格：主格、宾格和所有格。其中所有格表示所属关系，它有三种形式：由名词词尾 + 's 构成，由名词 + of + 名词构成，以及双重所有格。

1）名词 + 's

有生命的东西的名词一般用's，其构成规律如下：

（1）单数名词词尾加's，复数名词词尾如没有 s，也要加's。例如：

the boy's friend 男孩的朋友

the children's toys 孩子们的玩具

（2）表示几个人共有一样东西，只需在最后一个人的名字后加's。如表示各自所有，则需在各个名字后加's。例如：

Tom and Jason's room 汤姆和詹森共有的房间（一间）

Tom's and Jason's rooms 汤姆和杰森各自的房间（两间）

（3）若名词已有复数词尾-s，只加'。例如：

Ladies' room 女厕所

the students' English books 学生们的英语书

（4）复合名词或短语，'s 加在最后一个词的词尾。例如：

his mother-in-law's glasses 他岳母的眼镜

（5）有些表示时间、距离、重量、国家、城市等无生命的东西的名词，也可以加's 来构成所有格。例如：

today's newspaper　今天的报纸

ten minutes' walk　十分钟的路程

China's agriculture　中国的农业

注：

（1）'s 所有格所修饰的名词,如前已出现,就可以省略,避免重复。如:John's bike is better than Mike's. 约翰的自行车比迈克的好。

（2）表示"年代"意义,如:This happened in the 1960's. 这事发生在二十世纪六十年代。

（3）表示店铺或某人的家时,常在名词所有格之后省去 shop, home 或 house 等,如: the doctor's, the Smith's, the greengrocer's。

　2）名词 + of + 名词

　　无生命的东西的名词一般用"名词 + of + 名词"的结构。例如:

　　the windows of the house 房间的窗户

　　the cover of the book 这本书的封皮

　3）双重所有格

　　"of + 's"结构或"of + 名词性物主代词"的结构叫做双重所有格,通常表示"许多中的一个（或一部分）"之意,带有感情色彩,其中用于属格的名词或代词表示某个确定的人。在使用时应注意:

　　（1）作 of 宾语的名词必须是人,且是特指。例如:

　　a friend of hers 她的一个朋友

　　a photo of Tom's 汤姆的一张照片（照片上不一定是汤姆本人）

　　Cf. a photo of Tom 汤姆的一张照片（照片上是汤姆本人）

　　（2）双重所有格修饰的名词不和 the 连用,但可以和数词、不定冠词 a, an 以及 any, some 等词连用。例如:

　　a classmate of my mother's 我妈妈的一个同学

　　some classmates of my daughter's 我女儿的几个同学

Language Tips for Writing

　　以下是常用的用于描绘人的词语:

1. 外貌

1）脸:round 圆的;thin 瘦的;long 长的;square 方的;dimple 酒窝; oval face 鸭蛋脸;well-featured 五官端正的;handsome 英俊的;rosy 红润的

2）头发:straight 直的;curly 卷发的;crew cut 平头;pony tail 马尾;bald 秃头的;jet-black 乌黑的;fair 金色的;blonde 淡黄色的;golden 金黄色的;dyed 染色的

3）五官:

　　（1）眼睛:deep-set 深陷的;sunken 凹陷的;bulging/protruding 凸出的;eyelashes 睫毛; eyebrows 眉毛;watery 水汪汪的;sharp 锐利的;bright 明亮的

　　（2）鼻子:straight 挺直的;big 大的;small 小的;flat 扁平的;hooked 钩状的;high-bridged

高鼻梁的

（3）嘴：tooth 牙齿；even 整齐的；uneven 不整齐的；double chin 双下巴

4）身高：tall 高；lengthy 高且瘦；leggy 长腿；short 矮；small（指女孩）娇小；medium height 中等身材

5）胖瘦：chubby（指婴儿或小孩）圆圆的，胖胖的；overweight 超过标准体重的（中性词，相对 fat 更有礼貌一些）；round 圆圆的；fat 胖（较没有礼貌）；plump（指女性或孩子）丰满的；thin 瘦的；slim 苗条；skinny 非常瘦的；lean 清瘦而健康的

6）服饰：smart 潇洒的；conservative 不显眼的；elegant 优雅的；casual 随便的；fashionable 时髦的

7）容貌：good-looking 长得好看的；plain 长相一般的

2. 个性

diligent 勤劳的；kind 和蔼的，善良的；sincere 真诚的；respected 受人尊敬的；honest 诚实的；upright 正直的；pleasant 友善的；hot-tempered 性情暴躁的；generous 慷慨的，大方的；patient 有耐心的；reliable 可靠的；easygoing 容易相处的；amusing 有趣的；energetic 有活力的；active 活跃的；arrogant 自大的；amiable 和蔼可亲的；ambitious 有雄心的；confident 有信心的；cooperative 有合作精神的；creative 有创造力的；energetic 精力充沛的；expressive 善于表达的；knowledgeable 有见识的

3. 爱好

play chess 下棋；listen to pop music 听流行音乐；play piano 弹钢琴；read 阅读；play computer games 玩电脑游戏；watch television 看电视；play basketball 打篮球

Text B　Successful English Learning

Reading Strategies (1): Reading for the Main Ideas

在阅读文章时，快速而准确地把握文章的大意，不仅有助于读者在浩如烟海的材料中选取自己所需要的信息，而且有助于读者把握作者的整体思路，理解各段落间的逻辑关系，从而很好地捕捉文章的主要细节，加深对文章的理解。读者可以通过以下途径较好地掌握文章的主旨：

1. 提出有关主旨的问题

What is the topic of the passage?

What does the author want me to know about the topic?

What general statement expresses what the author wants me to know about the topic?

2. 快速阅读以下内容

1）文章的大标题（title）；

2）文章的小标题（headings）；

3）每一段的第一句和最后一句；

4）特殊印刷（special print），如：斜体，粗体；

5）特殊符号（special punctuation），如：引号，感叹号等。

文章的大、小标题往往是对文章整体或各部分的中心内容最简洁的概述。每一段的第一句和最后一句往往是段落的主题句。判断主题句是获取段落大意最为重要的途径之一。

以 Text B 为例，从文章的大标题，我们可以获知该文与成功学习英语有关。而该文的三个小标题则明确地告诉读者要走上英语学习的成功之路，要明确的三个问题，即：（1）要有明确的学习目的；（2）要投入足够的时间；（3）要掌握一些语言学习的方法。到此，该篇文章的主题思想就比较明确了。如果再看看一个小标题下的第一个句子（该段的主题句），该文的中心思想就更为明确了。

Word Study

1. indicate *v.*   表明，显示

例：Research indicates smokers have a higher risk of developing lung cancer.

研究表明吸烟者更容易患肺癌。

2. commitment *n.*   投入；承诺，许诺

例：Our commitment to the cause must be absolute. 我们为事业而献身应该是无条件的。

Each of us should make a commitment to fight against global warming.

每个人都应该作出承诺，与全球变暖作斗争。

3. occasional *a.*   偶尔的，临时的

例：I only go to the cinema occasionally. 我只是偶尔去看看电影。

4. improve *v.*   改进，改善，提高

例：If you want to improve your oral English, you should speak more and not be afraid of making mistakes.

如果你想提高你的英语口语能力，你就应该多说，而且不要怕犯错。

With the rapid growth of economy, the living standard of the Chinese people has been greatly improved.

随着经济的迅速增长，中国人民的生活水平也得到了大幅度的提高。

5. professional

a. 职业的，专业的

例：If you want to be a qualified technician, first of all, you must master the required professional skills.

如果你想成为一名合格的技术员，首先必须掌握所需的专业技能。

n. 自由职业者，专业人员

例：She is a real professional. 她是一个真正的专家。

　　Can you name any tennis professionals? 你能说出一些职业网球运动员的名字吗？

6. purpose *n.*

1）目的，意图

例：What's your purpose for doing so? 你这样做的目的是什么？

2）用途，效果

例：This medicine is cheaper, but will serve the same purpose.

　　这种药要便宜一些，但能起到同样的效果。

on purpose 故意，有意

7. program *n.*

1）计划，方案，大纲

例：This training program is widely welcomed. 这个培训计划受到广泛的欢迎。

2）节目；节目单

例：What's your favourite TV program? 你最喜欢的电视节目是什么？

3）程序

例：He is good at writing computer programs. 他擅长编写计算机程序。

8. simply *ad.*

1）（强调某说法）确实，简直

例：The scene there is simply wonderful. 那里的景色简直美极了。

2）（强调简单）仅仅，只

例：You need to do nothing, but simply sit there and enjoy the fruits and TV program.

　　你什么也不用做，只需坐在那儿，享用各种水果和看电视。

9. complex *a.* 复杂的，难懂的

例：This is a rather complex problem. 这是一个相当复杂的问题。

10. organize *v.* 组织

例：This weekend, we'll organize a Mid-Autumn & New Students Welcome party.

　　这个周末，我们将组织一个中秋暨迎新晚会。

11. series *n.*

1）一系列，连续

例：The government will adopt a series of measures to solve the problem.

　　政府将采取一系列措施来解决这个问题。

2）系列（丛书、产品等）

例：They are publishing a new series on general science next month.

　　下个月他们将出版一套新的科普方面的书籍。

12. involve *v.*

1）牵涉，使陷入，使卷入

例：Don't involve me in your dispute. 不要把我牵扯到你们的争论当中。

2）包含，含有

例：The ten week program involves intensive training in listening and speaking.

　　这个十个星期的计划包含听说方面的强化训练。

　　Every investment involves risk. 每一项投资都是有风险的。

13. communicate　*v.*

1）交流，通讯，交际

例：How did you communicate with each other at that time when there was no E-mail at all?

　　还没有电子邮件时你们是怎么相互交流的呢?

2）传送，传递（想法、感情、思想等）

例：We can communicate our emotions in many different ways.

　　我们可以以许多不同的方式来传递我们的感情。

14. sense　*n.*

1）意识，观念

例：He is a man with a strong sense of responsibility. 他是一个很有责任感的人。

2）感官，官能

例：The dog has a keen sense of smell. 狗拥有很敏锐的嗅觉。

3）感觉

例：I had the sense that Jane was worried about something. 我感觉珍妮有心事。

　　Mom always gives me a sense of security. 妈妈总是给我安全感。

　　in a sense 从某种意义上说

　　make sense 讲得通，有意义，言之有理

　　make sense of 理解……，弄懂……

15. require　*v.*

1）需要，依靠

例：The room requires cleaning. 房间需要清洁了。

　　Pets require much care and attention. 宠物需要悉心照料。

2）要求，命令

例：Do you know what this position requires? 你知道这个职位有什么要求吗?

16. error　*n.* 错误，差错

例：The fire was caused by human error. 这火是人为造成的。

　　He cannot forget the errors of his youth. 他不能忘记他年轻时的过失。

　　Cf. mistake 与 error 都可表示错误的意思，但 error 更正式，有时强调违反某一标准做的错事，或道德上的错误。如：the errors of his youth. 在一些固定搭配中两者不能混用。如：an error of judgment 判断错误，by mistake 错误地。

17. develop　*v.*

1）发展，开发，研制

例：The western areas of China are developing rapidly. 中国西部地区正在快速发展。

They are engaged in developing new products recently. 最近他们正忙于开发新产品。

2）成长，发育

例：The child is developing normally. 这个孩子发育正常。

Key to Exercises

Text A

Getting the Message

Ⅱ. C

Vocabulary and Structure

Ⅰ. 1—j　　　2—h　　　3—g　　　4—a　　　5—i

6—b　　　7—e　　　8—c　　　9—f　　　10—d

Ⅱ. 1. specially　　2. is；comfortable with　　3. but　　4. like

5. for example　6. such as

Ⅲ. 1. The trial is expected to carry on for two months.

2. His bravery gave him the will to carry on（with）his work.

3. Does the price include the room only, or breakfast as well?

4. Schools should teach computer skills as well.

Ⅳ. 1. 交谈的话题非常普通，往往与情景有关——人们会从所处的环境开始谈起，如天气、所在的房间、吃的食物等。

2. 询问对方职业的话题也是很常见的，对于极其看重工作的美国人来讲尤其如此。

3. 了解这些可谈与不可谈的话题，有助于来自于不同文化的人们在与美国人初次见面时感觉更自在一些。

Ⅴ. 1. People usually greet each other when they meet for the first time.

2. I'm well aware of these problems.

3. All roads lead to Rome.

4. In China, people place a high value on friendships between each other.

5. He intends to talk to young people about the danger of AIDS.

Speaking

1. 1）**Liu Qian met an old schoolmate of hers on campus.**

　　Liu Qian：　　Hi, Wang Mei. I haven't seen you for a long time. How's everything going?

　　Wang Mei：　Pretty good, thank you. What about you?

　　Liu Qian：　　Just OK. Only we have too much spare time here. What do you like to do in your spare time?

　　Wang Mei：　Sometimes, I go to the library. Somtimes, I just listen to music or do some sports.

　　Liu Qian：　　That's interesting. Where are you heading?

　　Wang Mei：　I'm heading for the bookshop.

　　Liu Qian：　　Oh, really? I'm going to the post office, the same direction. Let's go together.

Wang Mei：   <u>All right，let's go.</u>

2)**At a welcome party，Zhou Yong met lots of new faces. She went up and tried to talk with them.**

Zhou Yong：   Hello，<u>I'm</u> Zhou Yong, a freshman from Class 2.

Li Jiao：   I'm Li Jiao, a sophomore from Class 1. <u>Nice to meet you.</u>

Zhou Yong：   Nice to meet you, too. So <u>where are you from</u>?

Li Jiao：   I'm from Chongqing. <u>What about you?</u>

Zhou Yong：   I'm from Yunnan. <u>Have you ever been to Yunnan</u>?

Li Jiao：   Yes，I've been to Lijiang, with my family. Lijiang is really a very wonderful place. Actually，it's one of the most beautiful places I've ever been to.

Zhou Yong：   I can't agree with you more.

Listening

1. B   2. A   3. B   4. C

5. A   6. A   7. C   8. B

Grammar

Ⅰ. 1. Chinese，Americans   2. sheep，people

3. pieces，paper   4. children's story

5. potatoes   6. shoes

7. Leaves   8. photos

9. boxes   10. vegetables，vegetable

Ⅱ. 1. A   2. D   3. C   4. A   5. A

6. D   7. D   8. B   9. A   10. B

Text B

1. T   2. F   3. F   4. F   5. T

Translation of the Texts

Text A

美国人的闲聊

美国人第一次碰面时,通常都会以"闲聊"开始他们的交谈。交谈的话题非常普通,并且往往与情景有关——通常人们都是从谈论周围的环境开始,如天气、所在的房间、吃的食物等。闲聊之所以重要,是因为沉默会让美国人感觉不自在。然而,了解在美国文化中哪些是可以接受的话题,哪些是不能接受的话题,却是非常重要的。

与情景相关的话题,比如天气,在许多文化中都是可接受的,不过显然这类话题不能讨论很久。询问对方职业的话题也是很常见的,对于极其看重工作的美国人来讲尤其如此。个人的兴趣爱好也可以询问。交谈常常以称赞开始。最后,在美国这样的国度里,由于人们频繁搬迁,因而询问对方是哪儿的人也是很常见的。

但是,也有许多话题是不适于开始对话的。比如:人们认为宗教属于个人的隐私。政治则是另一个通常不为人所接受的话题。另外两个立刻就会让美国人不舒服的话题是年龄和收入。美国人非常看重青春,所以许多美国人都不愿透露自己的年龄。至于经济方面的问题,收入和财产的价格也是个人的私事,不能作为与美国人开始交谈的话题。

　　了解这些可谈与不可谈的话题,有助于使来自不同文化的人们在与美国人初次见面时感觉更自在一些。听美国人闲聊常常使外国人对美国人开展谈话的能力做出错误的判断。然而,文化影响着人们相互间的交流。了解谈话的特点有助于更好地了解美国人。

Text B

英语学习的成功之道

　　语言领域的研究显示,要想成为一名成功的语言学习者,可做的事情很多。对语言文化的好奇、日常学习以及抓住每一个说英语的机会使用英语,这些都是迈向成功的非常重要的条件。

◇对学习目标要有一个明确而现实的认识。

　　要知道你的目标是什么。你学英语只是为了应付偶尔的交谈吗?你想提高你的英语写作和会话的能力吗?你是因为职业的原因需要用英文写作吗?学习英语的动机有很多,你的动机就是你学习的目标。

◇对学习一种语言所需的时间应实事求是。

　　承诺一夜之间就能让你获得成功的培训项目纯属无稽之谈。语言学习是一个不断积累的过程,你会发现你在不同的技能方面提高的速度也不尽相同。许多学生在被动技能方面(阅读和语法分析)的进步较快,而在主动的更复杂的技能(说,听讲座时做笔记)方面则进步较慢。

◇学习一些"语言学习"的技巧。

　　记住语言是一个复杂的、由有意义的声音组成的系统,这个系统由一系列的规则(语法)组织起来。每个学生都必须掌握足够的语音、语法、句子结构方面的知识才能懂得这种语言。语言也是一种行为方式,它关系到人类进行交流和为人所理解的需要。语言学习涉及动机、情感、自我意识和文化信仰。语言远远不只是声音、词和语法。语言学习需要犯错误。不要畏惧语言,也不要怕犯错。学会放松自己。"玩"一种新语言是语言学习的一个重要部分。

Scripts for Listening

Conversation 1　M: Hello, I'm Alex Lam. And this is my sister Nancy.

　　　　　　　W1: Hi, I'm Mary Nielson.

　　　　　　　W2: Sorry, what's your last name again?

　　　　　　　W1: Nielson. N-I-E-L-S-O-N. You can call me Mary.

　　　　　　　Question 1: Who is Nancy?

　　　　　　　Question 2: What's the name of the second speaker?

Conversation 2　W1: Good morning, Mrs. Smith.

　　　　　　　W2: Hello, Mrs. Williams. How are things with you?

　　　　　　　W1: Not too bad. I'm just awfully busy these few days. How about you? I haven't seen you for a long time.

　　　　　　　W2: Yes, I've just been to America. I just came back the other day.

　　　　　　　W1: I see. Did you enjoy yourself?

　　　　　　　W2: Yes, very much.

　　　　　　　Question 3: How are things going with Mrs. Williams now?

Question 4: Where has Mrs. Smith just been to?

Conversation 3   John takes part in a party and meets his old friend.

       M1: Hi, Bob, long time no see. How are you doing?

       M2: Everything is fine. Come here, I'd like you to meet a friend of mine. John, this is my friend Barbara. And Barbara, this is John, my good friend.

       M1: Nice to meet you.

       W: Nice to meet you, too.

       M1: You know? Bob graduated from Stanford University.

       W: Well, that's really impressive.

       Question 5: Who is Barbara?

       Question 6: Who graduated from Stanford University?

Conversation 4   W1: Linda, do you know Mr. Peterson?

       W2: No, Susan, I don't believe so.

       W1: (to Mr. Peterson) This is Linda White, my niece. Linda, this is Mr. Peterson, a friend of mine. He is working at Microsoft Company.

       M: Glad to meet you, Linda.

       W2: How do you do, Mr. Peterson? I've heard a lot about you.

       Question 7: What's the relationship between Linda, Susan and Mr. Peterson?

       Question 8: Has Linda heard of Mr. Peterson before?

Unit Two Higher Education

Text A College Life: A Worthy Experience

1. The Benefits of a College Education

The best reason to go to college is to learn more about the world you live in.

A college education will help you develop your skills in reasoning, tolerance, reflection, and communication. These skills will help you resolve the conflicts and solve the crises that come up in the course of a personal or professional life. A college education will also help you understand other people's viewpoints, and learn how to disagree sensibly.

Many college graduates feel that the greatest benefit of their college years is the expansion of their social horizons. Meeting new people, making new friends, companionship, and sharing new experiences lead to personal growth. The skill of meeting and sharing information with people is known as networking. College graduates say that contacts they made in college often helped them find the job they wanted. Others report that friends in college were tied to their own career climb. College graduates describe the value of these networks as having expanded their horizons from the tribal village to the global village.

2. About the Author

Renee DeCoskey is an American girl who has always enjoyed writing. She went to college majoring in English in 2001, and the next year took on a writing minor. She helped out with several on-campus publications, serving as a copyeditor and photographer for the newspaper and a proofreader and contributor to some of their other annuals. She was also very involved with the campus writing center. She is now teaching 9th grade English and working to set up a writing center in that high school. By the end of 2008, she should have completed work to obtain her M. A. in English, as well.

1. College education is a big step for anybody to take. With a good college education, you can find a great job and make good money. In fact, it's never too soon to think about what you

want to do with your college education. List the things you want to find in your college life.

2. Loneliness is a very powerful emotion, and it is very common among young people. It is the first time for many college students to leave their parents and families. Do you have any ideas about how to escape loneliness?

Sentence Analysis

1. Growing up in a small town, I sometimes felt stuck.

此句中,现在分词短语 Growing up in a small town 作状语,表示原因。如:Not knowing how to deal with the problem, he called his teacher for help. 因为不知道怎么处理这个问题,他打电话给老师寻求帮助。

现在分词或现在分词短语作状语还可表示时间、结果、条件、让步、行为方式、伴随状况等。如:

Having completed one task, we started on another one. 完成了一项任务后,我们又开始了另一项。

2. I end up going to college in a small town, too, though.

1) stuck 为动词 stick 的过去式和过去分词,意为"困窘的,迷惑的"。在此句中过去分词形容词 stuck 作表语。如:

John will help you with your work if you're stuck.

你要是在工作上遇到困难, 约翰会来帮助你的。

2) end up:以……告终,后面接 doing。如:

You could end up running the company if you father retired. 要是你父亲退休了,到头来这个公司能归你掌管。

3) though 在此句中表示转折,"但是,然而"之意。

3. College really provides you with a time to figure out what your interests are.

1) a time:一次机遇,一个时机,作"时间的抽象概念"解。

2) what your interests are 是不定式 to figure out 的宾语。英语中及物动词、非谓语动词(不定式、动名词、分词)、介词等都可有自己的宾语或宾语从句。如:

I understand what you have told me. 我理解你告诉我的事情。

Can you tell me how much we will spend during the trip?

你能告诉我们在这次旅行中要花多少钱吗?

The new book is about how the spaceship was sent up into space.

这本新书是关于这艘飞船是怎样发射到太空的。

4. Even if you're already aware of your interests, it lets you continue to narrow them down until you can start to shape them into a career.

1) even if 引导一个让步状语从句。让步状语从句表示"虽然","尽管","即使"等概念,让步状语从句还可由 although(尽管),though(尽管),even though(即使),however(无论怎样),whatever(无论什么),whoever(无论谁),whomever(无论谁),whichever(无论哪个),whenever(无论何时),wherever(无论哪里),whether(是否),no matter (who, what, where, when, etc)（无论……）等词语引导。例如：

Pascal went ahead with the experiment even though he knew it was dangerous. 尽管帕斯卡知道实验很危险,他还是继续做下去。

2) 句中的主句含有一个由 until 引导的时间状语从句。

until 既可以作介词也可以作连词的功能,但两者有所区别。作连词用时意思是 up to the time when 直到……时(为止),如：

Wait until the rain stops. 等到雨停了再说吧。

I won't stop crying until you let me go. 你不放我走我就一直哭。

until (till) 作介词时,用法如下：

(1)up to (a specified time) 直到(某一时刻)。如：

You'd better wait until tomorrow. 你最好等到明天。

Until now Lucy has always lived alone. 露西一直独自生活至今。

(2)up to the time of (a specified event) 直到(发生某事)。如：

The secret was never told until after the old lady's death. 这个秘密在老妇人去世后才说出来。

Don't open it until your birthday. 等到你过生日那天再打开。

3) 此句中,有 narrow down 和 shape into 两个短语动词,注意人称代词 them 在短语中的位置。

动词加小品词构成的起动词作用的短语叫短语动词(phrasal verb)。短语动词的构成有以下几种方式：

(1)动词 + 副词。这类短语动词为"及物动词 + 副词"结构,如果宾语是名词,则既可以放在副词的前面,又可以放在副词的后面;若宾语是人称代词或是反身代词,则要放在副词的前面。例如:carry out, pick up, give up, point out 等。

(2)动词 + 介词。这类短语动词为"不及物动词 + 介词"结构,而且不管宾语是名词还是代词,它们只能放在介词之后。这类短语动词有:look after, hear of, burst into, benefit from, laugh at, care for 等。

(3)动词 + 副词 + 介词,这类短语动词的宾语只能放在介词后面。例如:go in for, catch up with, break away from,look forward to 等。

5. You can choose your classes and, for the most part, can avoid subject matter that isn't appealing to you.

1) 句中的 that isn't appealing to you 是定语从句,修饰名词词组 subject matter。关系代词 that 在句中作主语,不能省略。

2) class *n.* 有课程之意。

比较 class 与 lesson 的用法:两者都可作"(一节)课"解。可以互换。如:

We have two classes in the afternoon. = We have two lessons in the afternoon. 我们下午有两节课。

class 和 lesson 有其他区别性含义,因此二者通常是不能互换使用的。如:

(1)class 可以作"课堂","班级","阶级"解,但 lesson 不可。如:

He works very hard in class. 他在课堂上学习很努力。

There are seventy-six students in our class. 我们班有 76 个同学。

(2)lesson 可以作"功课","(课本中的)一课"解,但 class 不可。如:

They are doing their lessons. 他们正在做功课。

Lesson Two is very interesting. 第二课很有趣。

(3)作课程科目讲时,常用 class。如:

There are 5 classes for us to choose from. 我们有五门课程可以选择。

3)subject matter:matter under consideration in a written work or speech;a theme. ,意为"主要内容;题材",这里指课程的主要内容,借指课程本身。

6.Because I had chosen a small liberal arts school, I got to know my professors really well.

get to know:get acquainted with, 开始了解;开始知道。如:

We, Chinese, want to get to know the earthquake. 我们中国人都想逐步了解地震。

How did you get to know this song? 你是怎么会唱这首歌的?

7.Even now, two years after I've graduated, they still remember me with great detail and ask how teaching is going, even though I never told them I was teaching.

two years after I've graduated 在本句中作为插入语,用来说明事件发生到 now 这一时段的具体时间。

本句出现了现在完成时、一般现在时、现在进行时、一般过去时、过去进行时。

I've graduated 用现在完成时,表示毕业这一动作已经完成,却对于现在产生了一定的影响。

句子的主体采用一般现在时态,作为一般的陈述。

and ask how teaching is going 使用一般进行时态,因为在朋友的印象中,作者一直在进行着教书的工作。表示该动作的持续进行。

even though I never told them 此处使用一般过去,表示此前未曾告知这些人。

I was teaching 处于 even though 一句的背景之下,表示教书工作在过去背景中的持续进行,故使用过去进行时态。

不同时态在一个句子中的使用,很好的体现了事物发展进行的时间顺序,自然明了,前后有序。

8.They just knew that's what I was planning on doing.

本句谓语动词 knew 后面跟了一个省略了连词的宾语从句,句中的 that 是代词,指代 teaching,作为宾语从句的主语。在宾语从句中,what I was planning on doing 是表语从句。

注意本句中时态的使用。knew 是一般过去时,is 是一般现在时,was planning 是过去进行时。之所以用一般过去时和过去进行时,是因为所讲情况是过去发生或存在的;用一般现在时,是因为所讲情况是说话人说话时的情况。例如:

The question is when he finished it yesterday. 问题是昨天他是什么时候结束的。

plan on doing something = plan to do something。如:

When do you plan on going to Geneva? 你打算什么时候去日内瓦?

9. It's a good feeling.

feeling 多指由感情、情绪(如 emotion 和 mood)或欲望引起的情绪状态。如:

feelings of hope and joy 希望和快乐的感觉

a feeling of inferiority 自卑感

feeling 使用单数表达感觉,而使用复数形式则指对某事的看法观感。如:

My own feelings are that she is quite a good friend. 我的感觉是她的确是个好朋友。

Do not hide our feelings in front of people. 不要在别人面前隐藏自己的感受。

10. Because you spend so much time around others in college, you make really strong and lasting friendships because, essentially, you're living together and you're part of the same community.

1)本句有两个原因状语从句。第一个修饰 you make really strong and lasting friendships 这个主句;第二个修饰 Because you spend so much time around others in college, you make really strong and lasting friendships。因此句子翻译为“在大学里,由于你与其他人相处的时间多,你能与他们建立起确实牢固和持久的友谊,因为你们基本上是生活在一起的,你是这个集体中的一部分。”

2)around 的用法:

(1)在表示“圆形运转,回到原处”,“环绕”,“周围”时,为美国人常用。如:

The earth revolves around the sun. 地球绕太阳运行。

New things are happening all around us. 新事物在我们周围不断发生。

(2)表示“到处”,“无目的地”,“附近”,“左右”等较为模糊的概念,例如:

The news that the movie star was coming spread rapidly around the cinema. 这位电影明星就要到来的消息很快地就在电影院里传开。

(3)表示“不止一处”,“在许多地方”,“在不同地方”。如:

The soldiers are standing around. 士兵们在到处站着。

3)副词 essentially 意为“根本上;本质上”,修饰整个句子。修饰全句的副词置于句中或句末时必须用逗点隔开,如无逗点隔开易被认为是修饰动词,而放在句首时则逗点可有可无。例如:

She, apparently, wants to do something to help the pitiful beggar.

显然,她想做些什么来帮帮这个可怜的乞丐。

11. Each year of college is another year of independence gained.

过去分词 gained 是后置定语。单个的过去分词作定语时一般前置。但是当单个的过去分词作后置定语时,往往有强调动词性质的作用。例如:

Things seen are mightier than things heard. 看见的东西比听说的东西更具有说服力。

Word Study

1. favorite　*a.*　特别受喜爱的,中意的

例:In high school, football was my favorite sport. 读高中时我特别喜爱足球运动。

Green tea is one of my favorite drinks. 绿茶是我中意的饮品之一。

2. memory　*n.*　回忆;记忆力

例:These pictures bring back the pleasant memories of Sydney's summer.

这些照片使人回想起在悉尼度过的那个愉快的夏天。

My sister has a good memory for numbers. 我姐姐善于记住数字。

3. grow　*v.*

1)成长,生长

例:I will have my hair cut because it has grown too long.

我要去理发,因为头发已经长得太长了。

2)扩大,增长

例:Their influence is gradually growing among the young people.

他们的影响在年轻人中逐渐扩大。

The tourism is growing rapidly in this city. 这个城市的旅游业发展迅速。

4. stuck　*a.*

1)困窘的,迷惑的

例:I was stuck in the last question of the test paper. 我被试卷的最后一道题难住了。

2)卡住的,困住的

例:Because of the heavy snow, about 8,000 people were stuck in the city, unable to leave this week. 因为大雪,本周约有8 000人被困在这座城市不能离开。

stick　*v.*　刺,扎;粘贴

5. provide　*v.*

1)提供,给予

例:Trees provide shade in summer. 夏季树木提供荫凉。

Please provide aid for them when they fall in trouble.

当他们遇到麻烦时,请给予他们帮助。

2)供给,供应

provide sth. for sb.

例:This travel agency provides very good service for its customers.

这个旅行社为它的消费者提供很优质的服务。

provide sb. with sth.

例:She always manages to provide her students with the latest information.

她总是设法给她的学生们最新的资讯。

6. figure *v.*

1)认定,领会到

例:They figured it was better to take action first. 他们认定还是先采取行动更好。

He figured out the whole plan at once after I told him in brief.

我简要地给他讲了之后,他马上就懂得了整个计划。

2)计算

例:She figures her living expenses carefully every month.

她每月都细心地计算她的生活费用。

7. interest *n.*

1)兴趣,爱好

例:It's important to raise the students' interest in using their skills.

提高学生运用技能的兴趣很重要。

His two great interests are music and sports. 音乐和运动是他的两大爱好。

2)利益

例:Their conflicts result from the different economic interests.

他们的冲突源于不同的经济利益。

8. continue *v.*

1)继续

例:The local government continues warning the public about the dangers from buying medicines over the Internet. 地方政府继续警告民众在网上购买药物的危险性。

2)持续

例:Cold weather may continue for a few more weeks. 寒冷的天气可能还要持续几周。

9. narrow

v. 1)使局限于

例:Henry narrowed his interest to poetry. 亨利把他的爱好局限于诗歌。

2)缩小

例:They decided to narrow the gap between imports and exports.

他们决定缩小进出口差额。

a. 狭窄的

例:The pants are too narrow for Tom. 这条裤子太瘦,汤姆穿不进去。

10. shape

v. 1)塑造

例：He shaped history as well as being shaped by it.

犹如历史创造了他一般，他也创造了历史。

2）使成为……形状，形成

例：Childhood experiences often play an important role in shaping one's character.

童年经历在形成一个人的性格方面常常起着重要作用。

n. 形状，外形

例：The sculptor worked the clay into the shape of a dragon.

雕刻家将泥土捏成一条龙的形状。

in good shape 完整无损，处于良好状态

keep… in shape 使……保持原形

out of shape 变形，走样，不成样子

shape… into 塑造，使形成

11. career *n.*   职业；事业

例：His career had been a success before he made the terrible mistake.

在犯这个可怕的错误之前，他的事业一直很成功。

12. choose   *v.*

1）选择，挑选

例：You may choose whatever you like. 你可以喜欢什么就选什么。

2）决定，情愿

例：As long as good service is provided, I choose to stay in small motels rather than in large hotels. 只要有好的服务，我情愿住在小汽车旅馆而不住大饭店。

13. avoid *v.*   避免；避开

例：I try to avoid driving home at rush hours. 我尽量避免在高峰时间驾车回家。

It's safer to avoid the manager when he gets angry. 经理发脾气时避开他要稳妥些。

14. appealing *a.*   吸引人的

例：A winter vacation is appealing to me. 冬天度假对我很有吸引力。

appeal v. 吸引；恳求，呼吁

15. graduate

v. 大学毕业；毕业

例：He will graduate from the University of New South Wales soon.

他很快要从新南威尔士大学毕业了。

n. （大学）毕业生

例：Jack is a graduate of Harvard University, a Bachelor of Science.

杰克是哈佛大学的毕业生，理学学士。

16. detail *n.*   细节；详情

例：My boss told me to pay more attention to the details in the work.

我的老板告诉我在工作中要多注意细节。

We will provide you with full details on the discounts available during Christmas. 我们将为你提供圣诞折扣的详情报告。

in detail 详细地

for further details 欲知详情（请查询,参阅……）

17. essentially *ad.*   根本上;本质上

例:His view of life is essentially the same as that of his father. 他的生活态度从根本上和他爸爸是一样的。

He's essentially a very social man. 他本质上是个非常合群的人。

18. support

n. 帮助;支持

例:Thanks to a lot of support from the local people, he won eventually in the election.
由于当地人的大力支持,他终于在选举中获胜了。

v. 支持

例:Even those who supported this politician thought he was dishonest. 甚至连那些支持这个政治家的人都认为他不诚实。

19. gain *v.*

1)获得

例:The department store tried to gain customers by giving them some little gifts.
这家百货公司试图以送小礼物来赢得顾客。

2)增加

例:I hope I may gain weight by doing more exercise.
我希望通过更多的锻炼可以增加体重。

20. capable *a.*   有能力的;能力强的

例:As we think you are very capable, we would like to offer you the position.
由于我们认为你具有相当高的能力,我们将为你提供这个职位。

These systems are capable of performing different tasks quickly.
这些系统能很快地执行不同任务。

be capable of 有能力;有才能

capacity *n.* 能力;容量,容积

21. secondary *a.*

1)中等教育的

例:He worked in a secondary school before he studied for Master's degree.
在攻读硕士学位之前他在一所中学工作。

2)次要的

例:Such considerations are secondary to our main aim of improving quality.

相对于我们提高质量的主要目的来说，这些想法都是次要的。

a secondary technical school 中等技术学校

a secondary cause 次要原因

secondary education 中等教育

secondary product 副产品

secondary organ 附属机构

Phrases and Expressions

1. grow up 长大,成长

例:The two children grew up in a healthful, caring environment.

这两个孩子在健康、充满爱心的环境中长大。

2. end up 最终成为;最后处于

例:He ended up as CEO of the corporation. 他最终成了这个公司的首席执行官。

If you drive like that, you will end up badly injured.

你如果照这样开车,迟早要受重伤的。

3. make friends 结交朋友

例:At the start of university, making friends seems like the most difficult thing.

刚上大学时,结交朋友似乎是最困难的事情。

4. figure out 弄明白,想出

例:Can you figure out what he has in mind? 你能弄明白他心里想的是什么吗?

I need to figure out a name for my new book. 我需要为我的新书想一个名字出来。

5. narrow down 缩小,限制

例:When he was 22, he began to narrow down his interest for the future research.

22 岁时他开始把他的兴趣局限于他未来的研究领域。

6. get used to 适应于,习惯于

例:It felt very strange not living with her family, but she got used to living in a rented room soon. 不与家人住在一起是种奇怪的感觉,但她很快适应了在租住房里的生活。

You'll soon get used to the food here. 你很快就会习惯这里的食物。

7. prepare sb. for sth. 使某人为……做好准备

例:You'd better prepare yourself for studying in college. 你最好为在大学读书做好准备。

8. be capable of 有能力;有才能

例:This new car is capable of going 140 miles an hour. 这种新车能开到每小时 140 英里。

9. make it 成功,达到目标

例:He was so eager to go to college, but couldn't make it.

他那么渴望上大学,可没能如愿。

10. base… on 以……为基础

例：The stories in this book are based mainly on traditions.

这本书里的故事主要是根据传说写成的。

Differentiations and Analysis of Words and Expressions

1. contintue to do sth. , continue doing sth.

两个短语都有继续的意思,但 continue to do sth. 意为做完一件事后继续做另一件事,而 continue doing sth. 意为继续做还没有做完的那件事。如：

After washing dishes, I continue to do my homework. 洗完碗,我继续做作业。

After a short rest we continued climbing the mountain.

经过短暂的休息,我们继续爬山。

2. until, till

由 till 或 until 引导的时间状语从句均表示"直到……才",一般情况下,两者可以互换,但是在强调句型中一般用 until。如：

I didn't go to bed until(till)my mother came back.

直到我母亲回来我才上床睡觉。

It was not until the meeting was over that he began to talk to me.

直到散会之后他才开始跟我讲话。

3. choose, select, elect

choose 用途最广,指一般意义上的选择,有时侧重意志和判断,多以个人的好恶为标准。select 指从同类的人或物中,在慎重权衡辨别后加以精选,多以客观优劣为标准。elect 指通过投票选择某人担任某职位。如：

You have chosen the biggest. 你选了最大的一个。

It is hard to select from his numerous works poems that are really representative.

要从他众多的著作中选出有代表性的诗作相当难。

We all elected him chairman. 我们一致推举他当主席。

4. avoid, prevent, escape

avoid 系消极用语,暗示有意识地躲避不愉快的或可能发生的危险事务或情况,而不是逃避实际的威胁。prevent 为积极用语,指采取预防性、限制性的措施,以对某些危害或不良事物的发生加以阻止或杜绝。escape 表示逃脱、漏掉,常用于抽象、借喻的情况中。如：

He deliberately avoided seeing his teacher. 他故意回避他的老师。

It's easier to prevent illness than to cure it. 防病容易治病难。

Her name has escaped my memory. 我记不得她的名字了。

5. be used to doing, used to do

be used to doing 指"习惯于,适应于",后加名词或动名词,而 used to do 指"过去常常

做……",表示过去习惯性的动作或状态,但如今已不再如此。如:

He is used to a vegetarian diet. 他习惯了吃素食。

Grandma used not to be so forgetful. 奶奶过去没有如此健忘。

6. get, gain, obtain

get 的概括性最强,为一般用语,get 指"以某种方法或手段得到某种东西"。gain 往往指在斗争中和竞争中达到目的和获得优势的意思,所得到的东西常有一定的价值,强调努力的一面。obtain 是较正式用语, 常指"通过努力工作、奋斗或请求而如期达到目的和得到所希望的东西"。如:

Did you get my email last week? 上周你收到我的电子邮件了吗?

We gained this victory after a bloody battle. 经过一场血战后,我们取得了这次胜利。

He obtained valuable experience through practice. 他通过实践获得了宝贵的经验。

7. capable, able

这两个词都有"能够"、"有能力"的意思。在用作定语时,able 表示"能干"的意思,语意比 capable 强;able 常指外来原因引起的现象,而 capable 常指经常性的现象。able 一般用作正面意义,而 capable 则是中性词,既可指好事,亦可指坏事。capable 除表示"有能力的"意味外,还可用以表示"有可能的"涵义,able 则没有这个用法。able 后面接不定式,意思是"能的"、"有能力的",capable 之后接介词 of 加名词或动名词。例如:

He is an able clerk. 他是个很能干的职员。

He is a capable clerk. 他是个还算能干的职员。

He is able to solve the problem by himself. 他有能力自己解决这个问题。

They are not capable of doing the work. 他们没有能力做这件工作。

That machine is capable of being restored. 那台机器有可能修好。

8. worth, worthy, worthwhile

worth 是一个只能作表语的形容词,意为"值……的"、"相当于……的价值的"、"值得的"。后接名词或动名词的主动形式。worthy 可作表语,也可作定语。作定语时意思为"有价值的"、"值得尊敬的"、"应受到赏识的";用作表语时意为"值得的"、"应得到的",其后接 of sth. ,也可以后接 to do sth. 。worthwhile 与 worthy 一样,可作表语和定语。表示某事因重要、有趣或受益大而值得花时间、金钱或努力去做,一般作"值得努力的"、"值得做的"、"有意义的"解。用作表语时,可接动名词或动词不定式。如:

The art gallery is worth visiting. 这个美术展览馆值得参观。

This social phenomenon is worthy of being studied. 这种社会现象值得研究。

This is a worthy English-Chinese dictionary. 这是一本有价值的英汉词典。

Helping old people is a worthwhile activity. 帮助老人是一件有意义的事。

It is worthwhile to ask him to join the club. 邀请他加入俱乐部是值得的。

Word Building

1. 名词后缀：-er, -or

名词后缀-er 表示"从事某种职业的人或某地区、地方的人"。例如：

school →schooler	bank →banker
observe →observer	London →Londoner

名词后缀-or 表示"做……的人或物"。

educate →educator	govern →governor（统治者）
conduct →conductor（售票员；导体）	direct →director

2. 名词后缀：-ty, -ity

抽象名词后缀-ty, -ity 表示"性质，状态"。例如：

opportune →opportunity	certain →certainty
safe →safety	proper →property（财产、性质）

3. 动词前缀：en-

前缀 en-加在某些名词前构成动词，表示"放进"、"放在……上面"、"使成……"。例如：

courage →encourage	root →enroot（使……植根于）
danger →endanger（危及）	slave →enslave（征服）

Grammar Focus

代词用来代替名词或名词词组，用以避免名词或名词词组的重复。代词必须与它所代替的名词在人称、数、性、格上一致。代词一般分为九类：人称代词、物主代词、反身代词、相互代词、指示代词、疑问代词、连接代词、关系代词、不定代词。

1. 人称代词（personal pronouns）

人称代词就是指代表示人或物的名词的词。在使用人称代词时应注意以下问题：

1）主格或宾格的使用

人称代词作主语时一般用主格，作动词宾语或介词宾语时用宾格。但当人称代词独立使用或与不定式一起使用充当主语时，常用宾格。例如：

— Susan, go and join your sister cleaning the yard.

— Why me? John is sitting there doing nothing.

— Who's there?

— Me, mother.

— I'm hungry!

— Me too.

当人称代词作表语时,在正式文体中一般要用主格,尤其是后面跟有 who, that 引导的从句时。例如:

It was she that cleaned the room.

但在非正式文体中,作表语的人称代词一般都用宾格。例如:

Dear, open the door, please. It's me.

It was her that cleaned the room.

2)人称代词的排列次序

当有多个人称代词一起使用时,通常的顺序是:

单　数	复　数
you, he and I	we and you/they
you and he	you and they
you/he and I	we, you and they

例如:

You, he and I should return on time. 你、我、他应该按时返回。

当有名词与代词同时使用时,代词一般放后,例如:

Betty and I have already been to Japan. 我和贝蒂已经去过日本了。

3)注意 it 的正确用法

it 充当人称代词时有很多种用法,要正确地理解它的用法意义。例如:

It's June 25th. 今天是 6 月 25 日。(时间)

It's 50 miles from Shanghai. 这里距上海有 50 英里。(距离)

It's pleasant to lie in the sun. 躺在阳光下真舒服。(形式主语)

It seems that the baby likes the drink very much.

好像婴儿很喜欢这种饮品。(在特定句型中充当无具体意义的主语)

It was Henry who picked up Mary last night.

昨晚是亨利接走了玛丽。(在强调句中充当结构词)

2. 物主代词(possessive pronouns)

物主代词是与名词一起使用或单独使用表示所有关系的代词。在使用物主代词时应注意形容词性物主代词和名词性物主代词的不同功能。前者一定要与名词一起使用,后者必须单独使用。例如:

Our office is on the first floor and theirs on the third.

我们的办公室在一楼,他们的在三楼。

Do you prefer his or mine? 你喜欢他的还是我的?

That's ours, not theirs. 那是我们的,不是他们的。

3. 反身代词(reflexive pronouns)

反身代词指以 self 和 selves 结尾的代词。反身代词主要用来表示主语发出的行为及于主语自身,或用来强调句中的某个词语。例如:

He hid himself behind a big rock. 他藏在一块大岩石后面。

He himself is a lawyer. 他本人就是一个律师。

4. 相互代词(reciprocal pronouns)

相互代词表示某种情况涉及两者或多者之间的相互关系,主要有 each other 和 one another。一般来说,each other 指两者间的相互关系,one another 指几个人之间的相互关系。例如:

They have misunderstood each other since they were in college.

他们从读大学时就彼此误解。

We can help one another. 我们可以互相帮助。

5. 指示代词(demonstrative pronouns)

指示代词是指明所指对象的代词,主要有四个:this, that, these, those。严格地说,只有当这几个词后面不跟名词时,它们才是指示代词。如果它们后面跟名词,它们应该是指示形容词或限定词。

this 和 these 一般指近处或将要说明的对象;that 和 those 一般指远处或已经说到的对象。

this 和 that 一般指单数的对象,these 和 those 指复数的对象。当指时间、程度等对象时,只能用 this 或 that。

指示代词的一个重要功能,是避免重复。例如:

The classmates from the south of China like swimming more than those from the north.

来自中国南方的同学比那些北方同学更喜欢游泳。

The best wool is that from Australia. 最好的羊毛是澳大利亚的羊毛。

6. 疑问代词(interrogative pronouns)

疑问代词指表示被询问的对象的词语,有 who, whom, whose, what, which 等。例如:

Who told you that? 谁告诉你的?

What do you want? 你要什么东西?

7. 连接代词(conjunctive pronouns)

连接代词指引出从句并代表人或物的词语。很多疑问代词都可以充当连接代词,引起主语从句,宾语从句和表语从句等。例如:

What caused the accident remains unknown. 是什么导致了这次事故还不知道。

I don't know who will be our head. 我不知道谁来做我们的领导。

8. 关系代词(relative pronouns)

关系代词是用来引起定语从句的代词,有 who, whom, whose, that, which 等。例如:

The teacher will punish those who were absent for class the day before.

老师要惩罚那些头一天缺席的学生。

The man told the police everything that he noticed on the spot.
那个人把他在现场看到的一切都告诉了警察。

9. 不定代词 (indefinite pronouns)

不定代词是所指对象不明确的代词,如 all, each, both, either, neither, one, none 等。例如:

I have two brothers; both are doctors. 我有两个哥哥,他们都是医生。

Tom has three cousins; all are professors. 汤姆有三个表兄,都是教授。

除了相当多的独立的不定代词外,还有相当多的复合不定代词,如 somebody, anyone, nothing 等。

修饰不定代词的定语要放在不定代词之后。例如:

I have something important to tell my mother. 我有重要的事情要告诉妈妈。

Language Tips for Writing

手机短信作为一种更便宜、更快捷、更方便、表达更清楚和没有时间障碍的一种交流方式,被越来越多的人们所接受。由于手机短信容量有限,短信通常都短小精悍,言简意赅。

作为一种新的语言表现方式,英文短信的语言具有以下的特点:

1. 话语范围与生活、工作和学习密切相关,具有实用的特点,语言简要明了;

2. 通常无空行、无分段,标点符号常常省略;

3. 口语化的词汇使用较多;

4. 语法方面一般使用一般现在时、主动语态、简单句和省略句;

5. 广泛使用缩略语,分为以下几类:

   1) 音似型,如 u 代表 you;

   2) 数字型,如 2 代表 to;

   3) 首字母型,如 BTW 表示 By the way;

   4) 主要字母型,如 hrs 表示 hours;

   5) 综合型,由主要字加上发音,如 thx 表示 thanks。

Text B   Mother Goes to College

Reading Strategies (2): Reading for Specific Details

细节是直接说明或论证中心思想的例证或事实,包括日期、数字、名称和概念等。准确、快速地捕捉细节信息,对于学生理解全文、把握主题起着相当重要的作用。读者通常采用寻读法快速查找文章的细节信息。寻读中,要善于发现"提示词"以及与"提示词"有联系的关键词,如人名、地名、时间等,尽可能迅速地在不连贯的、跳跃式的阅读过程中找到有用的信息。以下策略有助于查找和掌握细节信息:

1. 确定要查找的细节信息到底是什么。

2. 利用文章的副标题和段落编号来快速定位所要寻找细节的位置。

3. 利用问题或陈述句中的关键词寻找细节。如,在"Marriages are usually arranged between people of _____"中,"marriage"和"arrange"即是寻读时的关键词。

4. 查找日期时,注意数字、月份和星期等具体信息。

5. 如果需查找的是名字,在文章中寻找大写字母和缩略词,如 Co. , Ltd 等。

6. 如果寻找定义、术语、概念或评论一类的具体细节,需要特别注意引号、破折号、圆括号和逗号等标点符号。另外,斜体字和划线词也提示着此类细节的出现。

    以 Text B 为例,先看以下几个问题:

1) What did Sheri do before she started her study in the university?

2) How old are Sheri's three kids?

3) What did she study at the University of Denver's Women's College?

    从文章第二段可以快速找到关于谢莉工作的相关信息,"she took a job driving a truck… she switched to a desk job at the trucking company"。关于她三个孩子的年龄,可以在第六段寻读到数字 eight, seven 和 five,即为答案。至于她学的专业,从第七段中的"she earned a degree in business administration"便可知。

Word Study

1. dream

  n. 梦想;睡梦

  例:His dream was to become a scientist when he was a little boy.

    在他还是个小孩的时候,他就梦想成为一名科学家。

    I had a really weird dream a few days ago. 几天前我做了一个非常奇怪的梦。

  v. 做梦;睡梦

  例:I dreamt about you last night. 昨晚我梦见了你。

    He dreams of one day going to Tibet with his friends. 他梦想着有一天与朋友一起去西藏。

2. find *v.*

  1) 找到,发现

  例:I failed to find useful information in the library. 我没有在图书馆找到有用的资料。

  2) 发觉,感到

  例:I find it to have been a mistake. 我发觉这一直就是错的。

3. moment *n.* 片刻;瞬间

  例:Please wait a moment. He will be back soon. 请等一下,他马上回来。

at the moment 此刻,目前

for a moment 片刻

for the moment 暂时,目前

the moment that 一……就

4. pass

v. 流逝;经过

例:We sat in silence while the minutes passed.

　　随着时间一分一秒地过去,我们静静地坐着。

n. 通道;通行证

例:Is this the only pass to the valley? 这是去山谷的唯一通道吗?

5. close

a. 近的;亲密的

例:Our university is close to the Olympic Park. 我们大学靠近奥林匹克公园。

　　Many people have a close relationship with their pets.

　　许多人与他们的宠物有着密切的关系。

　　get close to 接近

v. 关闭;结束

例:He decided to close his store because it has been losing money.

　　他决定要关掉这家商店,因为它一直在亏损。

6. switch

v. 转换,改变

例:My friend Linda decided to switch to vegetarian diet. 我的朋友琳达决定改吃素食。

　　He kept switching jobs. 他不断变换工作。

n. 转变;开关

例:You couldn't turn on the light because the switch was broken.

　　你打不开灯,是因为开关坏了。

7. watch　*v.* 观看,注视;监视

例:Some were playing tennis, and others were watching.

　　一些人在打网球,另一些人在观看。

8. achieve　*v.* 达到;完成

例:He achieved success because he had worked very hard.

　　他取得了成功是因为他工作一直很努力。

　　achieve one's purpose/aim 达到目的

　　achieve sb's support 得到某人的支持

　　achieve fame 成名

　　achievement *n.* 成就,成绩

9. afford *v.* 买得起；提供

例：Obviously, she is not able to afford such an expensive car.

很显然，她买不起这么昂贵的小汽车。

His expression afforded his feeling. 他的表情表露出了他的感情。

10. encourage *v.* 鼓励；支持

例：When he failed in the game, his coach encouraged him to have another try.

当他在比赛中失利，他的教练鼓励他再试一次。

11. commute *n.* 通勤路程

例：My morning commute takes 45 minutes. 我早晨去上班要花 45 分钟。

v. 每天（乘车）往返上下班，定期往返

例：She was tired of commuting between the suburbs and the downtown.

她已经厌倦了在郊区和市中心来来往往。

12. stay *v.* 停留，留下；保持

例：I hope you enjoy your time when you stay in Philippine.

我希望你停留菲律宾期间过得愉快。

It was reported that the unemployment rate stayed below 5% in the city.

据报道这个城市的失业率保持在 5% 以下。

13. straight *a.* 整齐的；直的

例：You'd better put your room straight because your friends will come to see you soon.

你最好整理一下房间，因为你的朋友们就要来看你了。

The girl with long straight hair is my niece.

那个披着又长又直头发的姑娘是我的侄女。

14. merit *n.* 优点；美德

例：He obtained his position by merit and ability. 他获得这个位置是凭他的特长和能力。

15. note

v. 强调，着重提到；记下

例：He noted the importance of the task in the meeting.

他在会议上强调了这次任务的重要性。

n. 笔记；注释

例：Would you like to lend your lecture notes to your classmates?

你能把讲课笔记借给你的同学吗？

16. rewarding *a.* 值得做的；有益的

例：Collecting stamps is a very rewarding pastime.

集邮是一项很有益的消遣。

reward *v.* 报答；奖赏

Key to Exercises

Text A

Getting the Message

Ⅱ. C

Ⅲ.

1) First, I want to develop my interest in college. Second, I want to make some good friends during my college days. Finally, what the most important thing we can gain is that college life is the beginning of society, and it may prepare us for the real world.

2) Because you spend so much time living and studying with other students in college, you are sure to make wonderful friends who have much in common with you.

3) The best thing is college can prepare you for the real world because it is just like a small society, and you may develop your abilities as much as possible.

4) First, many young people are uncertain about a career path at the start of college. This is a time of exploration, and taking the time to explore the career they are really interested in. Second, At college, you'll surround yourself with people who can share different backgrounds, cultures and experiences, and make some lifelong friends with some of them. Finally, college education is very helpful for young people's personal growth and prepares them for society.

Vocabulary and Structure

Ⅰ. 1—g   2—d   3—j   4—h   5—a

6—b   7—e   8—i   9—c   10—f

Ⅱ. 1. lasting   2. narrow   3. experience

4. end up   5. based on   6. essentially

Ⅲ. 1. The company aims to provide green energy for the market.

2. These websites will provide all the information we need for us .

3. Because I was excited, I couldn't go to sleep.

4. Because he read so attentively, he forgot the time for lunch.

Ⅳ. 1. 我所喜爱的最美好的一些回忆是我的大学生活。

2. 即便你已经知道你的兴趣,它也会使你继续缩小兴趣的范围,到你开始把兴趣变成你的职业。

3. 大学所完成的最好的事情就是使你做好了进入现实社会的准备。

Ⅴ. 1. He's trying to figure out a way to solve the problem.

2. Are human beings the only animal capable of using tools?

3. They based their conclusions on the facts.

4. He couldn't graduate from the university without his families'support.

5. I'm not used to eating so late in the evening.

Speaking

1. 1) Li Min just met someone at a party, but he has to leave the <u>party early</u>.

Li Min: Excuse me, but I won't be able to stay <u>any longer</u>.

Lily: But you've just come.

Li Min: I'm very glad to have seen you and have had an enjoyable evening.

Lily: It's <u>a pity</u> for us to see you go.

Li Min: Goodbye. Take care of yourself. Don't forget to <u>keep in touch / write to me</u>.

Lily: Sure. Good-bye.

2) Wang Lin is seeing someone off at the airport.

Steven: Well, it's time to board the plane now!

Wang Lin: We're sorry <u>you have to leave</u>.

Steven: Thank you for <u>all the things</u> you have done for me during my stay here.

Wang Lin: It's our pleasure. Hope we'll be able to get together again before long.

Steven: I really appreciate you coming to <u>see me off</u>. Good-bye then.

Wang Lin: <u>Good-bye/So long</u>. Keep in touch.

Listening

1. B   2. A   3. C   4. B

5. C   6. A   7. B   8. C

Grammar

I. 1. Tom and <u>me</u> are responsible for this decision. (I)

2. The boss has managed to put <u>we</u> workers in a bad situation. (his/us)

3. <u>Anyone</u> here earns over a hundred dollars a day. (Everyone)

4. A student in that all-women's college should have no fear about <u>their</u> future. (her)

5. Either the classrooms or the reading room must have <u>their</u> floor cleaned. (its)

6. Nobody but <u>her</u> can solve this problem. (she)

7. We enjoyed <u>myself</u> very much tonight. (ourselves)

8. This room is bigger than <u>one</u> next door. (the one)

9. Let's clean their room first and <u>our</u> later. (ours)

10. Last night, he and <u>him</u> friends went to a big bookstore. (his)

II. 1. B   2. C   3. D   4. B   5. A

6. D   7. B   8. C   9. B   10. C

Writing

I. 1. See you in the library before you go to work.

2. My summer holidays were a complete waste of time. Before, we used to go to New York to see my brother, his girlfriend, and their three kids face to face.

II. 1. Cya at 2 p.m. 2 discuss winter hols.

2. Thx for gift u gave 2 me.

Text B

1. T   2. F   3. F   4. T   5. F

Translation of the Texts

Text A

大学生活：一段有价值的经历

我所喜爱的最美好的一些回忆是我的大学生活。由于在小镇里长大，我有时会感到困窘。尽管如此，我后来还是进了一所小镇里的大学。但这无关紧要，我在那里结交了一些极好的朋友，更重要的是，我对自己有了很多的了解。

大学确实为你提供了一段时间让你去弄明白你的兴趣所在。即便你已经知道你的兴趣，它也会使你继续缩小兴趣的范围，直到你开始把兴趣变成你的职业。你可以选课，通常你能避免那些对你没有吸引力的科目。由于我选择的是一所小规模的文科学院，所以我对我的教授们非常熟悉。即使到了现在，我已经毕业两年了，他们仍然非常清楚地记得我，还问我书教得怎样，尽管我从未告诉过他们我在教书。他们就是知道我一直打算干什么。这是一种不错的感觉。

在大学里，因为你用这么多的时间与周围的人在一起，所以你能建立真正牢固而持久的友谊，说到底，原因在于你们生活在一起，你们都是同一群体中的一员。有这样的互助体系确实是件很好的事情，尤其是当你正在逐步适应离开家，离开家人的时候。

大学所完成的最好的事情就是使你做好了进入现实社会的准备。大学生活的每一年都会增进你独立性。每一年你都会进一步地了解你自己以及你的能力。刚进校门时，你只不过一个大高中生，毕业时，你就成了一个有了目标、有事业的成年人，并且准备好切切实实地实现它们。

许多高中生说他们没有兴趣上大学，因为他们印象中的大学教育也是和中等教育体系一样的樊笼。他们应知道大学远远不是如此，而且，就教育、社交和个人发展而言，大学的的确确是一段值得为之努力的经历。

Text B

母亲上大学

谢莉·斯特雷里不知道生命之路会把她带向多远的地方——直到有一天她对孩子们的梦想帮她找到了答案……

从小到大，谢莉一刻也没有想过她能上得了大学。相反，她找了一份开货车的工作。时间一年年过去了，谢莉恋爱，结婚，生了三个孩子。因为她想离家近些，就换到了一家货车运输公司搞办公室工作。

但是，有一天下班后，谢莉在看孩子们玩耍时开始思索起来：我非常希望他们有成就，但我有能力给他们提供比如上大学那样的机会吗？

是她想到：首先需要上大学的正是她自己！

"去吧。"她的丈夫史蒂夫鼓励她说。于是谢莉在丹佛大学女子学院报了名。学院让她在周末上所有的课程，这样她还可以继续工作。

谢莉虽然很爱学习，但她也很想家：她不愿花两小时往返乘车去学习，于是周末就呆在了宿舍里。周末要是能和史蒂夫与孩子们在家该多好，她这样想着。但是，8岁的埃里克、7岁的瑞安和5岁的克里斯廷始终坚决支持妈妈。"尽最大的努力吧，"他们说。

谢莉尽了最大的努力，她的成绩全部是优秀，拿到了商业管理学位。现在她拿到了优秀生奖学金，在丹佛大学法学院学习！

"很不容易,"谢莉强调,"但是值得——对我、对我的家人都是如此。"

Scripts for Listening

Conversation 1　M: The train starts at 8:00. I'm afraid we have to hurry now.

W: We have 35 minutes to get there.

Question: What time is it now?

Conversation 2　M: It is raining outside. I'll have to be going.

W: Is it raining? What's the hurry? Not until you've had another drink.

Question: What does the women mean?

Conversation 3　M: It's been a pleasure to be with you. I think I have to catch the No. 2 bus to go home.

W: Well, if you've got to go, good-bye for now.

Question: How will the man go home?

Conversation 4　M: We are just in time for the train.

W: Yes. It's very kind of you to come all the way to see me off.

Question: Where did the conversation most likely take place?

Conversation 5　M: I really appreciate what you've done for me during my study in your university.

W: My pleasure. Hope you will come back to China again soon.

Question: What did the man do in China?

Conversation 6　W: So you are leaving tomorrow, Mr. London?

M: No. I'm leaving the day after tomorrow.

Question: When will Mr. London leave?

Conversation 7　M: Mary, did you call David to say goodbye last night?

W: Yes. I tried to get hold of him, but I couldn't get the telephone through.

Question: What happened when Mary called David last night?

Conversation 8　M: Wish you a good sleep. Good night.

W: Good night.

Question: When did the conversation take place?

Unit Three Being Mature

Text A   Am I Normal?

On Being Mature

What is mature? Is there any real test for maturity? Does being mature means having to wear modest clothing, hiding your true emotions from others, paying your bills, writing poetry that is meaningful to everyone else but yourself, or using all the big words sounding wise? Actually, the answer to the question can be varied from individual to individual.

Regardless, there are certain traits indicating that a person has grown up:

1. Think independently and have your own ideas.
2. Think positively and always have hopes in your heart.
3. Think both sides before you make any decisions.
4. Prepare yourself for your professional career.
5. Learn to adjust to new surroundings.
6. Respect the emotions of others.
7. Take on your own responsibilities.

1. One of the important points to be mature is to prepare yourself for your future career. As a college student, have you ever thought about how to prepare yourself for a new life at college?

2. Being mature doesn't simply mean getting older, but becoming sensible and skillful in coping with all kinds of situations. Can you give your classmates an example to illustrate a person who is physically mature, yet not mature mentally, or in other words, not mature in handling personal affairs?

Sentence Analysis

1. Now you're looking in the mirror, thinking only one thing: Am I normal?

   此句中,现在分词短语 thinking only one thing 作状语,表示伴随原因。如:

   I stayed up late last night, preparing for the lecture.

   Please fill in the form, giving your name, E-mail address, telephone number, etc.

   现在分词或现在分词短语作状语还可表示时间、结果、条件、让步、方式、原因等。如:

   Having completed one task, we started on another one. (时间)

   Not knowing her address, we couldn't get in touch with her in Paris. (原因)

   Turning to the right, you will find the path leading to the church. (条件)

   She came running towards us to tell us the exciting news. (方式)

   They stood there for an hour, watching the football game. (伴随)

   Her husband died of bird flu last year, leaving her with two children. (结果)

2. Height is just one of the thousands of features your genes decide.

   此句中,your genes decide 是定语从句,修饰先行词 features。该定语从句中省略了关系代词"that"或"which"。通常情况下,定语从句中作宾语的关系代词"whom"(指人),"that","which"(指物)可以省略。如:

   In the dark street, there wasn't a single person (whom) she could turn for help.

   Finally, the thief handed everything (that) he had stolen to the police.

   The first birthday gift (that/which) her parents gave her was an expensive necklace.

3. For example, eating an unhealthy diet can keep you from growing to your full potential.

   此句中,eating an unhealthy diet 是动名词短语做主语。又如:

   Working in these conditions is not a pleasure but a suffer.

   Collecting information is very important to any businessman.

   His complaining about everything is endless.

4. TV and magazines might make us think our bodies should weigh and look a certain way, but in real life, there are a lot of differences.

   此句中,think 是省略了"to"的不定式,作 make 的宾语补语。当不定式在 let, make, have, hear, look at, listen to, feel, observe, watch, notice, perceive (感觉到)等感官及使役动词后面作宾语补语时,不定式要省略 to。但是在被动语态中,则不能省略 to。例如:

   Whenever something is wrong with you, please do let me know.

   I will have the students write a passage about the benefits we get from Internet.

   Here in the company the workers were made to work 12 hours a day.

5. Some kids worry so much about their weight that they try unhealthy and dangerous things to

change it.

常由 so… that 或 such… that 引导结果、目的状语从句,掌握这两个句型的关键在于了解 so 和 such 与其后的词的搭配规律。such 是形容词,修饰名词或名词词组,so 是副词,只能修饰形容词或副词。so 还可与表示数量的形容词 many, few, much, little 连用,形成固定搭配。

He always studied so hard that he made great progress.

The scientist's report was so instructive(有启发性的)that we were all very excited.

It's such nice weather that all of us want to go to the park.

The furniture is so expensive that the young couple can't afford it.

He earns so little money that he can hardly feed his family.

We've come early so that the meeting can begin promptly.

He came in so quietly that he shouldn't wake his wife.

He saved such a lot of money that he could buy a new car.

此外,so… that 与 such… that 之间可以转换。如:

The boy is so young that he can't go to school by himself.

He is so young a boy that he can't go to school by himself.

He is such a young boy that he can't go to school by himself.

Word Study

1. normal

a. 正常的;标准的

例:It's normal for couples to argue now and then. 夫妻之间的吵闹是常事。

Weeping is a normal response to pain. 哭泣是痛苦的正常反应。

People who commit crimes like that aren't normal. 犯这种罪的人心理都不正常。

n. 常态;正常;标准

例:It is said that train services are now back to normal. 据说铁路交通已恢复正常。

The temperature was below normal for the time of year. 今年的气温低于往年。

abnormal *a.* 反常的,不正常的

normality *n.* 常态;正常

normally *ad.* 通常,正常的

normalize *v.* (使某事)正常,正常化

2. change

v. 改变;兑换

例:The leaves on trees change colour in the autumn. 树叶在秋天要变颜色。

Mary has changed a lot since I last saw her. 自从我上次见到玛莉以来,她改变了很多。

I need to change my dollars into Chinese Yuan. 我需要把美金换成人民币。

n. 变化;零钱

例:Doctors say there is favorable change in the patient's condition. 医生说病人的情况有所好转。

I've no small change on me. 我没有零钱。

change(sth.)to/into… 转换成

例:Britain changed to a metric system of currency in 1970. 1970 年英国已改用公制货币。

changeable a. 易变的;常变的

3. smart a. 漂亮的,时髦的;聪明的,精明的

例:My son looks very smart in his new suit. 儿子穿上新衣服显得很帅。

He's smart enough to know he can't run the business without her.

他太精明了,知道自己的事业离不开她。

4. obvious a. 显然的,明显的

例:His nervousness was obvious right from the start. 他从一开始就显得十分紧张。

It is obvious to everyone that one of the ways of reducing pollution in big cities is to use cars less. 大家都明白少用汽车是降低大城市环境污染的办法之一。

obviously ad. 显然;明白地

5. sprout v. (使)生长;发芽

例:Your son has sprouted a beard since we saw him last.

你儿子长胡子了, 我们上次见到他时还没长呢。

We can't use these potatoes; they've all sprouted. 这些土豆不能吃了,都出芽了。

It takes about a week for the seeds to sprout. 这些种子大约要一周后才会发芽。

6. otherwise

ad. 用别的方法;不同地

例:Obviously you think otherwise. 显然你的想法不同。

I'd like to go with you on Tuesday, but I'm otherwise engaged.

我很想星期二同你一起去,但是我有其他事情。

conj. 否则,不然

例:Do as you're told, otherwise you'll be in trouble.

叫你怎么做就怎么做,否则会有麻烦。

They got two free tickets to Sydney, otherwise they'd never have been able to afford to go. 他们得到了两张去悉尼的免费机票,否则他们怎么也支付不起。

7. stubby a. 粗短的,矮胖的

例:The little boy is pointing the toy train in the shop window with his stubby fingers.

那个小男孩一直用他又短又粗的手指着橱窗里的玩具火车。

The dog with a stubby tail is easy to be recognized. 这只尾巴短粗的狗很容易辨认。

8. skinny a. 皮包骨的,瘦削的

例:You're skinny enough without going on a diet! 你不必节食就够瘦的了!

Your daughter should eat more, she is much too skinny. 你女儿太瘦了,应该多吃点。

9. feature *n.*

1)特色,特点

例: Please list an interesting feature of city life.

请列举城市生活的一个有趣特点。

Many examples and detailed grammatical information are among the special features of this dictionary.

本词典别具特色,诸如例证多样,语法要点详尽等。

The most striking feature of Van Gogh's paintings is their bright colors.

色彩鲜明是凡·高作品最为显著的特点。

2)(*pl.*)相貌

例: Jenny is a girl of delicate features. 珍妮是一个长相秀气的女子。

10. decide *v.*　决定,拿定主意;裁决

例: With so many choices, it's hard for me to decide what to buy.

有这么多可选择的, 我真难决定买什么。

After a long discussion, the committee eventually decided the issue in his favour.

通过长时间的讨论,委员会最终作出了有利于他的决定。

It is difficult for the judge who will decide the case tomorrow.

法官明天很难判决此案。

You have a right to decide how to spend your holiday.

怎样度假,你有权自己决定。

decision　*n.* 决定;决心

11. referee *n.* 证明人,推荐人;裁判员

例: My English teacher is willing to act as referee for me in my job application. 我的英语老师愿意做我求职的推荐人。

Who is the referee in the match? 谁当这场比赛的裁判?

12. likely

ad. 很可能;可能的

例: I'd very likely have done the same thing in that situation.

在那种情况下,我很有可能像你那样做。

As likely as not she's forgotten all about it.

很可能她已经把这事忘得一干二净。

a. 可能的;有希望的

例: What is the most likely cause of the problem?

这件事情最有可能的起因是什么?

He is the most likely candidate for general manager.

他是最可能当选的总经理候选人。

It is likely to/that… 很可能……

例: It isn't likely to snow. 不大像要下雪。

It's very likely that she will quit the job in the hotel.

她很可能辞去宾馆的工作。

13. diet

n. 日常饮食;规定饮食

例: Too rich a diet is not healthful for you. 吃太多油腻的食物不利于身体健康。

To some extent illnesses are caused by poor diet.

在某种程度上,饮食欠佳会导致疾病。

The doctor says I've got to go on a diet. 医生说我得节食。

v. 只(准)吃某类食物或少量食物;(尤指为减轻体重)节食

例: You should be able to reduce your weight by careful dieting.

你应该通过节食来减轻体重。

According to the doctor, you ought to diet and take more exercise.

根据医生建议,你应该节食并多做运动。

go /be on a diet 节食

例: Linda always seems to be on a diet. 琳达好像一直在节食。

14. potential

n. 潜能,潜力

例:She has the potential to become a champion in the match of springboard diving. 她很可能荣获跳板跳水的冠军。

The region has enormous potential for economic development.

这个地区的经济有巨大的发展潜力。

Many foreigners studied the Chinese market to find the potential there for profitable investment.

许多外国人对中国的市场进行了研究,以寻求投资获利的可能性。

a. 潜在的,可能的

例:The book is a potential best seller. 该书很可成为一部畅销书。

Many potential customers are waiting for a fall in house prices before buying.

许多潜在的客户都在等房价下跌以后再购房。

exploit / fulfill / realize one's potential 发掘/发挥/认识自己的潜力

例:I don't feel I'm achieving my full potential in my present job.

我认为在目前的工作中,我还没有完全发挥我的潜力。

15. nutrient   *n.*   营养品;营养素

例:The plant absorbs nutrients from the soil. 植物从泥土中吸收养料。

A healthy diet should provide all your essential nutrients.

健康食品应该含有各种基本的营养素。

16. weigh   *v.*   称(……的重量);权衡

例:He weighed the stone in his hand. 他用手掂了掂这块石头的重量。

She weighs 50 kilos. 她体重为 50 公斤。

You'd better weigh the advantages of the operation against the risks involved.

你最好仔细考虑做这种手术的好处与危险。

weigh in（at sth.）（of a jockey, boxer, etc.）（指骑手、拳击手等）赛前测体重

例：He weighed in at several pounds above the limit. 他赛前量体重比规定限度重几磅。

c. f. weight *n.* 重量；分量

例：Apples are usually sold by weight. 苹果通常按重量卖。

She has grown both in height and weight. 她身高和体重都增加了。

17. vary *v.* 改变,（使）变化

例：My mother's mood seems to vary according to the weather.

母亲的情绪似乎随天气的变化而变化。

Generally prices vary with the seasons. 物价一般随季节而波动。

variation　*n.*　变化,变动

Phrases and Expressions

1. be full of 有很多,充满的

例：The basin was full to the brim with cold water. 盆子里装满了冷水。

The cinema is full of people. I'm afraid you'll have to wait for the next show.
电影院已客满, 很抱歉你只能等下一场了。

2. in fact 事实上, 实际上

例：In this world, men and nature relate to each other closely.

在这个世界上, 人和自然彼此间有着密不可分的联系。

They said she was a slow learner, whereas in fact she was not interested in the subject in
the least. 他们说她反应慢, 其实是因为她对这门学科一点不感兴趣。

2. act like/as 担任；充当……的角色, 起……的作用

例：I don't understand their language; you'll have to act as interpreter in the course of our
negotiation. 我不懂他们的语言, 谈判过程中你得当翻译了。

3. keep sb. from doing sth. 使……不做某事

例：His ex-husband had kept her from seeing his children。她的前夫不让她去看孩子。

I hope I'm not keeping you from your study. 希望我没有妨碍你的学习。

4. plenty of 许多

例：They always gave us plenty of food to eat while we stayed with them after the snowstorm.
雪灾后和他们呆在一块的日子里, 他们总是给我们很多东西吃。

No need to hurry — you've got plenty of time. 不必着急, 你们有充足的时间。

5. vary from...to... 由……到……情况不等

例：Test scores vary from class to class. 各班考试分数不尽相同。

The heights of the trees vary from one meter to two meters.

这些树子的高度从一米到两米不等。

6. in real life 在现实生活中

例：Things can not always go well with you in real life.

现实生活中事情不可能总是一帆风顺的。

7. worry about 担心，担忧

例：You've really got no need to worry about your weight. 你真的不必担心你的体重。

There's nothing to worry about. 没什么可愁的。

 Differentiations and Analysis of Words and Expressions

1. change, alter, modify, vary

　　这组词都有使事物发生变化，与原来不同的意思。除 modify 是及物动词以外，其他词既可作及物动词也可作不及物动词。change 的词义很广，用法最普遍，表示使某事物有任何改变；alter 表示使某事物在外观、性质、用途等方面稍作改变，通常指改变衣服的大小、松紧等；modify 用于物体时，表示结构或功能的部分改变。这个词还可表示态度、意见等的变化；vary 所指某事物或其部分的改变常为暂时的或反复的。例如：

Most English women change their names when they marry. 英国妇女大多因结婚而改姓。

He changed his mind completely. 他完全改变了主意。

Her expression changed when she heard the good news.

她听到这一好消息时表情就变了。

I'll have to alter the diagram. I've made a mistake. 我得修改图表，我出了点儿错。

She had to alter her clothes after putting on weight. 她胖了以后，衣服也得改了。

The car has been modified for racing. 这辆汽车已改装为赛车。

He has been forced to modify his position if he wants to be elected.

他要想当选就得稍稍改变立场。

It's better to vary your diet rather than eat the same things all the time.

你最好变换一下饮食，不要总吃同样的东西。

Political opinions vary according to wealth, age, sex etc.

政治见解因财富、年龄、性别等不同而有所区别。

2. be full of, be filled with

　　这两个词组的汉语意思相当，都是表示装满、充满的意思，只是要注意其不同的搭配。例如：

1）The dustbin needs emptying; it's full of rubbish. 垃圾箱该倒了，垃圾都满了。

2）Sophia is very lovely. She's always full of vitality. 索非亚很可爱，她总是充满活力。

3）The hole is filled with sand. 洞里满是沙子。

4）Please fill this glass with milk for me. 请把这个杯子给我斟满牛奶。

3. thin，skinny，slim，slender

　　这组词指人的体重低于标准时，thin 是最常用的词，该词可含贬义，指虚弱或不健康，常常与程度副词连用；skinny 是贬义词，表示皮包骨头、无力；slim 或 slender 都是褒义词，指为人心向往之的、相当轻的体重。slim 一词尤用于描述经节食或锻炼来减轻、维持体重的人。

1）She's gone terribly thin and weak since her operation. 她动过手术，所以非常瘦弱。

2）He looks much too skinny to be a weight-lifter. 他瘦骨嶙峋的，当不了举重运动员。

3）She kept slim by dieting and exercising. 她靠节食及锻炼来保持身材。

4）You have a beautifully slender figure. 你的体形十分苗条。

Word Building

　　在本课中出现较多的前缀、后缀有：

1. 形容词后缀：-ous

　　名词之后加上后缀-ous 构成形容词，意为"充满……的"、"具有……特征的"。例如：

danger → dangerous　　　　　　fame → famous

anxiety → anxious（忧虑的）　　　advantage → advantageous（有优势的，有利的）

2. 形容词后缀：-ic

　　名词后加上后缀-ic 构成形容词，表示"具有……的"、"与……有关的"。例如：

alcohol → alcoholic　　　　　　athlete → athletic（运动的、健壮的）

science → scientific　　　　　　scene → scenic（风景的）

3. 形容词后缀：-y

　　名词之后加后缀-y 构成形容词，表示"具有……特征的"、"多……的"。例如：

fun→funny　　　　　　　　　　skin→skinny

health→healthy　　　　　　　　thirst→thirsty

4. 名词后缀：-al

　　动词之后加后缀-al 构成名词，表示动作、过程、人物、事物等。例如：

propose→ proposal（提案，建议）　survive→survival（幸存；幸存者；残存物）

approve→ approval（认可）　　　arrive →arrival（到达，抵达；到达的人或物）

Grammar Focus

数词（numeral）

　　数词是英语中常用的一种限定词，表示数目的多少或顺序的先后。数词分为基数词和序数词。表示数目多少的数词叫基数词（cardinal numeral），表示顺序的数词叫序数词

（ordinal numeral）。除此之外,还有分数、百分数、小数和倍数。

一、数词的构成:基数词和序数词

基数词		序数词	
1	one	1st	first
2	two	2nd	second
3	three	3rd	third
4	four	4th	fourth
5	five	5th	fifth
6	six	6th	sixth
7	seven	7th	seventh
8	eight	8th	eighth
9	nine	9th	ninth
10	ten	10th	tenth
11	eleven	11th	eleventh
12	twelve	12th	twelfth
13	thirteen	13th	thirteenth
14	fourteen	14th	fourteenth
15	fifteen	15th	fifteenth
16	sixteen	16th	sixteenth
17	seventeen	17th	seventeenth
18	eighteen	18th	eighteenth
19	nineteen	19th	nineteenth
20	twenty	20th	twentieth
21	twenty-one	21st	twenty-first
22	twenty-two	22nd	twenty-second
23	twenty-three	23rd	twenty-third
30	thirty	30th	thirtieth
40	forty	40th	fortieth
50	fifty	50th	fiftieth
60	sixty	60th	sixtieth
70	seventy	70th	seventieth
80	eighty	80th	eightieth
90	ninety	90th	ninetieth
100	one hundred	100th	one hundredth
101	one hundred and one	101st	one hundred and first
200	two hundred	200th	two hundredth
1,000	one thousand	1,000th	one thousandth
2,000	two thousand	2,000th	two thousandth
10,000	ten thousand	10,000th	ten thousandth
1,000,000	one million	1,000,000th	one millionth
1,000,000,000	one billion	1,000,000,000th	one billionth

说明：

1. 基数词

1）英语基数词 1—12 是独立的单词，如 one，two，three 等。

2）13—19 的基数词是在基数词尾加-teen，其中 thirteen，fifteen，eighteen 的变化较为特殊。

3）20—90 的整数均以后缀-ty 结尾，如 twenty，eighty，ninety 等。

4）几十几的基数词由十位数词和个位数词构成，中间加连字符号"-"，如 twenty-one，fifty-nine 等。

5）三位数以上的基数词，百位和十位（或个位）之间一般用连词 and，如 one hundred（and）five，three thousand four hundred（and）nineteen。

6）英语中没有"万"这个词汇，1 万用 10 千，即 ten thousand 来表示；英语中也没有"亿"这个词汇，1 亿用 100 百万千，即 a hundred million 来表示。

2. 序数词

1）英语序数词 1—19 除第一（first）、第二（second）、第三（third）有特殊形式外，其余均由在基数词后加-th 构成。

2）有几个序数词加 -th 时拼法不规则，它们是：fifth，eighth，ninth，twelfth。

3）十位整数的序数词的构成方法是：先将十位整数基数词词尾-ty 中的 y 变成 i，然后加-eth。

4）基数词"几十几"变成序数词时，仅将个位数变成序数次，十位数不变。如 twenty-one 变成 twenty-first。

5）序数词的缩写形式：阿拉伯数字后加上序数词的最后两个字母构成。如：1st，2nd，3rd，4th，31st，82nd，93rd，94th 等。

基数词和序数词的使用：

1. 分数

分数的分子用基数词表示，分母用序数词表示。分子大于 1 时，分母用序数词的复数形式表示。如：

1/2 one half	1/3 one-third
2/3 two-thirds	1/4 one-fourth（one quarter）
3/4 three-fourths	4/5 four-fifths

2. 小数

小数点以前的数，用基数词的读法读出；小数点以后的数，将数字一一读出，小数点读作 point。如：

1.6　one point six	0.6　zero point six
19.015 nineteen point zero one five	0.006 zero point zero zero six

3. 百分数

百分数中的百分号% 读作 percent。如：

5% five percent	0.5% zero point five percent

56%　fifty-six percent　　　　　　　200%　two hundred percent

4.倍数

表示"两倍"用twice,表示"三倍"及"三倍以上"一般用"基数词＋times"的方式构成。如:

Twice three is six. 二三得六。(3 的 2 倍是 6)

His room is three times the size of mine. 他的房间的面积是我的房间的三倍。

This year's output increased three times. 今年的产量增加了两倍。

二、数词的用法

1.年、月、日的表示法

与汉语不同,英语中表示日期的顺序为:月—日—年(美式)或日—月—年(英式)。如:

2008 年 8 月 1 日写作:August 1st, 2008 或 1st August, 2006

"年"的表示

表示"年"用基数词,读时分成两部分,先读前面的两位数,再读后面的两位数。如:

1985 年读作:nineteen eighty-five

1992 年读作:nineteen ninety-two

1800 年读作:eighteen hundred

1905 年读作:nineteen and five

967 年读作:nine hundred sixty-seven

月、日的表示

"月"用英语中表示月份的名词,"日"用基数词或序数词表示都可以。如:

2 月 7 日写作:Feb. 7(th), 读作:February (the) seventh 或 February seven

10 月 1 日写作:October 1(st) 读作:October (the) first 或 October one

2.时刻的读法

6:00: six 或 six o'clock

9:30: half past nine 或 nine thirty

8:05: eight five 或 five past eight(分钟数在 30 分钟内:分钟数＋past＋钟点数,表示"几点过几分"。)

2:15: fifteen past two 或 a quarter past two

8:50: eight fifty 或 ten to nine(分钟数超过 30 分钟:(60 减去分钟数)＋to ＋下一个钟点数,表示"差几分几点"。)

1:45: a quarter to two 或 fifteen to two

3.编号问题

编号在英语中可用序数词或基数词表示。序数词位于名词之前,并加定冠词;基数词位于名词之后。书写时基数词可以用相应的阿拉伯数字表示。如:

the eleventh lesson ＝ lesson eleven 第十一课

the third part ＝ part three 第三部分

由于基数词简单,因此用基数词的情况较多。如:

Room 128

Page 110

Line 6

Bus No. 111

4. 货币的表示法

中国货币

中国货币单位是"元"(yuan)，一般没有复数形式，符号为¥。如：

15 元：15 yuan (RMB ￥＄15)

美国货币

美国货币的基本单位是"美元"(dollar)，复数是 dollars，符号为＄。如：

1 美元：1 dollar (US＄1)

20 美元：20 dollars (US＄20)

英国货币

英国货币的单位是"英镑"(pound)，复数是 pounds，符号为£。如：

1 英镑：1 pound (£1)

100 英镑：100 pounds (£100)

Language Tips for Writing

Here is something useful to express your good wishes or seasonal greetings with a postcard：

1. Good luck, good health and much happiness throughout the year.

恭祝新年好运、健康、快乐！

2. I do hope you have a most happy and prosperous New Year. 谨祝新年快乐幸福，大吉大利。

3. With the compliments of the season. 祝贺佳节。

4. May the season's joy fill you all the year round. 愿节日的愉快永远与你相伴。

5. Season's greetings and best wishes for Christmas. 祝福您，圣诞快乐。

6. Wishing happiness will always be with you in the coming New Year.

恭祝来年幸福和欢乐与你同在。

7. May the joy and happiness around you today and always. 愿快乐幸福永伴你左右。

8. Please accept my sincere wishes for the New Year. Hope you will continue to enjoy good health. 请接受我诚挚的新年祝福，顺祝身体健康。

9. Allow me to extend to you all my best wishes for your perfect health and lasting prosperity on the arrival of the New Year. 恭贺新年，祝身体健康，事业发达。

10. Please accept our best wishes for you and yours for a happy New Year.

请接受我们对你及你全家的美好祝福，祝你们新年快乐。

11. Season's greetings and sincere wishes for a bright and happy New Year!

致以节日的问候与祝福,愿你拥有一个充满生机和欢乐的新年。

12. Please accept my endless good wishes as a remembrance of our lasting friendship.

请接受我无尽的祝福,让它们成为我们永恒友谊的纪念。

13. Good luck and great success in the coming New Year. 祝来年好运,并取得更大的成就。

14. On the occasion of the New Year, may my wife and I extend to you and yours our warmest greetings, wishing you a happy New Year, successful career and happy family life.

在此新年之际,我同夫人向你及你的家人致以节日的问候,祝福全家新年快乐、事业有成、家庭幸福。

15. May everything beautiful and best be condensed into this card. I sincerely wish you happiness, joy and success.

愿一切最美好的祝福都能用这张贺卡表达,真心祝你幸福、快乐、成功!

Text B　How to Be a Young Adult

Reading Strategies (3): Skimming

　　Skimming(略读)是一种高效的、有选择性的、有针对性的快速浏览技巧,其目的在于了解文章的主旨大意或作者的写作意图。为了合理有效地运用这一策略,阅读者不需要逐字逐句地细读全文,而是有选择地跳过(skip over)一些不必要的细节,利用较短的时间粗略地阅读全文,以达到"事半功倍"的效果。

　　掌握略读这一技巧的关键就在于学会在阅读过程中区别文章的重要部分和非重要部分,全局部分和枝节部分。一些次要信息要大胆略去不读,迅速找出 topic sentence,即找出概括全段大意的句子。一般来说,快速阅读时我们只看文章的标题、下标题,文章的开头、结尾,以及每个部分或者段落的首句和尾句,并且关注文章中反复出现的关键词,反映段落中心思想的主题句,以便尽快地把握住全文的中心内容。

　　通过略读,我们经常回答以下问题:

1. 主旨类

1) What is the main idea (subject) of this passage?

2) What is this passage mainly (primarily) concerned with?

3) The main theme of this passage is _____.

4) The main point of the passage is _____.

5) Which of the following is the best title for the passage?

6) The title that best expresses the theme of the passage is _____.

7) On which of the following subject would the passage most likely be found in a textbook?

8) The purpose of the writer in writing this passage is _____.

9) Which of the following best describes the passage as a whole?

2. 态度类

1) What's the writer's attitude to...?

2) What's the tone of the passage?

3) The author's view is _____.

4) The writer's attitude in this passage is apparently _____.

5) The author suggests that _____.

6) According to the author, _____.

3. 推理类

1) The writer implies without directly stating that _____.

2) It can be inferred from the passage that _____.

3) The author strongly suggests that _____.

4) It can be concluded from the passage that _____.

5) The passage is intended to _____.

6) The writer indicates that _____.

以 Text B 为例,通过标题(How to Be a Young Adult)本身,读者可以迅速了解这篇文章的主旨。

又如练习册中阅读部分的第一篇文章,读者通过首句 In modern society there is a great deal of argument about competition. 可以预测本文的主要内容是关于人们对"竞争"的不同看法。第二篇文章的第一段的最后一句 How to make yourself safe while surfing? 则可知本文主要论及如何保证上网冲浪的安全性这一问题。

Word Study

1. approach

v. 接近,靠近

例:As you approach the village, the first building you see is the church.

接近那座乡村的时候,首先看到的就是教堂。

With winter approaching, many animals are storing food.

冬天临近了,许多动物也在开始储藏食物了。

n. 接近;方式

例:The fallen leaves suggest the approach of autumn. 地上的落叶意味着秋天的来临。

He decides to take different approaches to teach his son.

他决定采用不同的方式来教育儿子。

2. act

v. 采取行动(做某事),起作用;表演

例：There is no time left; we must act at once. 没有时间了,我们必须立刻行动。

He acts the part of Hamlet well. 他扮演哈姆雷特这个角色演得不错。

n. 行为,动作

例：We must judge a person by his action, not by what he says.

我们判断一个人, 要看他的所作所为, 而不是看他所说的话。

3. blame

n. 责怪,责备

例：It's no use trying to shift the blame onto other people. 推诿责任是无用的。

v. 把……归咎于

例：The driver was to blame for the traffic accident. 这起交通事故司机有责任。

blame sb. (for sth.) / blame sth. on sb. 责怪,指责,归咎于

be to blame (for sth.) /deserve to be blamed 对……应负责任,应受责备

4. admit　*v.*

1)承认,坦白某事物

例：You may not like her, but you have to admit that she's good at her job.

你也许不喜欢她,但你不得不承认她很擅长她的那份工作。

He admitted having stolen the watch. 他招认偷了那块表。

2)招收,容纳

例：Our college admits about 3,000 students every year.

我们学院每年招收大约 3 000 名新生。

The classroom admits only 250 people. 这间教室只能容纳250 人。

admittance 准许某人或某人获准进入(尤指私人场所);进入的权利

admission 承认,招认,坦白;进入或获准进入某建筑物,社团,学校等

5. grateful　*ad.* 感激的;感谢的

例：I am extremely grateful for the assistance your staff have provided.

对你的员工给我提供的帮助我感激不尽。

I would be most grateful if you could send me an invoice in due course.

如能如期收到发票,我们将不胜感激。

gratefully *ad.* 感激地;感谢地

6. complain　*v.* 抱怨,埋怨

例：He complained to the waiter that his meal was cold. 他向服务员抱怨说饭菜是凉的。

Employees complained bitterly about working conditions.

雇员对工作环境非常不满。

complaint *n.* 抱怨;埋怨;不满

7. duty　*n.*

1)责任,义务

例：It's not something I enjoy. I do it purely out of a sense of duty.

　那并不是我喜欢做的事，我纯粹是出于责任感才做。

2)（某人必须执行的）任务或行动

例：She goes on duty tonight at half past seven. 她今晚7点半开始值班。

3)关税

例：customs duties 关税

　　duty-bound 义不容辞

　　duty-free(指货物)免关税(的)

8. current

　ad. 当前的,现在的

　例：In its current state, the laptop is worth ￥5,000.

　　目前,这台手提电脑价值5千元人民币。

　　current affairs 时事

　n.（水、气等的）流，流动；电流

　例：The poor boy was swept away by the current. 那个可怜的小男孩被激流卷走了。

　　electrical current 电流

　currently *ad.* 当前；时下

9. accept　*v.*

　1)接受

　例：The university I applied to has accepted me. 我报了名的那所大学已经录取我了。

　2)同意,认可

　例：She has accepted your explanation as to why you didn't attend the meeting.

　　她已经认可你对没有参会的原因的解释了。

　acceptable *a.* 值得接受的；可容忍的

　acceptance *n.* 接受；认可；承兑,认付(票据)

10. responsible　*a.* 对……负责任, 承担……责任

　例：Undoubtedly, the airline is legally responsible for the safety of its passengers.

　　毫无疑问,航空公司对其乘客的安全负有法律责任。

　　Everyone is responsible for protecting environment. 保护环境人人有责。

　　be responsible to sb. 对(某人)负责

　　be responsible for sth. 对(某事)负责

　irresponsible *a.* 不负责的

　responsibility *n.* 责任,责任心

11. advice　*n.*

　1)忠告,建议

　例：On her doctor's advice Mr. Smith decided to take early retirement.

遵循医生的建议,史密斯先生决定早点退休。

2)(关于交易等方面的)通知

例:We received advice that the goods had been dispatched.

我们收到了关于货物已发出的通知。

act on/follow/take sb's advice 听从/遵从/接受某人的劝告

c. f. advise v. 劝告,建议;通知或告知某人

12. mature

　　a. 成熟的;(指想法、意图等)深思熟虑的

　　例:He's not mature enough to be given too much responsibility.

　　　　他还不成熟,不宜给他重任。

　　　　On mature reflection we have decided to decline their invitation.

　　　　经过反复思考,我们决定谢绝他们的邀请。

　　v. (使)成熟

　　例:Experience has matured him a great deal. 他经历这些事之后已经成熟多了。

　　maturity　*n.* 成熟;到期

Key to Exercises

Text A

Getting the Message

II. B

Vocabulary and Structure

I. 1—e　　　　2—a　　　　3—g　　　　4—f　　　　5—i

　　6—d　　　　7—c　　　　8—b　　　　9—j　　　　10—h

II. 1. referee　　　2. varies　　　3. decide　　　4. features　　　5. normal　　　6. worry about

III. 1. It is *likely* that young drivers have more accidents than older drivers.

　　2. It is *likely* that everybody will have a successful life career with vision, determination, self-respect, and hard work.

　　3. Her ex-husband had prevented her from seeing her children.

　　4. His leg injury may prevent him from playing in tomorrow's football game.

IV. 1. 然而,现实生活中的差异却很大。

　　2. 人的很多特性都是基因决定的,而人的身高只是其中之一。

　　3. 但基因并不决定一切。举例来说,不健康的饮食有碍你充分发育,成长到本来可能的高度。

V. 1. The film was so boring that I could hardly keep myself from falling asleep.

　　2. The basin was full to the brim with hot water.

　　3. The Smiths decided to go to Australia for their winter holidays.

　　4. My teacher thought it was abnormal for a girl to be interested in football.

　　5. Changing your eating habits is the best way to lose weight.

Speaking

II. 1. 1)F   2)A   3)B   4)C   5)E   6)D

2. *Sample conversation*：

Tom： Good evening, Prof. Smith, thank you for your correcting and suggestions. It is helpful to my term paper.

Smith： I'm happy that it is helpful to you.

Tom： Yes, it indeed took much of your time. I don't know how I shall express my gratitude to you.

Smith： It's my pleasure.

Tom： And I'm very grateful for all the help and encouragement you've given me.

Smith： I'm happy to be of any help. Don't hesitate to let me know any time you need me.

Tom： I will, Professor Smith. You are so kind.

Listening

1. C   2. B   3. A   4. C   5. B   6. C   7. A   8. B

Grammar

I. 1. thousands of   2. smaller and smaller   3. twos and threes   4. is

5. Three-fourths   6. early thirties   7. a fourth time   8. three kilometers'

9. Page Two   10. the twentieth

II. 1. B   2. A   3. C   4. B   5. D

6. A   7. A   8. A   9. C   10. B

Writing

I. *Sample*

Dear Anita,

I'm leaving for Chengdu tonight, and I am busy packing my luggage now. I'm afraid I have no time to say goodbye to you. Anyhow, thank you very much for everything you have done for me. I'll never forget my pleasant stay in Rockdale with you and the merry Christmas we spent together.

Most appreciatively,

Lily

II. *Sample*

Dear Jenny,

I am in Sydney now. The weather is fine, and we can enjoy the warm sunshine. Yesterday I went to Manly Beach with my friend, appreciating the beautiful scenery of the beach.

My host mom, Marika, is a very kind person, so my stay here is very pleasant. Don't worry about me.

Today, I am going to visit my sister and go shopping with her. By the way, I will bring you a gift.

See you soon and have a happy life.

Yours,

Joyce

Text B

1. F   2. T   3. F   4. T   5. T

Translation of the Texts

Text A

我是正常的吗？

自从你上次生日以来，很多事情已发生了变化。举个例，你比去年更聪明了，这是显而易见的。但可能还有一些其他的变化。或许你已经比班上其他同学高出几英寸了，当然也许是每个同学都长高了，只有你觉得自己还是很矮。现在，当你看着镜子里的自己，只有一件事萦绕心头：我正常吗？

人皆有异

首先，什么是正常呢？这没有一个统一的标准。否则，世界上就会充满了不正常的人了！下一次你去商场的时候，环顾一下四周。你会看到有的人个高，有的人个矮，有的人肩宽，有的人脚小，有的人大腹便便，有的人手指细长，有的人小腿敦实，有的人手臂瘦削……这下你懂了吧。

高与矮

人的很多特性都是基因决定的，而身高只是其中之一。事实上，因为你有父母双亲，你的基因就像一个裁判员，通常会让你的身高处于父母的身高之间。如果你的父母个子都很高，那么你同样也很有可能是个高个子。

但基因并不决定一切。举例来说，不健康的饮食会阻碍你充分发育成长，而充足的睡眠和足够的运动及营养将帮助你正常的发育成长。

称体重

每个孩子的体重也会有很大的不同。孩子们的体重和他们的朋友相比往往或多或少有些差异，而且这仍然可被视为正常。电视和杂志可能使我们相信我们的身材和体重应该合乎特定的标准，但在现实生活中却有很大的差异。

一些孩子太在意自己的体重，因而尝试不健康的和危险的方式去改变它。其实拥有健康的体重最好的办法是合理的饮食和大量的锻炼。

Text B

如何成长为一个年青人

现在你的少年时代即将结束，你很快将满二十了。既然你现在已正式成为成年人了，以下就教你如何开始做一个年青的成年人。

1. 如果你把事情搞砸了，不要撒谎或者推诿责任。承认你的错误，表示歉意并征求他人的意见，看看你可以做点什么事情来挽回局面或者弥补过失。

2. 找个工作，努力寻找直到找到为止。要有计划，不要再让你的父母无限期地供养你。

3. 当你找到一份工作，应该心存感激，努力工作，遵守公司制度。不要抱怨你的工作职责，待遇或薪水。

4. 收看大电台的新闻，了解一些政治和时事。

5. 阅读当地的报纸，当然不仅仅是体育或生活类版面。

6. 接受这样一个事实，就是大部分成年人实际上很可能清楚他们在谈论的内容，而且你甚至可以从那些糊里糊涂的人那里学到一些东西。

7. 与有责任感的、年纪比你大的人交朋友。向他们征求意见，并听取他们给你的建议。

8. 想一想五年之后你想拥有怎样的人生。对于如何达成你的梦想，要制订一个计划。

9. 避免饮酒。如果别人看到你喝醉了，大部分人会想到的第一个形容词绝不是"成熟"。

10. 把你的部分薪水存入银行。当你想要买房买车的时候会用得着的。

11. 按时偿还债务，这样会让你几年后的大型采购更容易获得批准。

12. 既然知道你无法控制其他人，那么对于别人对你的看法就不要太在意。

13. 尊重你的父母。当你需要帮助的时候，他们是最有可能伸手援助的。

Scripts for Listening

Conversation 1　M：Would you like a cup of coffee?

W：No thanks. I'd like a cup of tea, please.

Question：What does the woman prefer?

Conversation 2　M：I really can't thank you enough for the invitation。

W：It's my pleasure.

Question：According to the conversation, which of the following is true?

Conversation 3　M：Why don't you have a seat for a moment?

W：Oh, yes. Thanks.

Question：What will the woman do?

Conversation 4　W：You can go back to work, but you need to take some medicine to bring your fever down.

M：Thank you.

Question：Where does the conversation most likely take place?

Conversation 5　M：Your English is really fluent. Are you from America?

W：Thank you, sir, but I am from Canada.

Question：Where is the woman from?

Conversation 6　W：Tom, how is your study?

M：Thanks to your help, I really made some progress in English.

Question：Why does Tom thank the woman?

Conversation 7　M：Tomorrow is Mother's Day. What will you do?

W：I want to send Mom some flowers to express my gratitude.

Question：What will the woman do?

Conversation 8　W：I'm truly grateful for your help, sir.

M：Don't mention it.

Question：Which of the following is right?

Unit Four Ways to Success

Text A The Way to Success

Background Knowledge of the Text

No doubt, everyone wishes to be successful in life. All great man achieved success through four key factors. A famous English saying goes: "Genius is nothing but diligence!" Now we can say: "Success is nothing but confidence, diligence, devotion and perseverance."

"Self confidence is the first point of success." It is from Thomas Edison, the most famous inventor in the world. One without confidence, especially self-confidence can never be successful.

Without self-confidence, one is afraid to show their own ideas and can not make themselves understood. So others can never accept them and they can never have any chance to get a stage to show themselves. Throughout history, all the famous persons around the world are self-confident, for example Chairman Mao, who founded new China; Hua Luogeng, who made a large contribution to the Math Study in China; Thomas Edision, whose inventions have made great changes in our daily life. They all show their own bright points to the people, to the world and to the history.

The key factor to success is diligence, which simply means no waste of time. Diligence can help us to remove ignorance and overcome difficulties. Diligence can make a fool wise, and a poor man rich. If we idle away our time now, our future life will be a failure. Devotion, which means the concentration of our mind and effect in doing things, is another key factor to success. Whatever job we are doing, we must love it and do it whole-heartedly. Only when we set our mind on the job can we do it well. Furthermore, perseverance, or a strong will, is also necessary in order to make success a certainty. Without a strong will, we are likely to give up when we are confronted with some difficulties.

Warming-up Questions

1. In order to be successful, you should have such factors as diligence, confidence, optimism, cooperation with others and so on. In your opinion, what is the first and foremost element for

success? Why?

2. Hard work is very important and is the surest way to success for most people. Do you think so? Does luck often play an important role in success? Which is more important, luck or hard work?

Sentence Analysis

1. There are surely many factors related to this matter, among which are diligence, confidence, optimism, cooperation with others and so forth.

此句中 related to this matter 是过去分词短语作定语修饰名词 factors，同时用介词 among + which 引导一个非限制性定语从句来补充说明先行词 factors。

现在分词表示动作正在进行或表示主动；过去分词表示的动作已经完成，及物动词过去分词具有被动含义。例如：

the developing country 发展中国家

the developed country 发达国家

the rising sun 冉冉升起的太阳

the risen sun 升起的太阳

the driving gears 主动齿轮

the driven gears 被动齿轮

the exploiting class 剥削阶级

the exploited class 被剥削阶级

过去分词短语作定语时要放在被修饰词之后。例如：

We suddenly met a woman dressed in white.

非限制性定语从句和主句之间用逗号隔开，对主句的先行词起作进一步解释或附加说明的作用，如果把它省去，主句仍能表达明确、完整的意思；有时关系代词 which 还可以代表前面的整个句子。例如：

An investigation was made into the accident, in which five people were killed.

They have made another wonderful discovery, which is of great importance to science.

Tom didn't go to the show, which is a pity.

I said nothing, which made him angry.

2. On the contrary, a man who keeps talking big but never puts his plan into action would eventually amount to nothing, however ambitious he should be.

talk big 夸夸其谈

put one's plan into action 把计划付诸行动

amount to 达到，成为；共计；等于

who / which / when / where / what / how 等疑问词 + ever = no matter + who /

which / when / where / what / how 等疑问词，表强调，"无论……"，可引导让步状语从句。例如：

However hard I tried, I could not memorize the whole text. = No matter how hard I tried, I could not memorize the whole text.

However brilliant you may be, you can't know everything. = No matter how brilliant you may be, you can't know everything.

I don't care whoever comes. = No matter who comes, I don't care.

You have to hold on, whatever difficulties you meet. = No matter what difficulties you meet, you have to hold on.

3. Confidence, to some extent, is also of great importance contributing to a brilliant career.

be + of + *n.* = be + *adj.*

The meeting is of great importance. = The meeting is very important.

此句中 contributing to a brilliant career 是现在分词短语作定语。例如：

He is a promising young man.

The room facing south is our classroom.

Who is the man standing by the door?

4. An optimist is inclined to stand up against such misfortune and draw useful lessons from them to avoid more serious ones.

stand up against = stand up to 勇敢地面对；经得起

另外有：

stand up for 支持，维护

stand by 袖手旁观；站在……一边；遵守；做好准备

stand for 代表，象征

stand out 突出，显眼

stand up（使）站起；耐用；站得住脚

5. Hardly anytime can you imagine a purposeful man without any aid from others could fulfill his task perfectly; especially in modern society where projects become more complex than ever, people need to work together effectively.

此句中半否定词 Hardly 放在句首，句子中的 can you imagine 为部分倒装。当 never, no, not, few, little, seldom, hardly, barely, scarcely 等否定词、半否定词以及否定意义的词组 at no time, in no case, by no means, in no circumstances 等位于句首时，句子要采用倒装语序，将句子中谓语的一部分（如助动词、be 动词或情态动词）置于主语之前。若无助动词时则需根据情况在主语前加上 do, does 或 did。

Never have I been to New York. = I have never been to New York.

Hardly have I heard of such a silly thing.

Not until yesterday did he realize the importance of learning English.

At no time will China be a superpower.

No sooner had we reached the station **than** the train left. = **Hardly / Scarcely** had we reached the station **when** the train left.

Word Study

1. success   *n.* 成功,胜利;成功的人或物

例:Confidence is the key to success. 信心是成功的关键。

The play was a great success. 那出戏大获成功。

succeed *v.* 成功,取得成功;做到

例:His plan succeeded. 他的计划成功了。

I succeeded in getting the job. 我谋到了那份工作。

successful *a.* 成功的,有成就的

2. complicated   *a.* 复杂的,难懂的

例:The puzzle is too complicated for the children. (complicated = difficult)

这个谜语对小孩子来说太难。

I can't understand the complicated instructions. 我无法理解这些复杂的说明。

complicate *v.* 变复杂,使复杂化

例:The problem complicated beyond reason. 问题复杂到了荒唐的程度。

There is no need to complicate matters. 没必要使事情复杂化。

complication *n.* 复杂化,混乱,纠纷

例:a legal complication 法律纠纷

3. related   *a.* 有关的,相关的

例:Income tax rates are related to one's annual income. 所得税税率与个人年收入相关。

relative *a.* 相对的

relation *n.* 关系,联系

例:I can find no relation between crime and poverty.

我找不到犯罪与贫穷之间有什么联系。

4. confidence   *n.* 自信,信心;信任

例:You should build confidence in yourself. 你应该树立自信心。

We have perfect confidence in your ability to do the job.

我们完全相信你有能力做这份工作。

break one's confidence 辜负某人的信任

confident *a.* 有信心的,确信的

例:be confident of / about 对……有信心,对……有把握

She is confident of the future. 她对未来充满信心。

I feel confident that you will succeed. 我确信你能成功。

5. optimism *n.* 乐观;乐观主义

例:We look to the future with optimism. 我们乐观地展望未来。

optimistic *a.* 乐观的,乐观主义的

be optimistic about 对……抱乐观态度

6. cooperation *n.* 合作,协作;配合

例:The bridge was repaired by the two states acting in fruitful cooperation.

在两州富有成果的合作之下,大桥修建竣工。

The government sought the cooperation of the citizens in keeping the street clean.

政府寻求市民配合,以保持街道整洁。

cooperative *a.* 合作的,协作的

例:cooperative efforts 协同努力

7. accumulate *v.* 积累,增加;堆积

例:While growing up, you accumulate wisdom. 成长中积累智慧。

Dust soon accumulates in rooms that are not cleaned. 房间不打扫很快就会积满灰尘。

accumulation *n.* 积累,增加;堆积

8. eventually *ad.* 最后,终于

例:He eventually retired from business. 他终于退休了。

She eventually realized that she was wrong. 她终于意识到自己错了。

eventual *a.* 最后的,最终的

例:His mistakes led to his eventual dismissal. 他的错误导致他最终被解雇。

eventual success 最后的胜利

9. ambitious *a.* 有雄心的,有壮志的

例:I have an ambitious goal. 我有一个雄心勃勃的目标。

She is politically ambitious. 她有政治野心。

be ambitious for / after 渴望……

ambition *n.* 雄心,志向;野心

例:He was filled with ambition to become famous. 他一心想成名。

10. contribute *v.* 有助于,促成;贡献,捐献

例:Confidence contributes to a brilliant career. 自信有助于事业的非凡成功。

He contributed $ 10 to the charity every payday.

他每逢发薪日都捐10美元给慈善事业。

contribute food and clothing for the refugees 捐助食物和衣服给难民

contribution *n.* 贡献,捐献

例:make a contribution to public safety 为公众安全作出贡献

11. slip *v.* 溜走;滑动

例:Another month has slipped away. 不知不觉中又一个月过去了。

The thief slipped out of the apartment without a sound. 小偷毫无声响地溜出了公寓。

You let the chance of a lifetime slip by. 你错过了一生难逢的好机会。

He slipped down in the street. 他在街上滑了一跤。

12. hesitate　*v.* 迟疑,犹豫不决

例:I didn't hesitate to say it out. 我毫不犹豫地讲了出来。

She hesitated about whether to accept the invitation. 她对是否接受邀请拿不定主意。

hesitation *n.* 迟疑,犹豫不决

例:She agreed without hesitation. 她毫不犹豫地答应了。

He had no hesitation in deciding to go abroad. 他毅然决定出国。

13. tend　*v.* 倾向;朝某方向

例:Interest rates are tending upwards. 利率有提高的趋势。

tend to 倾向于,往往;有助于

例:Nowadays the young tend to selfishness. 现在的年轻人往往很自私。

These measures tend to improve the working conditions.

这些措施有助于改善工作条件。

tendency *n.* 倾向;趋势

14. essential　*a.* 必要的,不可缺少的;本质的

例:Clothing, food and housing are essential to us.

衣、食、住、行对我们来说是必不可少的。

Discipline is essential in the army. 军队必须有纪律。

There is an essential difference. 有本质上的差别。

15. misfortune　*n.* 不幸,厄运;灾难

例:Misfortunes seldom come alone. 祸不单行。

He is always ready to help people in misfortune. 他总是愿意帮助那些不幸的人。

He had the misfortune to break his right leg last week. 上周他不幸折断了右腿。

16. access　*n.* 接近,进入

例:He is a man difficult of access. 他是一个难接近的人。

The place is within easy access. 这地方很近。

The only access to the building is along that muddy track.

只有沿着那条泥泞小道才能到达那幢楼。

accessible *a.* 易接近的

17. purposeful　*a.* 坚定的,有毅力的

例:We must have a purposeful idea. 我们必须有坚定的信念。

purposeless *a.* 漫无目的,无意义的

18. fulfill　*v.* 完成,实现;满足

例:Everyone should fufill their responsibility to finish the task.

每个人都应该尽职尽责完成这项任务。

I can not fulill your needs. 我无法满足你的需求。

19. furthermore   *ad.* 而且,此外

  例:The house is too small, and furthermore, it's too far from the city.

     这房子太小,而且离市区太远。

20. aspect   *n.* 方面;方向,方位

  例:We must consider a problem in all its aspects. 我们必须全面地考虑问题。

Phrases and Expressions

1. in one's opinion 依照某人的看法

  例:In my opinion, he was driving the car too fast. 照我看来,他车开得太快了。

     In his doctor's opinion, he should be well enough to travel by next week.

     根据医生的看法,下星期他应该可以康复并出行了。

2. on the contrary 正好相反

  例:A: Have you nearly finished? 你快完成了吧?

     B: On the contrary, I have only just begun. 正好相反,我才刚刚开始。

     We had thought she would go with us. On the contrary, she set out alone.

     我们本以为她会和我们一起走,与之相反,她却独自出去了。

3. to some extent 某种程度上说

  例:To some extent, he has done you a favor. 某种程度上说他已经帮忙了。

     To what extent would you believe it? 你对那件事相信多少?

4. in general 一般来说,大体上

  例:I like fish in general, and salmon in particular. 总的来说我喜欢吃鱼,尤其是鲑鱼。

     In general / Generally speaking, the coldest weather comes in January.

     一般来说,最冷的天气在一月份。

5. in any case 无论如何,不管怎样

  例:In any case, you must finish the task today. 无论如何你今天必须完成任务。

     It may rain tomorrow, but we are going home in any case.

     明天可能下雨,但不管怎样我们打算回家。

in case 假使;以防万一

  例:In case he comes, let me know. 如果他来的话,告诉我一声。

     Keep the windows closed in case it (should) rain. 把窗户关上以防下雨。

in case of 假使,如果

  例:In case of fire, ring the alarm bell. 如果发生火灾,请按警铃。

in this /that case 既然这样/那样

例：In this case, you may go now. 既然这样，你现在可以走了。

in no case 决不，无论如何都不

例：In no case will China be the first to use nuclear weapons. 中国决不首先使用核武器。

6. be likely to 很有可能

例：It is likely to rain. 看来要下雨了。

He is likely to be promoted. 他可能晋升。

be unlikely to 不太可能

例：He is unlikely to win. 他未必会赢。

7. put forward 提出

例：The government put forward a new policy. 政府提出了一项新政策。

He put forward a plan for the committee to consider. 他提出一项计划让全体委员审议。

put aside 储存，留出	put away 把……收起，放好
put off 推迟	put on 穿上；上演
put out 扑灭，消灭	put up 提出，修建，建立
put up with 容忍，忍受	

Differentiations and Analysis of Words and Expressions

1. favor，favorite，favorable

favor 是名词，意为"恩惠；偏爱"，如：do sb. a favor = do a favor for sb. "帮某人忙"。

例：A mother shouldn't show too much favor to one of her children.

作为母亲不应该对某个孩子过于偏爱。

favorite 作名词时意为"最喜爱的人或物；亲信"。

例：That song is a great favorite of mine. 那首歌是我最喜爱的。

The king had his favorites at court. 国王在宫廷中有自己的亲信。

favorite 作为形容词时意为"特别喜欢的；最喜爱的"。

例：What is your favorite flower? 你最喜欢什么花？

Do you have any favorite hobbies? 你有特别的爱好吗？

favorable 是形容词，意为"合适的；赞成的"，如：make a favorable impression on sb. 给某人留下一个好印象；a favorable comment 好评。

例：This is a favorable time for a trip. 这是旅行的好时光。

The situation will develop in a direction favorable to the people.

形势将朝着有利于人民的方向发展。

2. consider，consideration，considerable，considerate

consider 是动词，意为"考虑；认为"。

例：consider one's suggestion 考虑某人的建议

He is considered to be an authority. 他被认为是权威。

consideration 是名词,意为"因素;考虑;体贴"。

例:Economic considerations forced her to leave college. 经济上的原因迫使她离开大学。

Cost is a major consideration in buying anything.

买任何东西时价钱都是要考虑的主要因素。

Consideration of others is the basis of good manners. 关心体贴别人是文明礼貌的根本。

considerable 是形容词,意为"值得考虑的,重大的,相当的"。

例:This is the considerable reason. 这是值得考虑的原因。

He is a considerable man in the scientific world. 他是科学界的名人。

To love him needs considerable courage. 爱上他需要相当大的勇气。

considerate 是形容词,意为"体贴的,关心的,体谅的"。

例:She has a considerate husband. 她丈夫很体贴人。

We should be considerate to elderly people. 我们应该关心上了年纪的人。

She is always considerate of others' feelings. 她总是体谅他人的感受。

3. imagine, imagination, imaginable, imaginary, imaginative

imagine 是动词,意为"想象;认为"。

例:Can you imagine these fat men climbing the mountain?

你能想象这些胖子攀登这座高山的情景吗?

I imagine he will come on time. 我认为他会准时来。

imagination 是名词,意为"想象,想象力"。

例:He is an artist of rich imagination. 他是一个富有想象力的艺术家。

imaginable 是形容词,意为"可想象得到的"。

例:This is the only solution imaginable. 这是唯一可想到的解决办法。

The doctors saved the patient by every means imaginable.

医生用一切可能的办法救病人。

imaginary 是形容词,意为"想象中的;虚构的,幻想的"。

例:This is an imaginary figure. 这是虚构的人物。

imaginative = imaginary 表示"想象中的;虚构的,幻想的"。

He told us an imaginative / imaginary tale. 他给我们讲了一个虚构的故事。

imaginative 还有另外一个意思:"爱幻想的,富有想象力的"。

例:He is an imaginative child. 他是一个爱幻想的小孩子。

Can you give us an imaginative answer? 你能给出一个富有想象力的答案吗?

4. effect, effective, effectively, efficient, efficiency

effect 作为名词时,表示"结果,效果;作用,影响"。

例:His protest had no effect. 他的抗议无济于事。

The medicine has much effect on me. 这种药对我很有效果。

effective 是形容词,意为"有效的,有效果的"。

例:We must take the effective measures to protect our environment.

我们必须采取有效措施保护环境。

How long is the effective date? 有效期多久?

effectively 是副词(由 effective + -ly 构成),表示"有效地"。

例:The kind of glasses can protect your eyes effectively. 这种眼镜能有效地保护你的眼睛。

efficient 是形容词,意为"效率高的,有能力的"。

例:The public need an efficient government. 公众需要工作效率高的政府。

She is an efficient secretary. 她是一个有能力的秘书。

efficiency 是名词,意为"效率"。

例:We must try our best to increase the efficiency. 我们必须尽最大努力提高效率。

Word Building

在本课中出现较多的前缀、后缀有:

1. 否定前缀:dis-, im-, il-:

否定前缀 dis-, im-, il-通常表示否定或相反的意义。例如:

cover→discover   agree →disagree

balance →imbalance   possible →impossible

legal →illegal   logical→ illogical

2. 名词后缀:a. + ness

名词后缀-ness 加在形容词后形成抽象名词,表示"性质"、"状态"、"精神"、"程度"等。例如:

happy →happiness   carful →carefulness

dark →darkness   kind →kindness

rude →rudeness   bitter →bitterness

3. 名词后缀:v. + ment

名词后缀-ment 加在动词后表示"行为"、"状态"、"过程"、"手段"、"结果"等。例如:

move →movement   retire →retirement

judge →judgement   develop →development

achieve →achievement   agree →agreement

4. 形容词后缀:n. + ful

形容词后缀-ful 加在名词后表示"充满的……"、"有……的"。例如:

success →successful   pain → painful

purpose →purposeful   power →powerful

peace → peaceful   hope → hopeful

Grammar Focus

一、冠词的用法

冠词(Article)是最典型的限定词,不能单独使用,也没有词义,它用在名词的前面,帮助指明名词的含义。冠词分为定冠词(the Definite Article)和不定冠词(the Indefinite Article)。定冠词 the 与指示代词 this, that 同义,有"这/那个"的意思,但较弱,可以和名词连用,表示某个或某些特定的人或东西;不定冠词 a(an)与数词 one 同义,表"一个"的意思。

1. 不定冠词的用法

a 用于辅音音素前,一般读作 /ə/,而 an 则用于元音音素前,一般读做 /ən/。例如;an honest boy, an umbrella , a useful book 等等。

1)表示"一个",意为 one 或 a certain,指某人或某物。例如: There's a pen on the desk. 桌子上有一支钢笔。

2)除表示"一个"这一数量外,很多情况下 a 与可数名词一起表示一类事物或者泛指概念。代表一类人或物。例如:

We can't say a boy is cleverer than a girl. 我们不能说男孩比女孩聪明。

不定冠词在表示"一"的概念时,是非强调性的,如果强调"一"这一数量,常常用 one。例如:

We have only one day left to finish the task. 我们只剩下一天时间来完成这个任务。

3)不定冠词用在表示数量、时间等名词前,表示"每一(单位)……的价格、速度、顺序等"。例如:

Tom drives at 60 miles an hour. 汤姆以每小时 60 英里的速度开车。

I go back home once a month. 我每月回家一次。

4)不定冠词用于单数可数名词前,表示不确定性,泛指人的职业、国籍、宗教等。例如:

He was a teacher in the past. But he is a businessman now.

过去他是教师,但现在他是生意人。

5)不定冠词用在人名或表示人的名词前,表示不确定性,即说话人不清楚或没有指明所提到的人到底是谁。例如:

A Tom Smith is waiting for you downstairs. 一个叫汤姆·史密斯的人正在楼下等你。

6)不定冠词用于 be of a(an)noun 结构中,表示"相同……的"。例如:

Tom and his sister are of a height. 汤姆和他的妹妹身高相同。

These sweaters are of a size. 这些毛衣大小相同。

7)不定冠词用于固定结构 quite / half / rather / many / what / such a(an)+ n. 或 so / too / how adjective + a(an) + n. 中,表示程度、数量或感叹等。例如:

It takes half an hour to get there. 到那里需要半小时。

He's quite a famous artist. 他是个很有名的艺术家。

Many a man would welcome such an opportunity. 许多人会很高兴有这样一个机会。

8）不定冠词用于某些词组、习惯用语或谚语中。例如：a little / a few / a lot / a type of / a great many / many a / as a rule / in a hurry / in a minute / in a word / in a short while / after a while / have a cold / have a try / have a good time/ take a walk / keep an eye on / all of a sudden 等。

2. 定冠词的用法

1）特指双方都明白的人或物。例如：

Take the medicine. 把药吃了。

2）上文提到过的人或事。例如：

He saw a man standing there. The man was the person that he was looking for.

他看到一个人站在那里。那个人就是他正找的人。

3）指世上独一物二的人或事物。例如：the sun 太阳, the earth 地球, the moon 月球, the world 世界, the sky 天空, the universe 宇宙

4）与单数名词连用表示一类事物, 例如：the dollar 美元; the fox 狐狸

The compass was invented in China. 指南针是中国发明的。

The wolf hunts by night. 狼夜间出来觅食。

5）用在序数词、形容词和副词的最高级, 及形容词 only, very, same 等前面。例如：

Where do you live? 你住在哪?

I live on the second floor. 我住在二层。

Is this the best choice he can make? 这是他能做出的最好的选择吗?

That's the very thing I've been looking for. 那正是我要找的东西。

6）用在形容词或分词前, 表示一类人或事物。例如：the rich 富人; the poor 穷人; the blind 盲人; the aged 老人; the living 生者

7）与复数名词连用, 指整个群体。例如：

They are the students of this school. (指全体学生)

They are students of this school. (指部分学生)

8）表示所有, 相当于物主代词, 用在表示身体部位的名词前。例如：

She caught me by the arm. 她抓住了我的手臂。

9）某些地理名词, 如江河、海洋、海峡、海湾、山脉、群岛、沙漠等之前要用定冠词。例如：the Yangtze 长江, the Thames 泰晤士河, the South Sea 南海, the Pacific 太平洋, the English Channel 英吉利海峡, the Persian Gulf 波斯湾, the Himalayas 喜玛拉雅山脉, the Philippines 菲律宾群岛, the Sahara Desert 撒哈拉沙漠

由普通名词和其他一些词构成的专有名词, 如国名、组织机构、建筑物、报纸、会议、条约等的名称前, 要用定冠词。例如：

the People's Republic of China 中华人民共和国

the United Nations 联合国

the Great Hall of the People 人民大会堂

the People's Daily 人民日报

10) 用在表示乐器的名词之前。例如:

She plays the piano. 她会弹钢琴。

11) 用在复数专有名词前,表示一家人或一对夫妇也可表示整个民族等。例如:

The Smiths moved to California. 史密斯夫妇/史密斯一家搬到了加利福尼亚洲。

The Americans are a nation on wheels. 美国人是一个车轮上的民族。

12) 用在惯用语中。例如:in the day, in the morning (afternoon, evening), the day after tomorrow, the next morning, in the sky (water, field, country), in the dark, in the rain, in the distance, in the middle (of), in the end, on the whole, by the way, go to the theatre 等。

3. 以下情况通常不用任何冠词:

1) 一般来说,国名、人名、街名、广场名、公园名、大学名、杂志等专有名词前不加定冠词。例如:England, Mary, Tian An Men Square, Hyde Park, National Day.

2) 泛指的复数名词,表示一类人或事物时,可不用定冠词。例如:

They are teachers. 他们是教师。

3) 抽象名词表示一般概念时,通常不加冠词。例如:

Failure is the mother of success. 失败乃成功之母。

4) 物质名词表示一般概念时,通常不加冠词,当表示特定的意思时,需要加定冠词。例如:

Man cannot live without water. 人离开水就无法生存。

5) 在季节、月份、节日、假日、日期、星期等表示时间的名词之前,不加冠词。例如:

We go to school from Monday to Friday. 我们从星期一到星期五都上课。

6) 在称呼或表示官衔,职位的名词前不加冠词。例如:

The guards took the American to General Lee. 士兵们把这个美国人送到李将军那里。

7) 在三餐、球类运动和娱乐运动的名称前,不加冠词。例如:have breakfast/ lunch/ supper; play football/ basketball / chess

8) 当两个或两个以上名词并用时,常省去冠词。例如:

I can't write without pen or pencil. 没有钢笔和铅笔,我就写不了字。

9) 当 by 与交通工具、通讯工具连用,表示一种方式时,不加冠词。例如:by bus, by train, by plane, by post 等。

10) 有些个体名词不用冠词。例如:school, college, prison, market, hospital, bed, table, class, town, church, court 等个体名词,不加冠词表示该名词的抽象含义;加冠词则表示具体地方或场所。如:

go to hospital 去医院看病

go to the hospital 去医院 (并不是去看病,而是有其他目的)

11) 固定词组中不用冠词。例如:at night, at home, at first, at last, at present, in fact, by chance, out of work 等。

4. 抽象名词和物质名词前有无冠词的区别

1) 当抽象名词和物质名词表示一般概念时,不用冠词(即使前面有修饰性词)。例如:

Knowledge begins with practice. 认识从实践开始。

Fresh air is very necessary for a patient. 新鲜空气对于病人是非常必要的。

2) 当抽象名词和物质名词表示某一特定概念时,特别是当它们有一限制性定语时,前面要加定冠词。例如:

What do you think of the music? 你觉得这音乐怎么样?

The air in the room is so bad that no one can stand it for 5 minutes.
房间里的空气很糟,以致于没有人能忍受五分钟。

3) 当抽象名词和物质名词表示"一种"、"一场"、"一次"、"一阵"或"一份"等意义时,要在前面加上不定冠词 a 或 an。例如:

Would you please give us an explanation? 你能不能给我们解释一下呢?

What a heavy rain! 多大的(一场)雨啊!

It's a wonderful coffee. 这是一种很好的咖啡。

4) 如果抽象名词被用以表示具有某一品质或带来某一情绪的具体事件、人物或东西,则其前面要用不定冠词。例如:

He did me a great favour. 他给我帮了一个大忙。

The English evening was really a great success. 这次英语晚会很成功。

She is a disappointment to us. 她令我们很失望。

二、限定词的用法

限定词是指用于修饰和限制名词的一类词,它们表明所修饰的名词的所属关系、数量关系、类别关系等。限定词的选择决定于随后的名词的类别,是单数名词、复数名词,还是不可数名词。

1. 常用的几类限定词

1) 有些限定词如 the, some, any, no, other, whose 以及 my, your 等物主限定词和名词属格(John's, my friend's)等能与可数名词单数、可数名词复数以及不可数名词等三类名词搭配。例如:the book, the books, some books, any money。

2) 有些限定词如 a/an, one, another, each, every, either, neither 等只能与单数名词搭配。例如:an apple, another book, such a book, every student, neither sentence。

3) 有些限定词如 both, two, three, many, (a) few, several, these, those, a (great) number of 等只能与复数名词搭配。例如:both workers, several students, many students, (a) few words, these / those books。

4) 有些限定词如 a bit of, a great amount of, a great deal of, (a) little, much 等只能与不可数名词搭配。例如:a bit of water, a great amount of labour, a great deal of work, (a)

little space, much noise。

5）有些限定词如 a lot of, lots of, enough, more, most, such, other 等可与复数名词和不可数名词搭配。例如：a lot of books, a lot of money, lots of chickens, lots of food, plenty of chairs, plenty of water, enough copies, enough coal, more articles, more time, most people, most work, such men, such bread, other men, other bread。

2. 限定词的顺序

在名词词组中心词之前如果有两个或两个以上限定词出现时，就会产生限定词的先后顺序问题。按其不同的搭配位置，限定词可分为：

1）中位、前位、后位限定词

限定词可分为中位限定词（central determiner）、前位限定词（predeterminer）和后位限定词（postdeterminer）。

中位限定词包括 a(n), the, zero; this, that, these, those; my, you; Mary's, my friend's; some, any, no, every, each, either, neither, enough; what(ever), which(ever), whose 等。

前位限定词包括 all, both, half; double, twice, three times; one-third, two-fifths; what, such, (a / an)等。

后位限定词包括 one, two, three; first, second, third; next, last, other, another; many, much, (a) few, (a) little, fewer, (the) fewest, less, (the) least, more, most; several, plenty of, a lot of, lots of, a great / large / good number of, a great / good deal of, a large / small amount of; such 等。

2）三类限定词的搭配关系

如果一个名词词组带有上述三类限定词，其搭配关系总是按照"前位——中位——后位"的顺序排列。例如：all the five teachers, all these last few days, those last few months。

中位限定词之间和前位限定词之间是互相排斥的，即一个名词中心词之前不可并用两个中位限定词或两个前位限定词。所以，"我的那本书"不是 my that book 而是 that book of mine，因为 my 和 that 同是中位限定词，不可同时并列。但后位限定词的使用却不受此限。例如：several hundred guests, the first two chapters, two more sheets, the next few weeks。

3. 限定词用法比较

1）many, much, a lot of, lots of, plenty of

以上单词都表示"多"的意思，但是 many, much 常用于否定句和疑问句，而 a lot of 等则常用于肯定句。例如：

I haven't seen many English films. 多数英文电影我没看过。（many 修饰可数名词）

Have you seen many English films? 多数的英文电影你都看过吗？（many 修饰可数名词）

I haven't done much work today. 我还没有做多少活呢。(much 修饰不可数名词)

Have you done much work today? 今天你已经做了很多活吗？(much 修饰不可数名词)

I have seen a lot of / lots of / plenty of / a great number of English films. 我已经看了多部英文电影。(number 修饰可数名词)

I have done a lot of / lots of / plenty of / a great amount of work today. 今天我已经做了很多活。(amount 修饰不可数名词)

many / much 既可作限定词,也可作不定代词(indefinite pronoun),a lot 也可单独用作名词词组。例如：

A：Have you done all these exercises? 所有练习题你都完成了吗？

B：No, I haven't done very many. 不,我完成得不多。

A：Have you done much work today? 今天你做了许多工作吗？

B：Yes, I've done a lot.

同样地,a good / great many 也可用于肯定句。例如：

I have read a great many English novels. 我已读过大量的英语小说。

2)(a) few, (a)little

表示"少"的意思,可用(a) few,(a) little,既可用作限定词,也可用作不定代词。a few,a little 表示"少量",带有肯定意义。例如：

Let's invite a few friends to come with us. 让我们来邀请几个朋友来和我们在一起。

Here are a few more books on this subject. 还有一些有关这个课题的书。

There are only a very few left. 只剩下一点点。

I had a little difficulty in solving the problem. 要解决这个问题,我遇到了一点困难。

Give me a little of that wine. 给我一点那种酒。

I'm trying to use the little French I have just learnt. 我正在试用我刚学的一点法语。

few / little 若不与 a 连用则表示否定意义,相当于 not many / much,not enough。例如：

I have very few chocolates left. 我只剩下很少一点巧克力。

I understood little of his speech. 他的演讲我几乎不懂。

要注意,quite a few, a good few, not a few 不表示"少",而表示"相当多"的含义,相当于 a great number (of)。例如：

Quite a few of us are getting worried. 我们相当多的人正在担心。

You'll have to wait a good few weeks. 你将不得不等上好几个星期。

3)some, any

表示"一些"的意思。some 常用于肯定句, any 常用于否定句或疑问句。例如：

There are some letters for me. 有几封信件是我的。

There aren't any letters for me. 没有我的信件。

Are there any letters for me? 有我的信件吗？

any 也常用于条件句以及带有否定含义的句子中。例如：

If you have any trouble, please let me know. 如果你有任何麻烦,请让我知道。

I forgot to ask for any change. 我忘了要一些零钱。

当说话人期待肯定回答时,some 也可用于疑问句,比如当说话人期待来信时,他可以问：

Are there some letters for me?

当表建议时,也可在疑问句中用 some。例如：

Would you like some chocolate cake?

当 some 与单数可数名词搭配时,some 相当于 a certain("某一")的含义；而 any 与单数可数名词搭配,则相当于 every("任何一个")的含义。例如：

Some boy has broken a window. 某个男孩打破了窗户。

Any child could answer that question. 任何一个孩子都可以回答这个问题。

Language Tips for Writing

以下是关于成功的一些表达方式：

How do you define success? 怎样给成功下定义？

Success is relative; not everybody wants to manage billion-dollar conglomerate, or become President of the United States, or win the Nobel Peace Prize. 成功是相对而言的,并非每个人都想经营上亿美元的大型企业,并非每个人都想成为美国总统或获得诺贝尔和平奖。

But how to achieve success? 但是怎样才能取得成功？

The best way to success is to begin with a reasonably realistic goal and make earnest effort to attain it, rather than aim at something so far beyond your reach that you are bound to fail.

成功的最佳方法就是先订一个合理而实际的目标并努力去实现,而好高骛远注定会失败。

It's also important to cultivate a habit of constant perseverance.

养成持之以恒的好习惯也很重要。

Try to think of success as a journey, not as a specific destination.

把成功看作一个过程而不是最终目的。

You have to believe in yourself, that's the secret of success. 成功的秘笈就是自信。

A person's success is by no means an accidental phenomenon, but through long struggle.

一个人的成功绝非偶然现象,而是通过长期的奋斗努力。

Text B   The Role of Luck in Success

Reading Strategies(1) : Reading for Inference

推理判断是阅读的重要能力之一。在阅读过程中读者常常需要在理解文字表面意义的基础上,通过判断和推理,领会作者的言外之意。这种推理判断既可以是局部的,即针对文章细节或局部内容进行的推理判断;也可以是篇章的,即通过隐藏在文章字里行间的线索推断上下文论述的主题、文章的来源等。这时可采取寻找主题句(篇首、篇尾,段首或段尾)的方法,也可以从作者的结论中,或整篇文章的行文基调中寻求线索。

在推断时应注意如下三点:

①一定要以文章提供的事实为依据,不要凭空想像。

②不能与文中的任何陈述相冲突。

③如文章较难,则应仔细阅读以确保对原文理解的准确性。只有在此基础上才能做出正确的推断。

例如在该课的学生练习册的第一段对话中,读者就可通过对最后一段,尤其是倒数第二句的细读,推断出血型的转换技术有利于避免给病人输血时偶发的输错血型的事故。

Word Study

1. role   *n.* 作用;角色

例:Words play an important role in everyday life.

语言在我们的日常生活中起了重要的作用。

He played the role of Hamlet. 他扮演哈姆雷特的角色。

2. luck   *n.* 幸运, 运气

例:She has a good luck. 她很幸运。

lucky *a.* 幸运的

例:a lucky person 幸运儿

unlucky *a.* 不幸运的

3. specific   *a.* 确切的;具体的;特定的

例:I have no specific aim. 我没有明确的目标。

There are two specific questions we must answer. 有两个具体的问题我们必须回答。

specification *n.* 详细说明

4. explain   *v.* 讲解,说明,阐述

例:The referee explained the rules. 裁判员讲解了比赛规则。

I came to explain the situation to you. 我是来给你说明情况的。

5. discovery   *n.* 发现;发觉

例:For fear of discovery he changed his lodging every night.

害怕被人发现,他每晚换一个住宿的地方。

discover *v.* 发现,发觉

例:She discovered she had lost her purse. 她发觉钱包丢失了。

6. accident   *n.* 意外,事故

例:He was killed in a traffic accident five years ago. 五年前他死于交通意外。

accidental *a.* 意外的,偶然的

7. major

a. 主要的,较重要的

例:the support of the major figures 重要人物的支持

v. 主修

例:He majors in computer. 他学计算机专业。

8. create   *v.* 创造;产生,引起

例:He likes creating music. 他喜欢创作乐曲。

Her arrival created a terrible confusion. 她的到来引起一场混乱。

creation *n.* 创造力;创造性

creative *a.* 富有创造力的

9. offer

v. 提供

例:He offered his seat to the elderly man. 他把座位让给了老人。

Television has begun to offer selected programs from some foreign countries.

电视已经开始提供一些选自国外的节目。

n. 提供(物),提议

例:He made an offer of money. 他主动表示愿意提供金钱。

10. rare   *a.* 极好的;稀罕的

例:This is a rare good wine. 这是极好的酒。

Snow is rare in this region. 这个地区难得下雪。

It is rare for a person in his position to make such a mistake.

他这样职位的人很少犯这种错误。

11. influence   *n.* 作用;影响(力)

例:How great is the influence of religion on society? 宗教对社会的影响有多大?

He had a great influence on my career. 他对我的事业有很大的影响。

She won't obey me. I have no influence over her. 她不会听我的，我对她没影响力。

12. ignore   *v.* 忽视,不理睬

例：You can't ignore the spelling mistakes. 你不可忽视这些拼写错误。

I was fined for ignoring the red light. 我因闯红灯而被罚款。

ignorance *n.* 忽视,忽略

13. achieve   *v.* 实现；获得,取得

例：She achieved the task. 她完成了任务。

All these cannot be achieved overnight. 这一切不是一夜之间可以实现的。

achievement *n.* 实现,成就

14. add   *v.* 附加,增加

例：She tasted her coffee and then added some sugar. 她尝了一下咖啡,然后加了些糖。

His remarks add to the proof that she is innocent. 他的话进一步证明她是无辜的。

add up to 共计,合计达

addition *n.* 加,加法；附加物

additional *a.* 附加的,另外的

Key to Exercises

Text A

I. successful, confident, above, Everyone, way, reality

II. B

III. 1. The most essential element to success is diligence.

2. When one hesitates for lack of self-confidence.

3. "Two heads are better than one." means that people in cooperation with others are likely to put forward better ideas suitable to solve the very problem.

4. No, I don't think so. Because people need to work together effectively in modern society where projects become more complex than ever.

Vocabulary and Structure

I. 1—b   2—d   3—a   4—j   5—c

6—e   7—i   8—f   9—g   10—h

II. 1. To some extent   2. put forward   3. on the contrary

4. slipped away   5. tend to   6. aspects

III. 1. No matter how hard he tried, he couldn't get a promotion.

2. No matter how difficult the task may be, I will carry it out.

3. This kind of tool is very useful.

4. The chance is very important to every one of us.

IV. 1. 每个人都渴望成功,但是如何取得成功却是个复杂的问题。

2. 任何良机都可能会在人因缺乏自信而举棋不定时悄然溜走。

3. 如果你失败一次便永远不再去尝试,那么毫无疑问你将被成功拒之于门外。

V. 1. Chinese people have full confidence that the 2008 Olympic Games will be a great success.

　　2. In her opinion, these history books seemed to be too heavy for her to carry alone.

　　3. In general, spring is a season which almost everyone likes.

　　4. None of us is likely to take a seat next to Professor Li.

　　5. In any case, I will book the tickets first.

Speaking

II. 1. James：Why do you look so upset? What happened?

　　Kathy：Where were you yesterday? I kept calling you on your cell phone all afternoon. But when I called, I only heard "The power is off". Any reason you had to do that?

　　James：Uh, I was attending an interesting lecture given by a well-known professor, so I had to turn it off. No wonder you couldn't reach me.

　　Kathy：I see. You know what yesterday was? It was my birthday.

　　James：Oh, I'm terribly sorry to have forgotten your birthday! I hope you excuse/forgive me.

　　Kathy：That's all right. I can understand.

　　James：I'll make up for it.

　　Kathy：No problem. Let's forget it.

　　James：Really, sorry about that.

　　Kathy：Have you ever heard the saying / proverb "Love means never having to say you're sorry"?

　　James：Aha! Ok, Ok.

Listening

1. A　　　2. C　　　3. A　　　4. B　　　5. C　　　6. B　　　7. B　　　8. A

Grammar

I. 1. The, the　　　2. an, the　　　3. /　　　4. the, /　　　5. an, the

　　6. /, the　　　7. a　　　8. /, the　　　9. The, /　　　10. the

II. 1. A　　　2. D　　　3. C　　　4. A　　　5. B

　　6. D　　　7. C　　　8. B　　　9. D　　　10. A

Text B

1. F　　　2. T　　　3. F　　　4. F　　　5. T

 Translation of the Texts

Text A

成功之路

　　每个人都渴望成功,但是如何取得成功却是个复杂的问题。当然与此相关的因素很多,诸如勤奋、自信、乐观、团队协作等等。

　　在我看来,勤奋是取得成功的首要因素。一个勤奋的人能够积累越来越多的经验,而正是这些经验将在很大程度上促成他今后的成就。与之相反,一个只会夸夸其谈却从不把计划付诸于行动的人,无论他有什么样的雄心壮志,也最终将一事无成。

在某种程度上说,自信对于促成非凡的事业也是相当重要的。任何良机都可能会在人因缺乏自信而举棋不定时悄然溜走。一般来说,一个自信的人往往能抓住一个又一个的机会,也正是这些机会最终将他一步步引向成功之路。

无论如何,乐观都是一个人成功必不可缺的因素。人几乎不可避免会在人生的某段时期遭遇失败。乐观主义者往往能直面厄运并且从中汲取教训,从而避免更大的挫折。如果你失败一次便永远不再去尝试,那么毫无疑问你将被成功拒之门外。

在我看来,团队协作同样也是取得伟业的重要因素。任何时候你都几乎无法想象,一个有雄心抱负的人能在无他人帮助下完满地实现他的目标,尤其在现代社会,分工比以往更复杂,更需要人们有效地合作。况且如谚语所言:"三个臭皮匠赛过诸葛亮。"团队的智慧可能想出更好的办法恰当地解决问题。

一个人想取得成功需要具备上述品质:勤奋、自信、乐观、团队协作精神。这些品质相互关联,都是成功的必备品质。每一个人在努力追求成功的艰难旅途中都需要依赖这些品质。

Text B

成功中的运气成分

"一个人成功了是因为艰辛努力,而与运气毫无关系。"你是否赞同上述观点?

有人认为成功来自艰辛努力,与运气无关。虽然我坚信勤奋对大多数人而言是取得成功的万全之策,但我却不赞同上述论断。因为不可否认运气在成功过程中起到重要作用。比如说许多重要发现都是偶然的。不乏这样的事例:研究工作者或发明家在工作中取得重大突破,而实际上当时他们正致力于解决另一问题或是想发明别的东西。

此外,还有一点值得一提的就是你仅需在恰当的时候出现在恰当的地方——也许就会遇到某人,而他刚好能为你提供一份好的工作或一个极好的机会。当然还有就是极少数撞大运突然获得意外成功的赌徒和中彩票的人。

尽管运气的成分不可忽视,但并不意味着一个人就应该依赖运气而无视努力的价值。我相信,一个人只要愿意付出努力,那么他最终一定能取得成功,不管有没有运气的眷顾。而且勤奋还常常是交好运必不可缺的因素,因为勤奋使人能够充分利用遇到的好运。如果科学家没有努力地积累知识和培养技能,那么当幸运的突破机会降临时他也觉察不到。因此,我建议不要指望运气能让你成功,而是要在付出努力的同时密切留意良机。

Scripts for Listening

Conversation 1　Richard：Are you a new student here?

Angela：Yes. How about you?

Richard：Me too. Oh, by the way, my name is Richard, Richard Fleming.

Angela：Hi, Richard. I'm Angela, Angela Gates.

Richard：Sorry. I didn't catch your first name.

Angela：It's Angela. Nice to meet you.

Richard：Nice to meet you. So, what do you major in?

Angela：Accounting.

Richard：Really! Where?

Angela：North Campus.

Richard: I'm studying Marketing on South Campus.

Angela: Hey, I'm afraid I have to go now. My class begins at eight.

Richard: See you later.

Angela: See you.

Question 1: What does the young woman (Angela) major in?

Question 2: Where does the young man (Richard) study?

Conversation 2   Teacher: Today we are going to discuss "Academic Essay Writing".

Michael: Excuse me.

Teacher: Ah... Michael! Late again!

Michael: I'm terribly sorry, Ms. Hopkins.

Teacher: What's the excuse this time?

Michael: I must have turned off my alarm clock and gone back to sleep again.

Teacher: If you had gone to bed earlier you wouldn't be late for school now.

Michael: Last night I did my homework until midnight.

Teacher: So, where is your homework?

Michael: Oh... I just don't know what to say. I can't tell you how sorry I am.

Teacher: This is the third time you've been late for my class and the sixth time you have forgotten to bring your homework this month.

Michael: Forgive me. I promise it won't happen again. Please accept my apologies.

Teacher: Okay. I hope this is the last time. Go to your seat.

Michael: Thank you, ma'am.

Question 3: What reason does Michael give?

Question 4: Where is Michael's homework?

Conversation 3   Waiter: Good evening, madam. Do you have a reservation?

Ms. Baker: No, I don't.

Waiter: Awfully sorry, there are no vacancies left now.

Ms. Baker: How long do you think I will wait?

Waiter: About 15 minutes, I think.

Ms. Baker: 15 minutes! That's too bad.

Waiter: I am sorry, Ms...

Ms. Baker: Are you sure there aren't any vacancies left?

Waiter: Well, I'll check again for you.

Ms. Baker: Okay, I will wait for a moment.

Waiter: Oh, I am so sorry for my mistake. There is a table available in the smoking section.

Ms. Baker: Good.

Waiter: But it is in the smoking section. Do you mind, Ms?

Ms. Baker: I think I have no choice now.

Waiter: Please follow me then. I will show you to your table.

Ms. Baker: Thanks.

Waiter: You're welcome. Your server will be with you right away to take your order. Sorry again for my carelessness.

Ms. Baker: Don't mention it.

Question 5: Why does the man apologize the second time?

Question 6: How does the woman feel about the man's apology?

Conversation 4 Woman: Excuse me, but is there a post office near here, please?

Michael: No, there's no post office near here... Well, wait a minute, there's one on King Street. Have you ever been there?

Woman: No, It's my first visit here. How can I get there?

Michael: You can go there by Bus No. 3.

Woman: How far is it from here?

Michael: It's about 20minutes' ride.

Woman: It's a long drive. Well, could you tell me where I can catch the bus?

Michael: There is a bus stop on Bridge Street, opposite the subway station.

Woman: Thank you very much.

Michael: You're welcome.

Question 7: What's the woman looking for?

Question 8: Where is the bus stop?

Unit Five Friendship

Text A   The Elements of Friendship

To have a true friend and to be a true friend to others are as important as anything you will ever do. If you allow yourself to just think about it, it really does make sense. Once you become aware of it, circumstances begin to change immediately, because one of the best ways to learn about yourself is to see yourself through your friends'eyes. Our friends are like mirrors who reflect back to us our good and bad traits. Once you put it into your head and heart that you have a true friend and you are a true friend to others, things will instantly begin to improve for you. This is a promise.

There is a list of some things that can help you have a true friend and to be a true friend to others. Much of what is needed to make this work is simply being aware of it as a goal.

- Stand up for your friend, his or her ideas, or what is right or wrong — even when you are the only one.
- Don't say bad things about your friends to other people or to yourself.
- Spend quality time with your friends and yourself.
- Plan something fun to do once a week.
- Exercise with your friends.
- Think of yourself as a friend. No one deserves to be treated with love and respect more than you do.

Do whatever it takes to remember that:

- Every week write down five things for which you are grateful to your friends. (This will change your life.)
- Take yourself lightly.
- Always ask yourself, "What would I want my best friend to do in this situation?"
- All in all, the end of the list is to have more inner peace, self-esteem and overall happiness.

Warming-up Questions

1. Everybody has friends who he or she has had for many years and who he or she has known for a short while. Friendship is like a very warm feeling when we think of it. It is also difficult to say what is "the best" of friendship. List one or two things that you think are the best things about friendship.

2. There are more and more foreigners living or working in China. Many people want to make friends with them. But what are the things we should observe if we really want to make friends with them?

Sentence Analysis

1. A friend is someone who you hang out with a lot, and someone you rely on.

   此句中 and 连接两个并列表语, you rely on 是一个定语从句, 修饰并列表语中第二个不定代词 someone, 省略了关系代词 who。关系代词 who 在定语从句中做宾语。在口语或非正式文体中, whom 可省略或用 who 来代替, 但在介词后面以及在非限制性定语从句中只能用 whom。例如:

   There are some people (whom / who) we like and others (whom / who) we dislike.
   有一些人是我们所喜欢的, 还有一些是我们所不喜欢的。
   The people (whom / who) I work with are all friendly.
   和我一起工作的人都非常友好。
   Mr. Zhang, who came to see me yesterday, is an old friend of mine.
   张先生昨天来看我, 他是我的一位老朋友。
   The person to whom you spoke is my teacher. 你说话的那个人是我的老师。

2. Honesty and trust are very important but so is caring.

   该句中 so is caring 在语法中被称为重复倒装。由 so (neither, nor) 指代前面一句的内容, 表示 "也是 (也不)" 的意义时, 通常位于句首, 并引起倒装。例如:
   Andy has finished his assignment, and so have I. 安迪已经完成了他的工作, 我也是。
   If Ann will not go shopping, neither (nor) will I. 如果 Ann 不去逛街购物, 我也不去。

3. The definition of support is to take sides with or to provide help.

   该句中动词不定式短语作表语。不定式作表语一般表示具体动作、目的、或将来的动作。例如:
   Your present task is to study and work. 你现在的任务就是学习和工作。
   What he wanted was to get the work done as quickly as possible.

他想做的就是尽可能快地完成工作。

4. Similarities in friendship will make the bond grow.

同三单元一样,该句中 make 为使役动词,后面要求跟不带 to 的不定式。

动词不定式在下面情况中都要省略 to:

1)在感官动词 see, hear, watch, notice, feel, look at, listen to 等及使役动词 make, let, have 等后作宾语补足语的动词不定式要省略 to。例如:

The boss often made the workers work for over 12 hours a day.

老板经常让工人们一天工作 12 小时以上。

注意:以上情况用于被动语态时,不定式符号 to 一定要补回。例如:

The workers were often made to work over 12 hours a day.

2)在动词 help 后作宾语补足语的动词不定式符号 to 可带可不带。例如:

I often help my mother (to) do housework. 我经常帮助妈妈做家务。

3)在 had better, would rather 后动词不定式不能带 to。例如:

You'd better not go out at night. 你最好别在晚上出门。

The boy would rather stay at home by himself. 这个男孩喜欢独自一人待在家里。

4)"Will (Would) you please + 不带 to 的不定式"。例如:

Would you please not do that again? 请你别再那样做了好吗?

5)当不定式作介词 but, except 的宾语,表示"除了……不/没有做……"时,不定式要省略 to。例如:

She does nothing but watch TV. 她除了看电视什么也没做。

She doesn't want to do anything except sleep. 她除了睡觉什么也不想干。

5. An example of similarities is two friends liking the same kind of music.

该句中,liking 是现在分词,作 friends 的后置定语。也可以将这句话改为:An example of similarities is two friends who like the same kind of music.

Like 的逻辑主语为 friends,用现在分词作后置定语表主动;如果后置定语的动词的逻辑宾语为其所修饰的名词,那么就应该用过去分词。例如:

This is a new apartment lived by a young couple.

这是一套新公寓,一对年轻的夫妇住在这里。

这句话也可以改成:This is a new apartment which is lived by a young couple.

Word Study

1. honest *a.* 真诚的;正直的

例:He is an honest and reliable man. 他是一个诚实可信的人。

To be quite honest with you, you can not pass the examination.

老实告诉你,你这次考试及不了格。

2. trust

n. 信任;信托

例:Our teacher always trusts us, so we don't want to break the trust. 我们老师总是很信任我们,因此我们不愿意失去他对我们的信任。

She hasn't placed much trust in his promises. 她不大信任他的诺言。

v. 1) 信任

例:I trust in God. 我信仰上帝。

Don't trust to chance. 不要碰运气。

2) 委托;相信

例:Can I trust you to get the money safely to the bank?
我能托你将这笔钱安全存入银行吗?

3. freedom   *n.* 自由

例:We should give people freedom to do what they think best.

我们应该给人们以用他们认为最好的方式处理事务的自由。

4. main

a. 主要的;最重要的

例:This is the main street of the town. 这是市内的主要街道。

n. 1) 主要部分

例:The result is, in the main, satisfactory. 结果基本上是令人满意的。

in the main 大体上,就一般而论,从全体来看

2) 干道,总管道,干线(通常写作 the mains)

例:My new house is not yet connected to the mains.

我的新房子(的水电)还没有接上干线。

5. similarity   *n.*

1) 相似,类似

例:Are there any points of similarity between the two men?

这两个人之间有没有什么相似之处?

2) 相似或类似之点

例:There are many similarities between China and Japan. 中国和日本有许多相似的地方。

similar *a.* 类似的;同样的

例:My wife and I have similar tastes in music. 我的妻子和我在音乐方面有相似的爱好。

6. without   *prep.* 无,没有

例:Tommy came into the room without anything in his hands.

汤米走进房间,手里什么也没有拿。

Without air and water, there would be no creature on the earth.

如果没有空气和水,地球上将不会有任何生物。

7. quality　　*n.* 品质;特质;才能

例:He is a man with many good qualities. 他有很多优点。

Give us a taste of your quality. 让我们瞧瞧你的才艺吧。

8. condition

n. 条件;要件

例:Ability is one of the conditions of success in life. 能力是人生迈向成功的条件之一。

You can go swimming on condition that you don't go too far from the river bank.

你可以去游泳,但条件是你不能远离河岸。

on condition (that)... 只有在……的条件下

in / out of condition 健康良好(不佳)

v. 决定;支配;限制

例:My expenditure is conditioned by my income. 我的支出受到我收入的限制。

9. integrity　　*n.*

1)廉正;诚实

例:He is a man of integrity. 他是一个正直的人。

2)完整

例:This Treaty was supposed to guarantee our territorial integrity.

这一条约应该可以保证我方领土的完整。

10. last

a. 1)最后的;末尾的

例:December is the last month of the year. 十二月是一年的最后一月。

last but not least 最后的但并非最不重要的

2)刚过去的

例:We had a quarrel last night / week / month. 我们昨夜/上周/上月吵了一架。

3)仅余的,留在最后的

例:This is our last hope. 这是我们唯一的希望了。

v. 继续;延续,持久;维持

例:How long will the fine weather last? 这好天气会延续多久?

11. concern

v. 1)与……有关系;影响;对……有重要性

例:Does this concern me? 这与我有关系吗?

He is said to have been concerned in the crime. 据说他与此案有关。

2)concern oneself with / in / about 忙于;从事;关心;关切

例:Students should concern themselves with study. 学生就应该关心学习。

3)be concerned about / for sb. / sth. 使烦恼,使操心

例:Don't let my illness concern you. 不要为我的病烦恼。

　　n. 1)关系;关联;关心之事

　　例:It's no concern of mine. 这事与我无关。

　　2)担心,忧郁

　　例:My teacher looked at me in concern. 我的老师担心地看着我。

12. supportive　*a.* 支持的;支援的;拥护的;帮助的;鼓励的

　　例:She has been very supportive during my illness. 我患病期间她帮了我很大的忙。

　　support　*v.*

　　1）支持;支撑;扶持

　　例:Is this bridge strong enough to support heavy lorries? 这座桥禁得起重型卡车通行吗?

　　2）维持;赡养

　　例:He has a large family to support. 他要养一大家人。

　　3)忍受,忍耐

　　例:I can't support your jealousy any more. 我再也无法忍受你的嫉妒了。

13. alike　*pred a.* 相似的;同样的

　　例:The two sisters are very much alike. 这两姐妹非常相像。

14. resemblance　*n.* 相似;类似

　　例:There's very little resemblance between them. 他们之间的相似之处很少。

　　resemble *v.* 相似,类似

　　例:They resemble each other in shape but not in color. 它们的形状相似,但颜色不同。

Phrases and Expressions

1. rely on ／ upon 依赖;依靠

　　例:He can always be relied upon for help. 他的帮助是永远可以依赖的。

　　　　You may rely upon my early arrival. 你放心好了,我会早到的。

　　　　You may rely upon it that he will be early. 你放心,他会早到的。

2. hang out 居住;闲逛;厮混

　　例:Where are you hanging out now? 你现在住哪里?

　　　　On holidays, we like to go to the forest cabin and let it all hang out.

　　　　假日里,我们喜欢去森林小木屋完全放松。

3. hold up

　　1)阻滞,延搁

　　例:They were held up by heavy fog. 他们被大雾延搁。

　　2)在一起

　　例:The country needs a leader who will hold the nation up.

　　　　那个国家需要一个能使全国团结在一起的领袖。

4. relate to

1)（在思想上或意义上）相关联

例：It is difficult to relate results with / to any known cause.

这些结果难以与任何已知的原因相关联。

2)与……有关系

例：She is a girl who notices nothing except what relates to herself.

她只注意与自己有关的事情。

5. care for

1)爱好；喜爱

例：Do you care for modern music? 你爱听现代音乐吗？

2)喜欢，想要

例：Would you care for a drink? 你想要喝一杯吗？

3)照顾，养活

例：Who will care for the children if their mother dies?

如果这些孩子的母亲死了，谁将照顾他们？

6. a couple of

1)一对；两个

例：Please arrange the tables in couple. 请把桌子两张两张地摆放好。

2)一对夫妇/情侣等

例：There are several married couples. 有好几对夫妇。

They are a nice couple. 他们是很美满的一对。

3)几个

例：He went out shooting and came back with a couple of rabbits.

他出去打猎，猎获了几只兔子。

7. take sides with 袒护；拥护

例：We are your faithful fans so we will always take sides with you.

我们是你忠实的拥护者，所以我们会永远支持你。

 Differentiations and Analysis of Words and Expressions

1. like, alike

like 和 alike 作形容词时意思相同，都表示"像"，但用法上稍有区别，like 可以做定语或表语。例：

The two girls are very like. 这两个女孩很相似。

Like causes produce like results. 相似的原因产生相似的结果。

alike 作形容词时只能做表语。例：

The two sisters are very much alike. 这两个女孩很相似。

All the roads were alike to him, and then he was lost.

所有的路对他来说都很相似,他迷路了。

2. so, therefore

so 和 therefore 都表示"所以",但在词性上有一定区别,so 是连词,therefore 是副词。例:

It is raining heavily, so we will not go camping now. 正下大雨,我们不去露营了。

It is raining heavily, and therefore we will not go camping now.

正下大雨,我们不去露营了。

3. beside, besides

beside 表示"在……的旁边","在近旁"。如:

Who's the girl sitting beside Philip? 坐在菲利普旁边的女孩是谁?

besides 表示"除……以外","除了"。如:

Besides apples, I bought some oranges. 除了苹果,我还买了一些橘子。

Word Building

1. 名词后缀:-y, -ship

名词后缀-y 表示"性质,状态"。

deliver→delivery   discover→discovery

honest→honesty   modest→modesty

名词后缀-ship 表示"样子,性质,状态"。

friend→friendship   leader→leadership

scholar→scholarship   fellow→fellowship

2. 形容词后缀:-ive

形容词后缀-ive 表示"有……的,富有……的"。

exclude→exclusive   mass→massive

imagine→imaginative   represent→representative

3. 否定后缀:-less

否定后缀-less 表示"没有……的"。

hope→hopeless   help→helpless

use→useless   care→careless

4. 表示反对意义的前缀:anti-

反对意义前缀 anti-表示"反对,防止"。

anti-war 反战   anti-virus 防病毒

anti-aircraft 防空的   anti-ballistic 反导弹的

Grammar Focus

介词是一种虚词,不能单独作句子成分,必须有名词或代词作它的宾语,构成介词词组。英语中的介词大致可以分为以下三类:

简单介词:at, after, in, on, to, with, up, out 等。

合成介词:into, outside, upon, without 等。

短语介词:according to, as to, due to, thanks to 等。

一、介词的位置

介词一般放在名词或代词前,例如:

My house is at the foot of the big mountain. 我的家就在这座大山的山脚下。

介词可放在疑问句或定语从句末,例如:

What are you talking about when I came in? 我刚进门的时候你们在谈论什么?

介词可以放在连接代词之前,甚至放在句首,例如:

With whom did you go skiing yesterday? 昨天你和谁去滑雪了?

二、介词的用法

介词的用法很复杂。首先要了解一些主要介词的基本意思,同时要注意和其他词汇的搭配,特别是动词、形容词和名词与介词的搭配,一定要熟记这样的固定搭配关系。例:

1. 和动词的固定搭配

agree about sth.	laugh at / about
agree with sb.	listen to
aim at / for a target	look after
apologize to sb. for sth.	look at
apply to sb. for sth.	meet with sb.
approve of	object to
arrive at / in	pay for
ask for	quarrel with sb. about sth.
begin with sth.	reason with sb.
believe in	refer to
belong to	rely on
borrow from sb.	reply to sb.
choose between	report on sb. / sth. to sb.
confess to	resign from (a job)
deal with	retire from (one's job)
depend on	search somewhere for sb. / sth.

differ from sb. / sth.

dream about / of doing

emerge from a place

fail in

insist on doing

knock at

succeed in doing sth.

suffer from sth.

trade with sb. in sth.

trust in

wait for

write to sb. about sth.

2. "动词 + 宾语 + 介词"结构的动词

absent oneself from (work)

accuse sb. of sth.

adapt sth. of sth.

add sth. to

admire sb. for sth.

advise sb. about sth.

appoint sb. as / to (a post)

arrange sth. for sb.

assess sth. at a price

associate sb. / sth. with

attach sth. to sth.

blame sb. for sth.

charge sb. with a crime

combine sth. with sth.

compare sb. / sth. with

congratulate sb. on sth.

convert sb. to sth.

defend sb. from sth.

translate sth. from / into

explain sth. to sb.

forgive sb. for sth.

hide sth. from sb.

identify sth. with / as sth.

include sth. in sth. else

inform sb. of / about sth.

insure sb. against sth.

interest sb. in sth.

invest money in sth.

lend sth. to sb.

neglect sb. / sth. for sb. / sth.

refer sb. / sth. to sb.

remind sb. of sb. / sth.

reserve sth. for sb.

repeat sth. to sb.

share sth. with sb.

steal sth. from sb.

stop sb. from doing sth.

excuse sb. for sth.

3. 与介词连用的形容词

absent from a place

afraid of

angry at / about

annoyed at / about

annoyed with sb.

anxious about / over

aware of

awful at (doing) sth.

bored by / with

free from

full of

good at (doing) sth.

happy about / at / over / with

interested in / by sb. / sth.

keen on (doing) sth.

kind to sb.

late for sth.

obliged to

capable of（doing）sth.

careless of sth.

contrary to sth.

different from / to

excited about / at / by / over

eager for sth.

fond of

faithful to

famous for（doing）sth.

pleased about / with

sad about

satisfied with

separate from

sorry about / for（doing）sth.

sorry for sb.

surprised about / at / by

thankful to sb. for sth.

worried about

4. 与介词连用的名词

absence from

advice against / to / about

adaptation to

addition to

admiration for

agreement to / with

aim at

anger at / about

annoyance at / with

apology to sb.

application to

approval of

arrival at / in

awareness of

association with

belief in

boredom with

capability for

carefulness of

certainty of / about

choice between

combination of

comparison with

congratulation on

objection to

pleasure about

conversion to

curiosity about

dependence on

difference from / to

dream of

description of

discussion with

division by

excitement about / at

excuse for sth.

explanation of

failure in

guess at

gladness about

interest in

insistence on

information about

insurance against

investment in

knock at

kindness to

marriage to sb.

meeting with

neglect of

satisfaction with

separation from

payment for

reliance on

reply to sb.

report on

retirement on

reminder of

reservation for

return of sth. to

search for

surprise about / at

share of / with

talk to sb. about

taste of sth.

trade in sth.

trust in

thankfulness to / for

translation into

use of sth. for

三、常用介词用法辨异

1. at, in, on

在时间上,at 指时间点,in 指时间段,on 指特定某日、或某日的早晚等,例如:in the morning / afternoon / evening, at night, on Monday morning, on a cold afternoon, on Thursday, in March, in 2007, in the summer, in the eighteenth century。例如:

I always wake up late in the morning and work late at night.

我总是早上起得晚,晚上工作到深夜。

We're giving David a surprise party on his birthday.

我们准备在戴维生日那天为他开一个惊喜庆祝会。

I was born in June. 我六月出生。

在空间上,at 指某一地点,in 指某一空间,指"在……上"或"在某一地带(包括水域)"。例如:

Henry's house is at the third crossroad after that big building.

亨利的房子在那栋大楼后面的第三个十字路口旁。

Scot was at school from 1989 to 1994 and after that he worked at a big company for several years.

斯科特 1989 至 1994 年在大学就读,之后他便在一家大公司工作数年。

on 和 at 不同,它强调的不是在某一点上,而是强调某一带,如 a river, a road, a frontier,此外,on 表示在某一事物的表面上。例如:

We are living on tropical zone now but we used to live on frigid zone.

我们现在生活在热带,但过去在寒带。

We spent the afternoon in a boat on the lake. 我们一下午都在湖上划船。

I think that picture would look better on the other wall.

我认为这幅画挂在那面墙上会好看些。

Would you read the passage aloud in class on page 82?

你能在班上读一下 82 页的那篇文章吗?

2. in, within

两者均指将来的一段时间,但 in 表示在一段时间之内,意为"在……期间,过……之

久”,强调时间的终点。例如:

The meeting is in twenty minutes. 会议 20 分钟后开始。

This is my first visit to China in four years. 这是我 4 年中第一次访问中国。

而 within 表示"在……时间之内,不出",不是强调时间的终点,而是说动作或状态在某一时限内都可能发生。例如:

The plane will arrive within half an hour. 飞机将在半小时内到达。

I have seen him within these three days. 我在最近 3 天内见过他。

3. above, over, on

都表示"在……以上",on 表示与某物表面接触;over 表示在垂直上方;above 表示在某物上方。例如:

There used to be a picture on that wall. 那面墙上曾经挂了一幅画。

There is a bridge over the river. 那条河上面有座桥。

The plane is flying above the clouds. 飞机飞行在云端上。

4. beside, besides

beside 表示"在……的旁边","在近旁"。例如:

Who's the girl sitting beside Philip? 坐在菲利普旁边的女孩是谁?

besides 表示"除……以外","除掉"。例如:

Besides apples, I bought some oranges. 除了苹果,我还买了一些橘子。

5. besides, except, but

三者都表示"除……以外",except 指不包括该项在内,从整体中减去;besides 指包括该项在内还有多少;but 与 except 同义,语气不及 except 强。例如:

I like all fruits except apples. (I don't like apples.)

除苹果之外,所有的水果我都喜欢。

I've eaten nothing but bread since Monday.

从星期一开始,我除了面包什么东西也没吃。

Everybody arrived besides Simon and Max. 只有西蒙和马克思没有到了。

6. due to, owing to, because of, thanks to

四个都是短语介词,都表示"因为"的意思。例如:

His absence was due to the heavy snow. 因为下大雪,他没有来。

The crop was poor, owing to the drought. 因为干旱,庄稼收成不好。

She was late because of the traffic. 因为堵车,她迟到了。

thanks to 意为"托福"、"多亏"、"幸亏"、"由于"。例如:

Thanks to you, I'm safe after the accident. 多亏了你,我没有出事。

7. despite, in spite of, regardless of

Max came to the meeting despite his serious illness.

尽管病情严重,马克思还是来开会了。

I went out in spite of the storm and strong wind. 尽管刮风下雨,我还是出门去了。

regardless 的意思为 without worrying about,即"未估计到"、"不顾……"、"不惜"、"不计"、"不论"。例如:

Regardless of the heavy snow, he climbed the mountain. 他不顾大雪还是去爬了山。

I'm buying the furniture, regardless of the cost. 我不问价格买下了家具。

四、复杂介词

复杂介词是指由两个或两个以上的单词构成的介词。

1. 由两个单词构成。例如:

The big auditorium was oddly silent except for a few scattered giggles.

除了些零星的笑声,整个大礼堂非常安静。

Previous to the conference we had discussed the matter among ourselves.

在开会之前,我们先讨论了我们之间的问题。

He will inquire again as to what your reasons are. 他还会询问你的原因所在。

2. 由三个单词构成。例如:

The next flight doesn't go direct to Rome; it goes by way of Paris.

下一趟航班不直达罗马,在巴黎中转。

In consequence of having to use after-burners more fuel is consumed.

因为不得不使用补燃器,所以要消耗更多的燃料。

By reason of his cleverness he could not be defeated in arguments.

正是因为他的聪明,辩论中没能将他击败。

3. 由四个单词构成。例如:

Read the paragraph at the bottom of the page. 请阅读这一页的最后一段。

He declined the invitation on the ground of a previous engagement.

他以过去的婚约为由婉言拒绝了邀请。

She is going to see her grandmother in the teeth of wind and storm.

她不顾大风大雨还是要去看望她的祖母。

Language Tips for Writing

一、英文书信结构六大要素

1. 信头(Letterhead)

信头包括发信人的地址和发信日期。如果使用已经印好信头的信纸,就只需加上发信日期。信头位于信的最上方,原则上地址首先按从小到大的顺序(正好与中文书信相反):门牌号码和街名或单位名占一行(太长可占两行),城镇名和邮政编码占一行,国名占一行。然后是发信日期,它是信头的最后一行,可以写成日月年(英式)也可写成月日年(美式),如:May 8,1996 或 8 May,1996。

2. 封内地址(Inside Address)

封内地址包括收信人的姓名和地址。封内地址必须和信封地址一致,否则就是出了差错,收信人此时可将信退回或按封内地址转寄。封内地址的第一行是收信人姓名,第二行职务,从第三行开始写收信人地址,写法原则上和写发信人地址一样。

3. 称呼(Salutation)

称呼应与亲近程度相吻合。最为正式的也是最不亲近的称呼为 Dear Sir(英式)或 Dear Gentleman(美式)。比较熟识的人应称其姓,最随便也是最亲近的称呼是直呼其名,一般用于亲朋好友,但应注意,只称名时不要加头衔,如:William. J. Hall 为全名,则应该称呼为:Mr. William. J. Hall 或者 Mr. Hall. 另外,如果对方为女性却不知应称 Mrs. 还是 Miss 时可称 Ms. 。称呼后面的标点英国人习惯用逗号,而美国人习惯用冒号(亲朋好友之间可用逗号)。

4. 正文(Body)

正文是信的主体,和中文书信的要求一样,正文的内容要主题突出、层次清楚、语言简洁、表达准确。

5. 结束语(Complimentary Close)

结束语是习惯的客套用语,它必须和前面的称呼遥相呼应。如果前面称 Dear Sir,则应选择下列结束语: Very sincerely yours, Very respectfully yours, Very truly yours, Sincerely yours 或 Yours sincerely, Respectfully yours 或 Yours respectfully, Faithfully yours 或 Yours faithfully。如果前面称姓,则应选择下列结束语: Sincerely yours 或 Yours sincerely, Truly yours 或 Yours truly, Yours ever 等。如果前面称名,则表示写信人与收信人的关系亲近友好,应选择下列结束语: Sincerely Yours, Love, All my love 等。

6. 签名和发信人姓名(Signature and Name Addresser)

签名是亲笔手写,只需签姓名,不需加头衔等。

一封完整的英文书信必须依序包含上述六个要素。如果信件有附件并有必要提醒收信人,可在第六个要素之后加上附件注记(Enclosure 或 Encl.)。如果整封信写好后又发现遗漏了什么,可在附件注记之后加上又启(Postscript)或其缩写(P. S.)进行补充。

Text B How to Mend a Broken Friendship

Reading Strategies (5): Identify Topic Sentences

我们常有这样的情况:句子都能看懂,但读完文章印象却不深,这就牵涉到对文章框架结构的整体理解。这一部分的阅读技巧就是如何找文章的主题句,从而学会对文章的整体理解。

寻找主题句法是阅读技巧中非常重要的方法之一。主题句就是表达中心思想和段落大意的句子。对于不同体裁的文章,阅读时要选择不同的办法查找主题。对于叙述性文章,注意抓住事件的发生、经过和结果,通过故事梗概、情节理解其中心思想;说明性文章,一般是通过举例、定义、分类、对比等方法来说明和解释某一事物的,因此主题句一般都在文章的起始段或归纳段中;议论性文章中一般提出两种观点并加以论述或比较,阅读时要特别注意文中的两种观点,抓其实质内容,议论文中的主题句很多情况下都是每个段落的第一句,有时也可能是段落的最后一句或当中的一句。

寻找主题句同时还要充分发挥提示词的作用。提示词是联系句与句之间或段落与段落之间的纽带,阅读中抓住提示词可有效预测下文,并掌握文章的脉络,提高阅读的速度。

例如学生练习册上该单元阅读练习中的 Passage 1 就属于议论文。每一段的第一句都是 topic sentence。第一段介绍全文要讲的主题:Failure is what often happens. 第二三段则讲 Although failure happens to everyone, attitudes towards failure are various. 主要论述每个人对待态度各不相同。最后一段总结全文说出作者自己的观点 failure is not a bad thing.

Passage 2 中,全文每段的 topic sentence 也都为段首句。

Word Study

1. amend *n.*

例:The travel agency should make amends to the tourists for the injury.

旅行社应该赔偿游客所受的伤害。

make amends 赔偿;补偿;赔罪

2. grudge

n. 恶意;怨恨;嫉妒;遗恨

例:He has a grudge against me. 他对我怀恨在心。

I owe that man a grudge. 我有充分的理由对那人怀恨。

v. 不愿给;吝惜

例:I don't grudge him his success. 我不嫉妒他的成功。

I grudge paying ＄2 for a bottle of wine that is not worth 50 p.

我不愿意为一瓶不值 50 便士的酒付 2 美元。

3. reclaim *v.*

1)改正;矫正

例:Please reclaim yourself from error. 请纠正你自己的错误。

2)要求归还

例:You may be entitled to reclaim some of the tax you paid last year.

你或许有权要求退回去年你交付的部分税金。

4. somehow *ad.*

1)以某种方式或方法;借某种手段;设法地

例:We must find money for the rent somehow. 我们总得设法找钱付房租。

2）为某种理由；说不上什么理由；反正

例：She never liked me, somehow. 她反正从来没有喜欢过我。

5. meanwhile *ad.* 其时；同时

例：Meanwhile the minutes kept ticking away. 其时,时间一分一分地过去。

6. conversation *n.* 谈话；会话

例：I saw him in conversation with a friend. 我看见他与朋友谈话。

No conversation while I'm playing the piano, please. 我弹钢琴时请不要和我说话。

7. awkward *a.*

1）笨拙的；不熟练的；不灵活的

例：The child is still awkward with his knife and fork. 这小孩还不大会用刀叉。

2）困窘的；局促不安的

例：There was an awkward silence in the hall. 大厅里弥漫着难堪的沉默。

8. cherish *v.* 珍爱；珍藏

例：One of our cherished privileges is the right of free speech.

我们所珍视的权利之一是言论自由。

Never cherish a serpent in your bosom. 永远不要施恩于忘恩负义之人。

9. identify *v.* 认同；认明；鉴定

例：Could you identify your umbrella among a hundred others?

你能在 100 把伞中认出你的伞吗?

His accent was difficult to identify. 他的口音很难辨出是什么地方的。

10. outrank *v.* 阶级高于；地位高于

例：Colonel Jones outranks everyone here. 琼斯上校比这里所有人的级别都高。

11. interaction *n.* 相互作用；相互影响

例：There should be a lot more interaction between the social services and local doctors.

社会公益服务机构和当地医生应该加强协作。

12. executive *a.* 有权执行决策、法律、命令等的；行政的

例：Bill Clinton once was the executive head of the State. 比尔克林顿曾是一国的行政首长。

13. heritage *n.* 遗产；继承物

例：These beautiful old palaces are part of our national heritage.

这些美丽的古老宫殿是我们民族遗产的一部分。

14. ironically *ad.* 说反话地；讽刺地

例：Ironically, the murderer was killed with his own gun.

饶有讽刺意味的是,杀人者被自己的枪所击毙。

15. outcome *n.* 结果

例：What was the outcome of your meeting? 你们会晤的结果如何?

Key to Exercises

Text A

Getting the Message

II. C

Vocabulary and Structure

I. 1—e   2—d   3—a   4—b   5—c

 6—j   7—h   8—g   9—f   10—i

II. 1. quality   2. honest   3. friendship   4. concern   5. hold up   6. bond

III. 1. Tom can speak English and French and so can Jack.

 2. If you won't go to Jim's birthday party, nor (neither) will I.

 3. Without the sun nothing would grow.

 4. He left the group of people without saying anything.

IV. 1. 友谊就是当朋友需要时你会在他们身边,或是有着共同的爱好,这样可以无拘无束地一起活动,或者是彼此间感觉放心。

 2. 真诚应该是友谊的基础。

 3. 支持的定义就是和朋友站在一边或提供帮助。

V. 1. He can always be relied on for help.

 2. We should improve what is called the quality of living.

 3. These two events were related to each other.

 4. She has been very supportive during my illness.

 5. I took sides with him in the dispute.

Speaking

III. 1. 1) Thank you very much. / It is very kind of you.

 2) Oh, yes. Thank you very much. / No, but thank you all the same.

 3) Ok, no problem.

 4) Yes, sure.

 5) Yes, of course I can.

 6) OK. No trouble at all.

 2. 1) Robert: <u>What's the matter / wrong</u> with your foot?

 Lisa: I fell down the steps just now.

 Robert: <u>Let me have</u> a look first. You might have broken a bone.

 Lisa: Oh, it hurts very much. Could I <u>bother you</u> to take me to the hospital?

 Robert: <u>Of course</u>, no problem.

 Lisa: Thank you. <u>It's very kind of you</u>.

 2) Black: Good morning. Are you hungry? <u>Would you like me</u> to make you something to eat?

 Julie: No, <u>there's no need</u>, Black. I'm not very hungry, but thank you <u>all the same</u>.

Black：Isn't there <u>anything I can do</u> for you?

Julie：Well, yes. <u>Would you mind</u> buying some fruits for me? Some apples, I think

Black：No, <u>of course not</u>. Anything else?

Julie：<u>That's very kind of you</u>, thanks a lot. Oh, there's just one more thing. <u>I wonder if</u> you could go to the post office for me.

Black：I'm sorry. <u>I'm afraid</u> I can't tonight. I have to meet Mort in ten minutes. But I could go tomorrow after work.

Julie：Oh, that's OK. <u>It doesn't matter</u>.

Black：I'll drop in and see you tomorrow then, Julie. See you, bye.

Listening

1. B   2. C   3. C   4. A   5. B   6. A   7. B   8. C   9. B   10. C

Grammar

I. 1. in   2. at   3. with   4. for   5. at   6. to

   7. upon   8. for   9. to   10. despite

II. 1. D   2. B   3. A   4. C   5. D   6. A   7. D   8. C   9. A   10. B

Text B

1. T   2. F   3. F   4. T   5. F

Translation of the Texts

Text A

何为友谊?

你上一次交朋友是什么时候? 朋友是那些诚实而且你能信任的人,是那些你经常和他们待在一起并可以依赖的人。友谊就是当朋友需要时你会在他们身边,并有着共同的爱好,这样可以无拘无束地一起玩耍,彼此间感觉轻松自在。友谊的主要内涵是真诚、信任、关爱和志趣相投。

没有真诚和信任,友谊不会持续很久。真诚的定义是"诚实和正直的品性"。真诚应该是友谊的基础。信任则是与真诚有关的另一个重要方面,你的朋友的确需要信任你。与真诚和信任一样,关爱也是非常重要的。

你需要关心你的朋友,这样你们的关系才会持续下去。关爱的定义是对别人关心或者充满兴趣。例如当你的朋友处于逆境真正需要你时,你也应该毫不犹豫地伸出援手。支持你的朋友就意味着和朋友站在一边或提供帮助。志趣相投和关爱一样也是非常重要的。

志趣相投能使友谊的纽带得以维系。志趣相投指的是品性相似。比如两个朋友喜欢同一类的事物如音乐、业余爱好等。这种共同性能使朋友们想在一起做更多的事情。

如果好友们希望友谊长存,他们总会彼此真诚、彼此信任、彼此关爱、志趣相投。真正的友谊地久天长!

Text B

如何修复破碎的友谊

没有比现在更好的时间来改善同老朋友之间的关系了。下面就教你如何忘掉怨恨、重新找到给你生活带来欢乐和笑声的友谊。

主动联系老朋友。爱达荷州双瀑布市邻街长大的丽莎·弗莱和波娜·特纳从不怀疑她们的友谊会长存。但是,在丽莎结婚搬到纽约并有了小孩后,她写给波娜的信突然没有了回音。"你认为我是不是哪里得罪了她?"丽莎问她丈夫。

同时,波娜也认为自己对丽莎已不再重要了。"她现在已经有了自己的家,"她对自己说,"我们不可能像以前那样亲密了。"

最后,丽莎鼓起勇气给她的老朋友打了一个电话。开始的谈话非常尴尬,但很快她们就坦承非常想念对方。一个月后,她们重逢了,很快又回到了以前亲密无间的融洽气氛中。

"谢天谢地,我终于还是联系你了,"丽莎说。"我们都认识到我们对于彼此还是像从前那么重要。"

我们都应该珍惜友谊。若干年前,一个民意调查机构拉普·斯塔奇全球公司要求 2007 人标出一两件对于他们最重要的事情,友谊的重要性远远超过了家庭、工作、衣服和汽车。

美国西部心理学协会的执行主席唐纳德·帕南说:"一份成熟的友谊是长期的经历和相互交往的结果,这种影响使我们更了解我们自己,并且令我们保持联系,实在是一份值得我们保护的财富。"

印第安纳州西拉斐特普渡大学的公共关系教授布兰特·R·布尔森说,"具有讽刺意味的是,越是好朋友,越容易起冲突。"其结果可能恰好是你不想面对的——朋友关系的终结。

Scripts for Listening

Conversation 1   W: Is there anything I can do for you?

M: Well, I'd like to buy some socks and a shirt — a white one with long sleeves, please.

Question: What is the most probable relationship between these two persons?

Conversation 2   M: Can I help you?

W: I want to open an account.

Question: Where does the conversation take place?

Conversation 3   M: Could you please tell me what room Robert Davis is in?

W: Yes, he is in the intensive care unit on the fourth floor. I suggest that you check with the nurse's station before going in, though.

Question: Where does this conversation most probably take place?

Conversation 4   W: What's the matter, Tom? You don't look happy.

M: I'm not. I'm worried about my physics test.

Question: What is Tom worried about?

Conversation 5   W: Could you tell me what time the film starts?

M: Yes, sure. At 7. You still have 15 minutes.

Question: What time is it now?

Conversation 6   M: I'd like to make a long distance call to New York, America.

W: Ten dollars for the first three minutes and two dollars for each additional minute.

Question: What is the woman's job?

Conversation 7   W: Can I help you, sir? Or would you like to see the menu?

M: No, thank you. I already know what to order. Just two steaks and a chicken soup and a salad.

Question: Where does this conversation probably take place?

Conversation 8　W：I can hardly breathe. Would you please put your cigarette out?

M：I'm sorry that I'm bothering you, but this is the smoking section. Why don't you ask the air hostess to change your seat?

Question：What does the woman think the man should do?

Conversation 9　W：Could I borrow this dictionary?

M：It's my roommate's, and he's not here right now.

Question：What does the man imply?

Conversation 10　M：Could you post the letter for me?

W：Well, the post office is very close to your office.

Question：What will the woman do?

Unit Six Sports

Text A Revival of the Olympic Games

Many people know that the first modern Olympic Games started in the country where the Games were originated in 1896. Before that time some countries in the world organized sports festival in small scales. Not many people know who proposed the idea to bring nations together and for what purposes of his idea were, who was the first president of the International Olympic Committee (IOC). This text tells us how the first modern Olympic Games were revived.

1. **Wenlock Olympian Society**　Much Wenlock, earlier known simply as "Wenlock", is a small town in Shropshire, England. It lies in the Bridgnorth district, on the A458 road between Shrewsbury and Bridgnorth. Nearby, to the northeast, is the Ironbridge Gorge. The population of the town's parish, according to the 2001 census, is 2605. The town is known for William Penny Brookes'version of the Olympic Games, founded in 1850; they gradually grew in importance and he renamed them the **National Olympian Games**. The Wenlock Olympian Society Annual Games are still contested in the town.

2. **Baron Pierre de Coubertin**　Baron Pierre de Coubertin (1863-1937), French aristocrat was the founder of the modern Olympic Games.

    He was born to a wealthy family in Paris on New Year's Day of 1863.

    As the member of a wealthy family, Coubertin did not face the pressure of having to make a living as a young man. He rode horses, rowed, boxed, fenced, and circulated in high Parisian society. Despite his easy life, (or because of it), he was haunted by the need to create some meaning, to have some greater purpose than merely chatting with other aristocrats or attending parties.

3. **Sorbonne University**　The historic **University of Paris** (French: *Université de Paris*) first appeared in the second half of the 12th century, but was in 1970 reorganized as 13 autonomous universities (University of Paris I—XIII). The university is often referred to as the **Sorbonne** or **La Sorbonne** after the collegiate institution (*Collège de Sorbonne*) founded about 1257 by Robert de Sorbon, but the university as such is older and was never completely centered on the Sorbonne. Of the 13 current successor universities, the first four

have a presence in Sorbonne, and three include Sorbonne in their names.

4. Presidents of the IOC

Presidents of the IOC
Demetrius Vikelas（1894-1896）｜ Pierre de Coubertin（1896-1925）｜ Henri de Baillet-Latour（1925-1942）｜ Sigfrid Edström（1942-1952）｜ Avery Brundage（1952-1972）｜ Lord Killanin（1972-1980）｜ Juan Antonio Samaranch（1980-2001）｜ Jacques Rogge（2001-current）｜

Warming-up Questions

1. For months before the **Olympic Games**, runners relay the Olympic Flame from Olympia to the opening ceremony. Is that true? As we know the 29th Olympic Games was held in Beijing from August the 8th, 2008, but do you know when the era of the Modern Olympic Games started and who revived them?

2. The fact that the Olympic Games take place every four years is known to all. But have the Olympic Games been held every four years continuously since the first Modern Olympic Games started? If not, for what reason and in which years were the games canceled?

Reference answer to question 2：The Olympic Games have been held every fourth year starting in 1896, except in 1916, 1940, and 1944 due to the World Wars.

Sentence Analysis

1. …which were established in the nineteenth …

　　which 引出非限制性定语从句,修饰 the National Olympic Games,在从句中作主语。关系代词在从句中作主语时,从句的谓语动词应与从句所修饰的先行词保持一致。该句的先行词 the National Olympic Games 为复数,故从句的谓语为复数。如从句的先行词为单数,从句的谓语应为单数。例如:

　　The dictionary that/which is on the shelf can not be borrowed away from the library.

　　书架上的那本词典不能借出图书馆。

　　Do you know the boys who are standing over there? 你认识站在那边的男孩吗?

　　但在非限制性定语从句中,当关系代词修饰整个主句时,从句谓语动词为第三人称单数,且总是用关系代词 which。例如:

　　He has not a telephone, which makes it difficult to get in touch with him.

　　他没有电话,很难与他联系上。

　　Liquid water changes to vapor, which is called evaporation.

液态水变为蒸汽,这就叫做蒸发。

2. The interest in reviving the Olympics as an international event grew …

　　该句中介词短语作后置定语修饰 The interest。介词短语作定语时一般后置。例如:

　　The students from this area usually study English very hard.

　　来自这个地区的学生学英语通常非常努力。

　　The cat under the chair is sleeping. 椅子下面的猫正在睡觉。

　　The water in the river is very clean, and you can directly drink it.

　　这条河的水很洁净,可直接饮用。

3. …, to have the youth of the world compete in sports, rather than fight in war.

　　"have + sb. +不带 to 的不定式"表示"使/让(某人)做(某事)"之意。例如:

　　I will have you know that I have been working in this company for 20 years.

　　我要让你知道我已经在这个公司工作了 20 年了。

　　We can't have the machine run idle. 我们不能让马达空转。

　　"have + sth. +过去分词作(宾语补足语,不作后置定语)"表示"让…… 受到……"、
"让人把…… 弄……"、"使得……"的意思。例如:

　　We must have the table repaired at once. 我们必须马上请人修桌子。

　　He had his experiment report typed out yesterday. 昨天他让人把实验报告打出来了。

4. To organize the Games, the International Olympic Committee (IOC) was established, with
the Greek Demetrius Vikelas as its first president.

　　该句中 with 引出的是"with +名词(代词)+ 介词短语"的复合结构,表示伴随状况。
with 后的逻辑主语为 the Greek Demetrius Vikelas,它与句子的主语不同,其后的 being 省
略了。介词短语 as its first president 为逻辑主语的补语。例如:

　　My mother came into my room with a newspaper in her hand.

　　我妈妈手里拿着一张报纸进了我的房间。

Word Study

1. **century**　*n.* 世纪,百年

　　例:The book appeared at the beginning of the eighteenth century.

　　这本书出版于十八世纪初。

　　The war broke out towards the close of the fifteenth century.

　　这场战争发生在十五世纪末叶。

2. **game**　*n.* (有规则的)体育运动;比赛项目;游戏

　　例:The boys usually like ball games, such as basketball or tennis.

　　男孩通常喜欢诸如篮球或网球等之类的球类运动。

　　They are going to the baseball game. 他们要去看棒球比赛。

Many college students like to play computer games. 许多大学生喜欢玩电脑游戏。

3. festival *n.*

1)（音乐、戏剧、电影等的）节

例：the Edinburgh Festival 爱丁堡艺术节

the Cannes Film Festival 戛纳电影节

A Beer Festival is held in this city every year. 这个城市每年都举行啤酒节。

2）节日

例：Almost every Chinese family celebrates the traditional Spring Festival.

几乎每个中国家庭都会庆祝传统的春节。

4. establish *v.* 建立；创立

例：Trading relationship was established between the two countries in 1986.

这两国间的贸易关系建立于 1986 年。

Our college was established in 2000. 我院创立于 2000 年。

5. similar *a.* 相似的；类似的 ~（to sb. /sth.)/ ~ in sth.

例：The color of her dress is similar to that of mine. 她的裙子的颜色和我的相似。

These two words are similar in spelling but different in meaning.

这两个词拼写相似，但意义不同。

similarity *n.* 相似

6. organize *v.* 组织；筹备

例：The meeting was badly organized. 会议组织得很糟糕。

She is organizing a party for her coming birthday. 她正在筹备即将到来的生日聚会。

organization *n.* 组织

7. scale *n.* 规模；程度

例：Because of the low salary, the bus drivers in this country organized a strike on a large scale. 由于工资低，这个国家的公交车司机组织了大规模的罢工。

8. certainly *ad.*

1）无疑；确定；肯定

例：I do not know certainly whether he will come. 我不能确定他是否会来。

2）（用于回答问题）当然；行

例：Did he win a prize last term? Certainly he did. 上学期他得奖了吗？当然得了。

certain *a.* 确实的，无疑的；必然的；某一

9. revive *v.*

1）（使）复兴，复活；（使）恢复健康

例：These trees will soon revive in water. 这些树见了水很快就会活过来。

A drink of coffee may revive her. 喝杯咖啡也许会让她精神恢复过来。

2）重新使用；使重做

例：They are making great efforts to revive old customs. 他们正极力恢复旧风俗。

10. ruin *n.*

1）残垣断壁；废墟

例：The old mill is now little more than a ruin. 老磨坊现只剩下一点残垣断壁了。

2）毁坏；破坏；毁灭

例：A large number of temples fell into ruin before liberation. 解放前,许多寺庙都毁了。

Drink was your mother's ruin. 酗酒毁了你的妈妈。

11. uncover *v.*

1）发现；揭露；揭发

例：The young lady uncovered the corruption of the official.

这个年轻女人揭发了官员的腐败行为。

2）揭开盖子

例：The mother uncovered the pan and was going to prepare supper for her children.

妈妈揭开锅盖准备为孩子们做晚饭。

cover *v.*

1）盖,覆盖

例：Lies cannot cover up facts. 谎言掩盖不住事实。

The top of the mountain is covered with snow all year round.

这座山顶成年覆盖着积雪。

2）包括,涉及

例：The survey covers people in different age groups. 该调查涉及不同年龄组的人群。

12. defeat

n. 失败；战败

例：The troops were scattered after a serious defeat. 该部队大败后就散了。

They finally had to admit defeat. 他们最后只得认输。

v. 击败；战胜

例：He defeated all competitors. 他把所有竞争者都打败了。

13. receive *v.* 接到；收到 ~ sth. (from sb. /sth.)

例：I haven't received an e-mail from my younger brother for two weeks.

我有两周没有收到我弟弟的电子邮件了。

The professor received a warm welcome from the students.

这位教授受到学生的热烈欢迎。

14. society *n.* 社会

1）社会（以群体形式生活在一起的人的总称）

例：They discussed what roles young people would play in today's society.

他们讨论了年青人在当今社会中应起什么样的作用。

She is excellent in the society of ladies. 她在女界中很优秀。

2)（尤用于名称）协会；社团；学会

例：Nowadays many college students actively take part in different activities organized by different societies. 现在许多大学生积极参加不同社团组织的不同活动。

15. compete *v.* 竞争；对抗 ～（with/against sb. ）（for sth. ）

例：The two shops are competing against each other for more customers.

这两家商店正相互竞争以争取更多的顾客。

She doesn't want to compete with her friends. 她不想与她的朋友竞争。

competition *n.* 竞争

16. recovery *n.*

恢复；痊愈 ～（from sth. ）

例：He is quite beyond recovery. 他完全不能恢复。

I congratulate you on your recovery from illness. 我祝贺你痊愈。

recover *v.* 康复

例：Her mother is still recovering from her operation. 她妈妈仍处在手术后的恢复中。

17. present

v. 提出；提交 ～ sth.（for sth. ）～ sth.（ to sb. ）

例：He will present his final report to the committee next week.

他将于下个星期向委员会递交最终报告。

a. existing or happening now 现存的；当前的

例：He is the present manager of this company. 他是这个公司现任经理。

n. a thing that you give to sb as a gift. 礼物；礼品

例：I got a lot of presents on my birthday. 我生日时收到了很多礼物。

18. audience *n.* （戏剧,音乐会或演讲会等的）观众,听众

例：The audience was/were clapping for 10 minutes. 观众鼓掌长达 10 分钟。

The lecturer draws large audiences. 这演说家吸引了众多的听众。

19. total

a. 1）总的；总计的

例：The total number of the students in this college is 3 ,566.

该校的学生总人数为 3 ,566。

2）完全的；彻底的

例：The classroom is in total darkness. 教室里一片漆黑。

n. 总数；总额；合计

例：Add up these figures and see if the total is correct.

把这些数目加起来,看总数是否正确。

v. 总数达；总计

例：The visitors to this famous touring place last year totaled 2 millions.

去年到这个著名游览胜地的观光者总计达 200 万。

20. standard

n.（品质的）标准，水平

例：The company produces the products according to the related Chinese national standard.

公司按有关中国国家标准生产产品。

The living standard of the Chinese people has been raised. 中国人的生活水平提高了。

a. 标准的

例：she wants to learn standard pronunciation. 她想学习标准的发音。

21. public

n. 民众；平民；百姓

例：The public is the best judge.（The public are the best judges）公众是最好的裁判。

a. 1）[only before noun] 大众的；公众的；平民的；百姓的

例：The waste from the factory may be a danger to public health.

　　工厂排放的这种废弃物可能危及公众的健康。

　　2）[only before noun] 公共的；公立的

例：There are three public libraries in the city. 这座城市有三个公共图书馆。

The schools here are mostly public schools. 这里的学校大部分是公立学校。

22. propose　*v.* 提议；建议（*formal*）

例：What plan will you propose at the meeting? 你将在会议上提什么计划呢？

Some teachers proposed changing the name of the college.

有些老师建议更改学院的名称。

23. allow　*v.* 允许；准许

例：Her parents won't allow her to swim by herself. 她的父母不允许她独自游泳。

Students are not allowed to bring food into the classroom. 不允许学生将食物带入教室。

Phrases and Expressions

1. at the same time

1）同时

例：He was singing and dancing at the same time. 他又唱又跳。

2）（用以引出必须予以考虑的相对情况）然而，不过

例：There is much point in what you say, but at the same time we adhere to our own opinion.

你所说的话颇多中肯的地方，不过我们仍坚持己见。

2. search for sth./sb.　查找；搜查

例：The lady has searched for her lost purse here and there but she can't find it anywhere.

这位女士到处寻找丢失的钱包,但没找到。

They searched for the missing man. 他们寻找走失的人。

3. think of

1) 想出;构思出

例:She has thought of a plan of how to hold her birthday party.

她想出了怎么举行生日聚会的计划。

2) [no passive] (尤与 can 连用) 记得;想起

例:I can think of at least three occasions when he arrived late. 我记得他至少迟到过三次。

I can't think of the student's name at the moment. 我一时想不起这个学生的名字。

4. rather than 而不是

例:I think I'll have an apple rather than a banana. 我想我要个苹果,不要香蕉。

He will go to the library rather than go shopping after class. 下课后他去图书馆,不去购物。

5. in one's eyes/in the eyes of 在某人看来

例:Rich and poor are equal in the eyes of the law. 从法律上看,穷人和富人都是平等的。

Every child is beautiful in its mother's eyes. 在母亲的眼光中,她的每个小孩都是美丽的。

6. take place (尤指根据安排或计划) 发生,进行

例:When does the concert take place? 音乐会何时举行?

His death took place last night. 他在昨夜去世了。

7. less than (比较数量、距离等) 小于,少于

例:It takes less than an hour from here to the airport by car. 乘车从这里去机场不到一个小时。

It is less than five minutes' walk to get to the cinema. 到电影院走路不到 5 分钟。

Differentiations and Analysis of Words and Expressions

1. similar, same

similar 意为"相似的,类似的",指大体上相似但非同样;而 same 则指"同一的,一样的;相同的,一模一样的"。例如:

The two brothers appear to have similar problems.

这俩兄弟好像有类似的问题。(并非完全一样。)

We lived in the same bedroom for four years when we were in college. 上大学四年我们住在同一寝室。(此句如将 same 改成 similar,其后的 bedroom 一词就应为复数。)

2. ancient, old

ancient 是 modern 的反义词,意为"古代的"。old 是惯熟的用语,ancient 是庄重的用语。

old 一般用来指存在很久的人或物。例如：

The ancient China is attracting more and more foreigners.

古老的中国正吸引着越来越多的国外游客。(此句中 ancient 是庄重的用语。)

This is an old house. 这是一座旧房子。(指存在很久的东西。)

3. search for, seek for, look for

search for 语气最强的用语,指用极大的注意去搜查。例如：

They searched for him, but in vain. 他们寻找他,但没找到。

注意：search 后加 for 和不加 for 意思全然不同。例如：

search a house 指搜查家中的东西。

search for a house 指查找房子的所在地。

seek for 语气比 look for 强,且较为庄重,特别含有需要时间和劳力的意味,在日常惯用语中很少用到。例如：

We were seeking for the lost sheep the whole morning.

整个上午我们都在寻找丢失的羊。

look for 为通俗的和日常的用语。例如：

They are looking for the lost child everywhere. 他们正四处寻找这个丢失的小孩。

4. goal, purpose, object, aim, end

goal 指经过考虑和选择,需经坚持不懈的努力才能达到的最终目标。例如：

We should set ourselves new goals in the new term, and try to achieve them.

我们应在新的学期给自己订些新的目标,然后力图实现。

purpose：(目的)一般的用语,常和 aim 替用,但 purpose 往往指的是心理的活动(mental acts)。

例如：What is the purpose of your manager's visit? 你们经理的来访目的是什么?

object 指眼前的对象或目的,含有较强的具体的意味,往往指存在事物(things)中的,但实际上该词又常常和 purpose, aim 通用。注意该词和 objection(反对)的区别。例如：

The object of my visit is to consult you. 我的来访目的是向你们咨询。

Her sole object in life is to become a travel writer.

她人生的唯一目标就是当游记作家。

aim 指存在于心中的目标,该目标或善或恶,依人的品性而定。例如：

He has a high aim in life. 他胸怀大志。

end 常指终极目的(ultimate object or purpose)例如：

He has gained his end. 他已达到了他的目的。

He does everything for his own political ends.

他所做的一切都是为了达到他自己的政治目的。

Word Building

英语中有些词可以根据其词尾来判别词类。例如：

1. **动词后缀:-en**　一般通过在形容词后加 en 转变为动词,表示"使……"。

　　a. + **en**→*v.*

soft→soften（使软化）　　　　　　　hard →harden（使硬化）

short→shorten（缩短）　　　　　　　deep→deepen（加深）

2. **形容词后缀: -y**　一般通过在名词后加 **y** 转变为形容词,表示"有……的","充满……的","似……的","带……的"之意。*n.* + **y**→*a.*

hair→hairy（多毛的）　　　　　　　noise→noisy（喧闹的）

milk→milky（乳状的,乳白色的）　　　water→watery（水分多的）

英语中有些词可以通过加前缀改变词义。例如：

1. **前缀:mid-**　一般通过在名词前加 **mid** 构成名词和形容词,表示"在中间,居中"。

day→midday（中午）　　　　　　　night→midnight（午夜）

summer→midsummer（中夏,夏至）　　winter→midwinter（中冬,冬至）

2. **前缀:mis-**　一般通过在动词或名词前加 **mis** 改变词义,但词类不变,表示"错误地"或"错误的"。

　　1）*v.*

understand→misunderstand（误解）　　judge→misjudge（错误地判断）

apply→misapply（误用）　　　　　　behave→misbehave（行为不端）

　　2）*n.*

behavior→misbehavior（不端正的行为）　calculation→miscalculation（误算）

fortune→misfortune（厄运）　　　　　application→misapplication（误用）

Grammar Focus

一、形容词的概念及其分类

形容词表示人或事物的性质和特征。可分为：

1. 性质形容词(adjectives):往往伴随名词出现,说明名词的情况、性质和特征。例如：

a fat man（一个胖人）　　　　　　　a live rabbit（一只活兔）

a bad egg（一个坏鸡蛋）　　　　　　a long journey（长途旅行）

2. 数量形容词(adjectives of quantity):说明数量"多少"的词,位于名词前。例如：

two eyes 两只眼睛　　　　　　　　　twenty books 20 本书

注：

1）"much"和"many"也是数量形容词,不过表示的数量不像 "one，two，three" 等那么确切。"much"和单数名词一起用,"many"和复数名词一起用。否定和"not"连用。例如：

I have not many friends in this city. 我在这个城市没有许多朋友。

There wasn't much rain this morning. 今晨没下多少雨。

2）"no"也可用作数量形容词,其后接名词。例如：

No students were in the classrooms last night as it was very cold.

由于天气非常冷,昨晚没有学生到教室去。

3）指示形容词(demonstrative adjectives)："指示"名词的形容词。

this，these 用于指近处的人和物。

that，those 用于指远处的人和物。

this，that 后跟单数名词。

these，those 后跟复数名词。例如：

These cars are new. 这些轿车是新的。

I like that flower. 我喜欢那朵花。

4）疑问形容词 (interrogative adjectives)：疑问形容词和名词一起提出问题。例如：

What book are you reading? 你在看什么书？

Which boy can answer this question? 哪个男孩能回答这个问题？

Whose house is that? 那是谁的房子？

5）物主形容词(possessive adjectives)：表示所属关系的词,均与名词连用并前置。例如：

I bought a jacket for my son yesterday. 昨天我给我儿子买了一件夹克衫。

Their school is not big. 他们的学校不大。

二、形容词的句法作用

1. 作定语：形容词在句中的主要作用是作定语,其位置一般位于所修饰的名词前。例如：

Those are *clever* boys. 那些是聪明的孩子。

The *ugly* woman is wearing a *beautiful* dress. 这位难看的女人穿着一条漂亮的裙子。

One day a *poor* woodman was cutting a *big* piece of wood near a *wide* river.

一位贫穷的樵夫正在一条大河附近砍一块大木头。

注:1)名词前如有好几个形容词(或几个名词)作定语修饰时,其顺序通常按以下的规则：

(1)限定词(包括冠词、物主、指示、不定代词等)→表示说话人评价的形容词→表示大小、形状、新旧的形容词→表示颜色的形容词→表示国别、来源、材料的形容词→表示用途或目的的形容词或分词、名词等类别词→名词中心词。(各修饰词:即形容词,可有缺项,但顺序不变)。例如：

a beautiful new brown French leather jacket 一件新的漂亮的法国的棕色皮茄克

a lovely，long，cool drink 一大杯可口的冷饮

　　　　a tall, ancient oak-tree 一棵高大的老橡树

　　　　long red and white poles 红白色的长杆

　　(2) 表示数目的词通常位于形容词前,定冠词、指示代词后。(数词不与不定冠词或形容词性所有格连用)

　　　　twelve little boys 十二个小男孩

　　　　the third tall girl 第三个高女孩

　2) 在下述情况下,形容词作定语时要后置。

　　(1) 由 any, some, no, every 等构成的合成代词,其定语应后置。例如:

　　　　This is something <u>important</u> to your study. 这对你的学习很重要。

　　　　There is nothing <u>new</u> in their conclusion. 他们的结论没有新东西。

　　(2) 具有表语作用的形容词应后置。例如:

　　　　All the people <u>present</u> (= who were present) agreed on doing the test.
　　　　到场的全体人员都同意做试验。

　　　　In our factory the only fuel <u>available</u> (= that was available) was coal.
　　　　我们工厂里唯一可用的燃料是煤。

　　(3) 如形容词后带有其他的修饰语构成较长的形容词词组时通常总是后置,例如:

　　　　This is a problem <u>easy to understand</u>. 这是一个容易理解的问题。

　　　　She is a woman <u>capable of doing many things</u>. 她是一位能做许多事情的妇女。

　　(4) 两个意义相近或相反的形容词由连词连接,在加强语气时应后置。例如:

　　　　We all speak well of your room, <u>tidy and clean</u>.
　　　　我们都说你的房间好,又整齐,又清洁。

　　　　People, <u>old and young</u>, are all enthusiastic. 人们不论老少都满腔热情。

　　(5) 有些形容词习惯于放在名词后,但为数不多。例如:

　　　　sum <u>total</u> 总额

　　　　money <u>due</u> 应付而未付之款

2. 作表语:形容词作表语时一般位于连系动词(如 be, become, smell, get, taste, look, seem, turn, sound 等)之后。例如:

Our bedroom is not <u>big</u> but <u>clean</u>. 我们的寝室不大但却干净。

The weather has turned <u>cold</u>. 天气变冷了。

The suggestion sounds <u>good</u>. 这个建议听起来不错。

3. 作补足语

作宾语补足语,例如:

He painted the gate <u>yellow</u>. 他把大门漆成黄色。

The farmers have got everything <u>ready</u> for the spring farming.
农民们做好了春耕生产的一切准备。

We consider the test <u>important</u>. 我们认为这项试验重要。

注:带有宾语补足语的句子,改为被动语态表示时,则句中原来的宾语变为主语,原来说明直接宾语的宾语补足语,就变成说明主语的主语补足语了。例如:

These chemicals must be kept <u>dry</u>. 这些化学制品必须保持干燥。

The oil tank was found <u>empty</u>. 这个油箱被发现是空的。

To study English well is considered <u>necessary</u>. 人们认为有必要学好英语。

三、名词化的形容词

有些形容词前加定冠词,可用作名词,在句中作主语、宾语或表语。名词化的形容词可代表一类人或事物,但不能像名词一样有所有格's的形式。例如:

<u>The rich</u> normally look down upon <u>the poor</u>. 富人通常瞧不起穷人。(作主语,宾语)

<u>The sick</u> are taken good care of in the hospital. 病人在这所医院受到很好地照顾。(作主语)

Who have freedom of speech in this company? It's <u>the rich</u> only!

在这个公司谁有言论自由? 只有富人!(作表语)

Language Tips for Writing

1. 有关奥运和运动的一些词汇:

1) 奥运会常见词汇:

Olympic Games, Olympics 奥林匹克运动会;Winter /Summer Olympics 冬季/夏季奥林匹克运动会;the International Olympic Committee(IOC)国际奥委会;the bidding cities 申办城市;the candidate cities 候选城市;host the 2008 Olympic Games 主办2008年奥运会;the Olympic spirit 奥林匹克精神;the International Olympic Day 世界奥林匹克日;the Green Olympics 绿色奥运;the Scientific Games 科技奥运

2) 球类项目词汇:

football 足球;basketball 篮球;volleyball 排球;rugby 橄榄球;tennis 网球;table tennis 乒乓球;baseball 棒球;handball 手球;hockey 曲棍球;golf 高尔夫球;cricket 板球;ice hockey 冰球;badminton 羽毛球

3) 田径运动(Track and Field)

(1) 径赛项目(Track Events):

track /lane 跑道;ring 圈;ground/field 场地;run the 100 meters/ the relay 跑100米/跑接力赛;starting block 起跑器;baton 接力棒;the 400 metre hurdles 400米跨栏赛;race 跑;middle-distance race 中长跑;long-distance runner 长跑运动员;sprint(AmE: dash)短跑

(2) 田赛项目(Field Events):

do the long jump/ the high jump/the pole vault 跳远/跳高/撑杆跳高;triple jump 三级跳; throw the javelin/the discus/the hammer 投掷标枪/掷铁饼/掷链球

2. 常用句型

1）play tennis/basketball /football…“打网球/篮球/踢足球……”,例如:

I usually play football on Saturdays. 我常在周六踢足球。

2）play sb. /against sb. “与……比赛/对垒”,例如:

We are going to play against them next week. 我们下周同他们比赛。

3）be in training for… (BrE)/practice for…(AmE) “为……进行训练”,例如:

The team are in training for their big match of this season.

The team are practicing for their big match of this season.

这个队正进行本赛季大赛前的训练。

4）go swimming/rock climbing/fishing… 某项体育运动或活动的名称以-ing 结尾时常与动词 to go 连用,例如:

My father usually goes fishing once a week. 我父亲通常一周钓一次鱼。

Have you ever been rock climbing? 你攀过岩吗?

Text B   A Woman at the Wheel

Reading Strategies (6): Reading for Detecting the Author's Purpose

　　作者写作时有不同的目的:告知读者信息、说服其改变主意或采取某些行动,或是引起某种情感的响应。作者在写一篇文章时也可同时有两个以上目的。在此情况下,读者应确定哪一个目的更为重要。如作者想告知信息,那么语言和内容应是客观的(不含任何看法),如作者想说服读者或想引起某种情感的响应(如幽默文章中),那么语言和内容应是主观的(含有作者的看法)。作者往往通过提出事实和见解说服读者接受某一观点。读者应分析作者用以支持其观点的推论,可通过归纳、情感词及作为事实陈述的见解找出作者论点的依据。读者还应通过了解文章的组织结构,更清楚地了解作者的写作目的,因作者选择的文章组织结构部分原因往往基于其特别目的。以课文 B 为例,虽然文中作者并没有直接告诉我们女赛车手可以和男赛车手一样获胜,但通过一些情感词的运用及作为事实陈述的见解,如:She is *small* but strong and she is a *good* racing driver. She is the only woman whom you might see at the wheel of a modern racing car… She *won* her third race — and after that everyone knew her name! 及最后一段中 It is possible that she will win one or two important races. 等,我们可以推测出作者的写作意图:尽管赛车这项运动要获胜对一名男选手都不容易的事,女选手通过努力同样能获胜,并能让男选手改变对女选手的看法。

Word Study

1. race   *n.*

1）速度竞赛

例：There is a car race near our town every year. 在我们镇附近每年都有一场车赛。

2）人种，种族

例：An increasing number of people in the country are of mixed race.

这个国家混血人口越来越多。

the black races 黑色人种

2. powerful   *a.* 强有力的，强大的

例：The ship has powerful motors. 这艘船有大功率的马达。

The world's most powerful nations had a meeting last week.

世界最强大的国家上周开了个会。

3. team   *n.* （游戏或运动的）队

例：There are several sports teams in our school. 我们学校有几个运动队。

Pupils normally enjoy team games. 小学生通常喜欢参加集体游戏。

4. spare

a. 备用的；多余的；剩下的

例：The man who is going to take part in a horse race has a spare horse.

参加赛马的这个人有一匹备用马。

Do you have a spare room? 有空房间吗？

v. 节约；吝惜；省掉；让给；抽出

例：Can you spare this book for a little while? 你能把这本书借给我一会吗？

He spares no expenses. 他不节省费用。

in one's spare time 在业余时间

spare no efforts to do sth. 不遗余力地做某事

5. except   *prep.* （用于所言不包括的人或事物前）除……之外

例：Yesterday evening all the students in this class went to see the film except her.

昨晚这个班的所有学生除她外都去看电影了。

Except that he speaks too fast he is an excellent teacher.

除了他说话太快，他是个非常优秀的老师。

6. save   *v.*

1）攒钱

例：He has saved little money though he earns a lot. 尽管他挣得不少却没攒什么钱。

2）救,拯救

例：The doctor saved my mother. 医生救了我妈妈的命。

7. cost

v. 需付费;价钱为

例：I didn't buy the dictionary because it cost too much. 我没买那本词典因为太贵了。

n. 费用,价钱

例：What is the cost of having my bike repaired? 修自行车的费用是多少?

Nowadays the cost of living is much higher than before.

现在的生活费用比以前高许多。

8. win

v. （在比赛、赛跑、战斗等中）获胜,赢

例：Our side won the match. 我们这方赢了这次比赛。

The book won him a reputation. 这书使他得名。

n. （比赛、竞赛等中的）胜利,赢

例：Our team has had three wins and two defeats this season.

这个赛季我们队的战绩三胜二负。

They haven't had a win so far this season. 他们这个赛季迄今还没赢过。

9. mind

n. 头脑;大脑

例：He is a man with a mind of the first class. 他是个头脑非常清醒的人。

We are both of one mind. 我们两人意见相同。

v. （尤用于疑问句或否定句,不用于被动句）对（某事）介意

例：Would you mind my shutting the window? 你介意我关窗户吗?

—Would you like to have tea or coffee? 喝点儿茶还是咖啡?

—I don't mind. 什么都行。

Phrases and Expressions

1. care for 照看

例：She has been caring for the old lady for three years. 她已照料老太太三年了。

The woman cared for my dog while I was away. 我不在时,她替我照看狗。

2. change one's mind 改变决定（或看法、主意）

例：I was going to see a film tonight, but I've changed my mind.

我原打算今晚去看电影的,但我改变主意了。

She is going to get married with this man and she hasn't changed her mind yet.

她要和这个男人结婚,没有改变主意。

3. have a look 看一看

例：May I have a look at your old photos? 我能看看你的老照片吗？

The police had a quick look at the driver's license. 警察很快地看了一下司机的驾照。

Key to Exercises

Text A

Getting the Message

Ⅱ. C

Vocabulary and Structure

Ⅰ. 1—g   2—d   3—a   4—f   5—h

6—b   7—j   8—e   9—c   10—i

Ⅱ. 1. audience   2. took place   3. was organized   4. rather than   5. thought of   6. allowed

Ⅲ. 1. The reason for the little girl's happiness was that her mother bought a new dress for her.

2. My reason for choosing computer as major is that I like it very much.

3. My mother didn't start to watch TV until she had washed dishes.

4. He did not come until the class was over.

Ⅳ. 1. 后来法国和希腊组织了类似的赛事，但都是小规模的，当然也不是国际性的。

2. 19 世纪中期，德国考古学家发现古代奥林匹亚的残垣断壁后，人们又开始对复兴奥林匹克作为国际性赛事产生了兴趣。

3. 然而，奥委会却做出了不同的决定：第二届奥运会在法国巴黎举行。

Ⅴ. 1. I would cook rather than clean the room.

2. The number of the students in this school is less than 300.

3. She established her own company with the help of her father.

4. He proposed that we go to see the teacher because he was ill.

5. Great changes have taken place in Chengdu in recent years.

Speaking

Ⅱ. 1. 1) The man wants to go to the nearest computer shop.

Yu Tao：Pardon me. Could you <u>please</u> tell me where the nearest computer shop <u>is</u>?

Liao Yue：Sure. Go <u>down</u> the street.

Yu Tao：Do I <u>take</u> the second on the right?

Liao Yue：No, you want the first on the <u>left</u>.

Yu Tao：Thanks a lot.

2) The woman wants to find Sichuan University.

An Ni：<u>Excuse</u> me. Would you mind <u>telling</u> me how to get to Sichuan University? I'm a <u>stranger</u> here.

Zheng Hao：Certainly. You should <u>take</u> the No. 12 bus opposite the road.

An Ni：How many <u>stops</u> shall I have from here?

Zheng Hao：I'm not so <u>sure</u>, but you can ask the conductor.

An Ni：Thank you <u>so much</u>.

Zheng Hao：That's all right.

Listening

1. C　　2. A　　3. B　　4. B　　5. C　　6. B　　7. B　　8. A

Grammar

Ⅰ. 1. red-green　　　　2. useful　　　　3. small yellow　　　　4. big, brown　　　　5. sweet
　　6. His, interesting　7. cold　　　　8. white　　　　　9. frightened　　　10. What

Ⅱ. 1. D　　　　2. B　　　　3. A　　　　4. A　　　　5. C
　　6. C　　　　7. B　　　　8. D　　　　9. A　　　　10. B

Text B

1. T　　2. F　　3. T　　4. T　　5. F

Translation of the Texts

Text A

复兴奥林匹克运动会

　　17 世纪时英国举行了奥林匹克体育运动赛事，随后在 19 世纪成立了国家奥林匹克运动会并延续至今。后来法国和希腊组织了类似的赛事，但都是小规模的，当然也不是国际性的。

　　19 世纪中期，德国考古学家发现古代奥林匹亚的残垣断壁后，人们又开始对复兴奥林匹克作为国际性赛事产生了兴趣。同时，拜伦·皮埃尔·德·顾拜旦在追溯法国人在普法战争（1870—1871）中失败的原因。他认为法国人之所以失败，原因在于缺乏恰当的体能训练，并因此寻求改进这种情况的办法。1890 年他参加了温洛克奥林匹克协会的年度运动会。顾拜旦也想出了一个方法让世界各国更加紧密地聚在一起，让世界上的年轻人在体育运动中竞争，而不是在战争中争斗。在他看来恢复奥林匹克运动会可达到这两个目的。

　　1894 年 6 月 16 至 23 日在巴黎索邦大学召开的代表大会上，顾拜旦向来自世界各地的代表们介绍了他的想法。在大会的最后一天，决定首届现代奥林匹克运动会于 1896 年在发源地雅典举行。为了组织奥运会，成立了国际奥林匹克委员会（IOC），希腊人德米特留斯·维凯拉斯担任首届主席。

　　参加首届当代奥林匹克运动会的运动员总数不到 250 人。以现代标准来衡量，这个数目似乎太小了，但在当时却是有史以来举行的最大国际体育运动赛事。希腊的官员和民众也热情高涨，甚至提出垄断奥运会举办权的想法。然而，奥委会却做出了不同的决定：第二届奥运会在法国巴黎举行。巴黎奥运会首次允许妇女参与竞赛。

Text B

握方向盘的女人

　　赛道旁的修理加油站非常繁忙。赛车手和机械工程师们正忙于检查动力十足的赛车。引擎是赛车最重要的部件，修理加油站的机械工程师都是男的，正忙着检查引擎。每个赛车队都有自己的修理加油站，站里有赛车用的燃油、修理场地、备用部件等。赛车手除一人外都是年轻男人，这人叫里拉·罗姆巴蒂。

　　罗姆巴蒂小姐是一位年轻的意大利妇女，个头虽小但却强健，并且是一位优秀的赛车手。在现代车赛上她是你可能见到的唯一的女性。

　　她说："我一生都爱速度快的车。当一名赛车手是我不变的追求。"她以前在她父亲的肉店工作。有时候她驾驶她父亲的拉肉的卡车。这当然让她有了驾驶经验。那时她尽可能多地攒钱。随后在 1965 年，她买了第一辆赛车，这辆车不大，价值约为 500 英镑。她驾驶它参加了两次车赛，而她的父母全然不知。第三次车赛她获胜了——此后她的名字便人人皆知了！

　　从那时起，里拉·罗姆巴蒂拥有几辆赛车，每一辆车都比前一辆大，速度也更快。开始男赛手不喜欢与女赛手比赛，但由于在车赛中她表现非常优秀他们不得不改变看法。现在罗姆巴蒂小姐驾驶的已是世界上跑得最快的车了。

看一下汽车赛季的报纸,你肯定会看到她的名字。她有可能会赢一两次重要的车赛。

Scripts for Listening

Conversation 1   M: Excuse me, please. Could you tell me how to get to the town centre?

W: First right, second left. You can't miss it.

M: Is it too far to walk?

W: No, it's only about a couple of hundred yards.

M: Thank you.

W: That's all right.

Question 1: Where is the man going?

Question 2: How far is it to the town centre?

Conversation 2   W: Excuse me, but I'm trying to find a cinema.

M: Take the third turning on the right and go straight on.

W: Should I take a bus?

M: No, you can walk to it in under five minutes.

W: Thank you very much indeed.

M: That's quite all right.

Question 3: After how many turns will the woman go straight on?

Question 4: How can the woman get to the cinema?

Conversation 3   M: Excuse me, can you tell me the way to Tianfu Square?

W: Certainly. Go down this street and turn left at the first crossroads. Then after walking for about five minutes, you'll see it.

M: Thank you very much.

W: You are welcome.

Question 5: At which crossroads will the man turn left?

Question 6: How long will the man walk?

Conversation 4   W: Excuse me. Could you tell me the way to the station, please?

M: Turn round and turn left at the traffic-lights.

W: Will it take me long to get there?

M: No, it's no distance at all.

W: Many thanks.

M: Not at all.

Question 7: Where does the woman wants to go?

Question 8: How far is it to get to the station?

Unit Seven Leisure Time

Text A The Problem of Leisure

Leisure or free time, is a period of time spent out of work and essential domestic activity. It is also the period of discretionary time before or after compulsory activities such as eating and sleeping, going to work or running a business, attending school and doing homework, household chores, and day-to-day stress. The distinction between leisure and compulsory activities is loosely applied, people sometimes do work-oriented tasks for pleasure as well as for long-term utility.

For an experience to qualify as leisure, it must meet three criteria:

1. The experience is a state of mind.

2. It must be entered into voluntarily.

3. It must be intrinsically motivating of its own merit. (Neulinger, 1981)

Types of leisure

Active leisure activities involve the exertion of physical or mental energy. Low-impact physical activities include walking and yoga, which expend little energy and have little contact or competition. High-impact activities such as kick-boxing and soccer consume much energy and are competitive. Some active leisure activities involve almost no physical activity, but do require a substantial mental effort, such as playing chess or painting a picture. Active leisure and recreation overlap significantly.

Passive leisure activities are those in which a person does not exert any significant physical or mental energy, such as going to the cinema, watching television, or gambling on slot machines. Some leisure experts discourage these types of leisure activity, on the grounds that they do not provide the benefits offered by active leisure activities. For example, acting in a community drama (an active leisure activity) could build a person's skills or self-confidence. Nevertheless, passive leisure activities are a good way of relaxing for many people.

Warming-up Questions

1. What did you do during your spare time when in senior high school? Is there any difference from what you do in college? List as many leisure activities you do as you can.

2. In your understanding, what is the relationship between leisure and work? Discuss it with your classmates.

Sentence Analysis

1. Of course there were always a privileged few who had leisure; but most men had to work 12, 14, or even 16 hours a day, six days a week.

此句包括两个并列分句,由并列连词 but 连接。常见的并列句有以下几种:

1)用来连接两个并列概念的连接词:and, not only… but also…, neither… nor…等,and 所连接的前后分句往往表示先后关系或递进关系。前后分句的时态往往保持一致(若第一个分句是祈使句,那么第二个分句用将来时)。例如:

The house was broken into and a lot of things were stolen.

这住宅被破门而入,许多东西被偷走了。

Neither has he called on her, nor will he do so. 他既没有拜访她,也不打算拜访。

Think it over again and you will find a way out. 再仔细考虑考虑,你会找到出路的。

2)表示在两者之间选择一个,常用的连接词:or, otherwise, or else, either… or…等,前后分句的时态往往保持一致关系,若第一个分句是祈使句,那么第二个分句用将来时。例如:

Either you or I am wrong. 要么是你要么是我错了。

We can go to the movies, or we can watch TV. 我们去看电影或者看电视。

3)表明两个概念彼此有矛盾、相反或者转折,常用的连接词:but, yet, still, however, while 等,前后分句时态一致。例如:

Peter went to the picnic, but Mary stayed at home. 彼得去野餐,但是玛丽却呆在家里。

My younger sister is reading a book in the study, while my brother is surfing the internet. 我妹妹正在书房看书,而我弟弟却在上网。

4)说明原因,用连接词 for,前后分句时态一致。例如:

He must have been ill, for he didn't go to work yesterday.

他一定是生病了,因为他没来上班。

5)表示结果,用连接词 so,前后分句时态一致。

He doesn't want to be late for class, so every morning he gets up early.

他不想上课迟到,因此每早起床很早。

2. As late as 1840 the average factory worker labored 72 hours a week.

在此句中 average 为形容词,意为"一般的, 通常的, 平均的";除此以外,还可作名词,意为"平均, 平均数";还可作动词,意为"平均, 均分;求平均值"。例如:

His average scores in the finial exam is more than 85. (*a.*)

他期末考试的平均分超过 85。

We average 8 hours' work a day. (*v.*) 我们每天平均工作 8 小时。

The average of 4, 8, and 60 is 24. (*n.*) 4、8 和 60 的平均数是 24。

on the/an average 平均,按平均数计算;一般地说

例如:On the / an average, there are 20 boys present each day. 每天平均有 20 个男生出席。

3. It is a particularly difficult problem for the sick, the aged, and those who have retired from earning a living.

earn one's living: to make a living 谋生

例如:They have no idea what it is like to earn one's living in industry or commerce.

他们不知道如何在工业和商业中谋生。

It's not easy to earn a living if one doesn't have any skills in the modern society.

现代社会,一个人如没有任何技术是很难谋生的。

4. We do not work to get leisure and the pleasures leisure brings us; rather, we use leisure wisely so that work itself can become awarding and enjoyable.

此句中,分号之后的并列分句带有 so that 引导的目的状语从句。

so that 既可以引导目的状语从句,又可以引导结果状语从句,区别是:

1)so that 引导的目的状语从句中常会有情态动词 can, could, may, might, will, would 等,而 so that 引导的结果状语从句中一般没有情态动词;

2)So that 引导的目的状语从句之前不用逗号,而 so that 引导的结果状语从句与主句之间往往有逗号相隔开(即略作停顿)。请比较:

He worked hard at his lessons so that he could gain high grades in the exams.

他努力学习功课,争取考试能获得好成绩。

He worked hard at his lessons, so that he gained high grades in the exams.

他努力学习,结果考试获得了好成绩。

5. The feeling of success at doing one's daily work — whether it is a job, maintaining a home, or going to school — depends largely on coming to it each day with fresh energy and active interest.

1)此句中,应提醒学生 whether 引导的同位语从句;例如:

The question whether they ought to stop working or not was discussed among the workers.

2)注意 depend on 的用法:

depend on：rely on；count on 依靠，依赖

例如：Our success depends（relies）mainly on your assistance.

　　　我们的成功取决于你们协助。

　　　Children must depend on their parents. 孩子们必须依赖他们的父母。

Word Study

1. **leisure**　*n.* 空闲；闲暇（定语名词），常用来修饰另一个名词：

例：Fishing is a popular leisure activity. 钓鱼是一项大众闲暇活动。

　　He has no leisure to do some reading these days. 这些天他没有空闲时间读书。

leisure time 空闲时间

leisure travel 休闲的旅行

at（one's）leisure：当某人有自由时间时；在某人方便时

例：I'll return the call at my leisure. 方便时我就会回电话。

2. **limit**

n. 界限，限度；（*pl.*）范围

例：There is a limit to everything. 凡事都有限度。

　　There is a limit to the amount of money I can afford.

　　我能付得起的钱数是有限的。

the limit of one's powers 某人的权力限度

reach the limit of one's resource 到达山穷水尽的地步

within the city limits 在城市范围内

v. 限制，限定

例：The Constitution limits the President's term of office to four years.

　　宪法规定总统的任期为四年。

　　Her mother limits the amount of food that she eats. 她母亲限制她的饭量。

3. **put**　*v.*

1）放，安置

例：Open the bag and put the money in. 打开袋子，把钱放进去。

2）使处于（某种状态）

例：She put her books in order. 她把书整理好。

3）表达

例：I want to know how to put this in French. 我想知道如何用法语来表达这件事。

　　　put an end to sth.；bring sth. to an end 结束……

例：Such a practice must be put an end to. 这种做法必须制止。

4. **enjoy**　*v.*（接名词或动名词作宾语）

1）欣赏，喜爱

例：The twin brothers always enjoy going to the concert.

　　这一对双胞胎弟兄对听音乐会总是兴致勃勃。

　　I enjoy my job. 我喜爱我的工作。

2) 享有,享受

例：He enjoys very good health. 他有健康的身体。

　　With a car he can enjoy his leisure by making trips to the country or seaside on the weekends. 有了小汽车,他就可以在周末到乡村或海边度假享受空闲时间。

enjoy oneself 享乐,过得快乐/愉快;尽情地玩

例：Did you enjoy yourself at the party? 宴会上你玩得痛快吗?

enjoyable a. 可爱的,令人愉快的,有趣的

enjoyably ad.

5. use

n. 1) 使用,应用

　　例：Something will have to be done about the use of cars.

　　　　必须对车辆的使用加以限制。

　　　　He is quite skilled in the use of the bow and arrow. 他对弓箭的使用很娴熟。

　　2) 利用,运用

　　例：The phrase has been in wide use from before 1950's.

　　　　这个词组从50年代前起就被广泛运用了。

　　Let's make full use of our time. 让我们充分利用好时间。

　　3) 用途,效用,用处

　　例：What is the use of waiting for her if she has decided not to come?

　　　　如果她决定不来,等她有什么用?

　　It's a tool with several uses. 这是多用途工具。

　　It's no use arguing with him. 和他吵是没有用的。

　　an electronic device with many uses 一种多功能电子仪器

v. 1) 用,使用;利用

　　例：Mr. is used before the names of men. Mr.用在男性姓名前。

　　　　How do you use a telephone? 你怎样使用电话?

　　2) 利用,运用

　　例：He used mathematics to work out the problems. 他利用数学来解决了这些问题。

　　3) 用或消费;

　　例：She rarely used alcohol. 她很少喝酒。

make use of 利用,使用

put to use 使用

use up 用完,用光

6. particularly   *ad.* 特别,尤其

例:Rice grows well in their county, particularly in their village.

他们县里的稻谷长得很好,他们村的尤其好。

It is particularly hot today. 今天特别热。

What are you particularly interested in? 你对什么特别感兴趣呢?

7. aged   *a.*   年老的;老年人特有的

例:The sick and the aged need our help. 病人和老人需要我们帮助。

an aged man 老人

8. retire   *v.*

1)退休

例:Men can retire from work at 60 in China. 在中国,男性 60 岁时可以退休。

2)引退

例:He is now retiring from political life and has gone abroad.

他即将退出政治生活,并已出国。

retire from the world 离群索居;退隐(出家当和尚)

3)(正式用语)就寝

例:He retires to bed at about 10:00 every evening. 他每晚大约 10 点睡觉。

retire to bed / to rest 就寝

retire for the night 就寝,上床去睡

9. so   *ad.*

1)[表示方式]这样,那样,如此,因此

例:Hold the pen so. 这样执笔。

You must not do so. 你一定不要那么做。

2)[表示程度]到那个程度,那样,如此地

例:Don't speak so fast. 别讲得那么快。

so important an event 这么重要的一件事

3)[表示强调]非常,很,极,十分

例:I'm so glad to hear from you. 接到你的来信,我非常高兴。

It's so kind of you. 你太好了;太感谢你了。

4)[代替表语或谓语,使用倒装语序]也……

例:You are an engineer, so is she. 你是工程师,她也是工程师。

Mary can speak Chinese, so can her brother.

玛丽会讲汉语,她的兄弟也会。

10. feeling   *n.*   感觉;情绪;同情

例:I never like to hurt people's feelings. 我从不愿意伤害别人的感情。

feeling of responsibility 责任感

soft feeling 柔软感；手感柔软

show much（no）feeling for 对……深表(毫无)同情

11. daily *a.* 日常的，每日的

例：The price rising have seriously affected the daily lives of millions of people.

物价上涨已严重地影响了数百万人的生活。

daily life 日常生活

daily necessities 日常必需品

a daily record 日常的记录

daily newspapers 日报

daily capacity 日产量

daily routine 例行公事

12. whether *conj.*

1）是否（接名词从句）

例：We should find out whether the museum is open. 我们该查明博物馆是不是开门。

2）不管，无论（接让步状语从句）

例：I shall go, whether you come with me or stay at home.

不论你来还是留在家中，我都要去。

Whether we help him or not, he will fail. 不论我们帮助他与否，他都将失败。

13. maintain *v.*

1）维持

例：He failed again and again simply because he had maintained his defeatist attitude.

因为他一直坚持失败主义的态度，所以失败了一次又一次。

maintain good relations 维持良好的关系

2）赡养；供给

例：He worked hard to maintain his family. 他努力工作来养家。

3）保养；维修

例：The car has always been properly maintained. 这汽车一直保养得很好。

14. largely *ad.* 很大程度上，主要地

例：There are few towns in this area；it is largely land for farming.

这个地区城镇很少，主要是农田。

This error is largely due to my oversight. 这个错误主要是由于我一时疏忽造成的。

15. energy *n.*

1）活力；精力

例：Young people usually have more energy than the old. 年轻人通常比老年人有活力。

to be full of energy 精力充沛，精力旺盛

to devote all one's energies to a job 全身心投入工作

2）能，能量

例：The energy crisis is becoming more and more severe. 能源危机变得越来越严重。

the sources of energy 能源

energy budget 能源预算

16. recreation　*n.*　娱乐；消遣

例：Football is the boys' usual recreation after school.

踢足球是男孩子们放学后通常的娱乐活动。

My favourite recreation is chess. 我最喜欢的娱乐是下国际象棋.

Some films combine education with recreation. 有些影片把教育同娱乐融合在一起。

recreational　*a.*　消遣的；娱乐的

17. necessarily　*ad.*

1）必要地

例：You should necessarily go to the party. 你一定要参加这宴会。

2）必然地

例：The study of a foreign language is necessarily difficult. 学习外语必然困难。

necessary *a.* 必要的，必需的，必然的

necessity *n.* 必要性，需要，必需品

18. meaning　*n.*

1）意义；含意

例：It doesn't seem to have much meaning. 似乎无多大意义。

the meaning of a sentence 句子的意思

2）重要性；价值

例：He says his life has lost its meaning since his wife died.

他说妻子死后他的生命就失去了价值。

the meaning of life 生命的价值

19. activity　*n.*

1）活动

例：We'd better take more activities in school. 我们最好多参加一些校内活动。

practical activities 实践活动

social activities 社交活动，社会活动

2）活跃；活动性

例：The classroom was full of activity; every child was busy.

教室里充满了活跃的气氛，每个孩子都忙个不停。

be in activity 在活动中

with activity 精力充沛地

20. spirit　*n.*

1）精神；灵魂

例：Don't let your spirits droop. 不要萎靡不振。

the spirit of the age 时代精神

a man of spirit 精神饱满的人

the fighting spirit 斗志

a broken spirit 消沉的意志，心灰意懒

2)［pl.］情绪，心情，兴致

例：After hearing the good news, we were all in high spirits.

　　听了好消息后，我们所有人都兴高采烈。

in good spirits 精神好，高兴，兴致好

in high /great spirits 情绪极高，兴高采烈，兴致勃勃

in low/poor spirits 意志消沉，垂头丧气，怏怏不乐

be down in spirits 情绪低落

in spirits 愉快地，活泼地

Phrases and Expressions

1. to the limit（of）到极点，到顶点

例：He tried my patience to the limit. 他把我逼得忍无可忍了。

　　Our resources are stretched to the limit. 我们的资源已接近枯竭。

2. come to sth.（to 是介词）

1）恢复知觉

例：The fainting victim came to. 昏倒的受害者恢复了意识。

2）合计，总计

例：By the end of the year, the total money collected had come to over 80 million dollars.

　　到年底，集资总数已超过 8 000 万美元。

3）突然想起

例：After speaking about half an hour, he came to a sad story of his family.

　　大约谈了半个小时以后，他突然想起了家里的一段伤心事。

come about 出现；发生

come across 偶然遇到或找到

come along 进展；出现；赶快

come around / round 恢复，还原；来，再来

come by 取得；从旁走过

come down 传承；降低

come on 催促；快速运动（常用于祈使语气）；进步，进展

come out 发行或发表；结果是；出现，显露

come through 经历……仍活着

come to an end 结束

come to the point 回到正题上来

come true 实现,达到

come up 出现,走近

come up to 等于;合计

come up with 提出;提供

3. go together [口]经常作伴;形影不离;陪同;相配

例:Gossip and lying go together. 闲话谎言,形影相随。

Shall we go together then? 那么我们一块去好吗?

These colors go well together. 这些颜色很协调。

Beer and cheese go well together. 啤酒与奶酪一起吃味道很好。

4. speak of

1)谈及,说到

例:When speaking of Beijing opera, he is very excited. 谈起京剧,他十分激动。

We often speak of seven continents. 我们经常谈到七大洲。

2)值得一提

例:It's nothing to speak of. 那不值得一提。

Her performance was nothing to speak of. 她的表演没什么可称道的。

They speak well of him. 大家很称赞他。

speak ill of sb. 说(某人)的坏话

Speak of the devil, and he appears. 说曹操,曹操到。

5. make use of

1)利用

例:First of all, we must make use of our present equipment.

首先,我们必须利用现有设备。

We must make good use of our time. 我们要很好地利用时间。

2)使用

例:We had better make use of something inexpensive.

我们最好使用某种便宜的东西。

6. contribute to

1)捐献

例:He offered to contribute to the Red Cross. 他主动提出向红十字会捐款。

2)作出贡献

例:He did not contribute anything to his family. 他对他家庭并无任何贡献。

This new discovery will contribute to all humanity.

这个新发现将对全人类作出贡献。

3)起作用,有助于

例：Proper rest and enough sleep contribute to longevity.

适当的休息和足够的睡眠有益于长寿。

 Differentiations and Analysis of Words and Expressions

1. lively, alive, living

1) lively 有"活泼的、快活的、生动的"等意思，可以指人或物，可做定语或表语；但与其他两个词不同，它没有"活着的"意思。例如：

Young children are usually lively. 小孩子们通常是活泼的。

He told a very lively story. 他讲了一个生动的故事。

2) alive, live, living 都有"活的、有生命的"意思，与 dead 意义相反。但 live 通常只作前置定语，且一般用于动物；alive, living 不仅可做定语（alive 只能置于名词后；living 一般置于名词前，也可置于名词后），也可以作表语。例如：

This is a live (= living) fish. (= This is a fish alive.)

这是一条活鱼。（指动物，且作定语时，三者均可用）

Who's the greatest man alive (= living man)?

谁是当今最伟大的人物？（指人，不能用 live。）

The fish is still alive (= living) 那条鱼还活着。（指动物作表语时不能用 live）。

3) living 主要指在某个时候是活着的，而 alive 指本来有死的可能，但仍活着的。而且，做主语补足语或宾语补足语时，只能用 alive；作比喻义（如"活像……"、"活生生的"等）解时，要用 living。例如：

The enemy officer was caught alive.

那位敌方军官被活捉了。（做主语补足语，不用 living）

We found the snake alive. 他发现蛇还活着。（做宾语补足语，不用 living）

He is the living image of his father. 他活像他父亲。（比喻义，不用 alive）

4) 只有 living 前加 the 方可表示"活着的人"，做主语时，视作复数。例如：

The living are more important to us than the dead.

活着的人对我们来说比死去的人更重要。

2. interesting / interested

1) interesting 意思是"令人感兴趣的、有趣的"，可用做表语，其主语通常是物，也可以用作定语，既可修饰人也可修饰物。例如：

Here is an interesting family photo. 这儿有一张有趣的家庭照片。

My father bought me an interesting story-book yesterday.

昨天我爸爸给我买了一本有趣的故事书。

The story is very interesting. 这故事很有趣。

He is very interesting. 他这个人很有趣。

2) interested 意思是"对……感兴趣"，常用于 be/become interested in 这一结构，其主语应该是人，而不是物。它还可以用作定语，只修饰人，不能修饰物。例如：

I am interested in English. 我对英语感兴趣。

Even before he was ten he became very interested in science.
他甚至在十岁以前就对自然科学很感兴趣。

I feel quite interested in the interesting story. 我对这一有趣的故事很感兴趣。

类似的形容词有：exciting（令人兴奋的），excited（感到兴奋的），

surprising（令人吃惊的），surprised（感到吃惊的）。

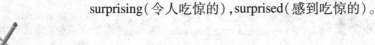

Word Building

在本课中出现较多的前缀、后缀有：

1. 名词后缀：-er；-ness

1）名词后缀：-er

表示"……的人"，用来指执行某一特殊动作的人、某地区、地方的人；"研究……的人"、"从事……职业的人"。例如：

swim→swimmer   run→runner

New York→New Yorker   southern→southerner

garden→gardener   write→writer

2）名词后缀：-ness

（在形容词、分词后形成抽象名词）表示"性质"、"状态"、"精神"、"程度"。例如：

bitter→bitterness   tired→tiredness

up-to-date→up-to-dateness new→newness

2. 形容词后缀：-able，-ful，-less

1）形容词后缀：-able

（附在动词或名词后构成形容词）表示"能够……的，适于……的，值得……的，有……性质的，有……趋向的"。例如：

change→changeable   comfort→comfortable

enjoy→enjoyable   peace→peaceable

2）形容词后缀：-ful

（加在名词之后，构成形容词）表示"充满……的"、"多的"；"赋有……性质的"。例如：

shame→shameful   beauty→beautiful

（加在动词之后，构成形容词）表示"容易……的"。例如：

forget→forgetful

3）形容词后缀：-less

（附在名词或动词之后）（构成形容词）表示"无"、"缺"、"没有"。例如：

fear→fearless   care→careless

3. 副词后缀：*a.* / p. p + -ly→*ad.*

（在形容词或分词之后，构成副词）表示"方式"、"状态"、"时间"、"地点"、"顺序"、"程度"、"方向"、"方面"等。例如：

bold→boldly　　　　　　　　great→greatly

unexpected→unexpectedly　　smiling→smilingly

economical→economically　　noble→nobly

scientifical→scientifically

Grammar Focus

一、副词

1. 副词的种类

　1）方式副词（大部分是形容词＋ly构成）：如 quickly, clearly, freely, carefully, calmly 等。

　2）时间副词：如 now, then, ago, before, just now, recently, already, immediately 等。

　3）地点副词：如 here, there, left, away, home, out, up, back, above, near 等。

　4）频度副词：如 always, often, usually, sometimes, ever, rarely, never, seldom, hardly 等。

　5）程度副词：如 much, a little, very, so, enough, greatly 等。

　6）疑问副词：如 when, where, why, how 等。

　7）关系副词：如 when, where, why 等。

2. 副词的功能

　1）作状语：修饰形容词、副词、动词、介词短语、句子等。

　例：Their living conditions were very terrible. 他们的生活条件非常差。

　　　They felt greatly surprise. 他们感到非常吃惊。

　　　He runs very fast. 他跑得很快。

　　　Obviously, they are going to win the match. 很明显,他们将赢得这场比赛。

　　　Seriously, I like to work with you. 我愿意与你共事,我是认真的。

　2）作表语

　例：I must be off now. 我必须得马上离开了。

　　　The meeting is over. 会议结束了。

　　　How long will you be away? 你将离开多长时间?

　3）作定语

　例：The two rooms upstairs are my sister's bed-room. 楼上两屋子是我姐姐的卧室。

　　　It is important to read the directions below. 阅读以下的说明书是很重要的。

　4）作宾语补足语

　例：We saw her off two days ago. 两天前我们给她送行。

　　　Let me out. 让我出去。

3. 副词的位置

　1）修饰形容词、副词、介词短语和名词短语的副词,位于被修饰成分之前。

　例：They worked very hard. 他们很努力地工作。

　　　That girl is quite pretty. 那女孩十分漂亮。

　　　It's completely dark. 天完全黑了。

注意:enough 作副词时,放在被修饰成分之后。

例:He studies hard enough. 他学习足够努力。

2)地点副词、方式副词和多数时间副词(表示频率的除外)位于被修饰动词之后,如带宾语,则位于宾语之后。

例:She dances very well. 她舞跳得很好。

He left the office angrily. 他生气地离开了办公室。

Please wait for me at the school gate. 请在校门口等我。

We will go to Chengdu tomorrow. 明天我们将去成都。

We shall have a meeting in the classroom this afternoon. 今下午我们将在教室里开会。

3)频度副词在句中位置有以下两种情况:

(1) 在 be 动词、情态动词及第一个助动词之后

例:She is always kind to us. 她对我们总是很亲切。

I can never forget the day. 我永远不会忘记那天。

The work has never been done. 从未作过那份工作。

(2) 在实义动词之前

例:He often goes to school early. 他常常很早去上学。

二、形容词、副词的比较级和最高级

1. 形容词、副词的比较级和最高级的构成

1)大多数单音节形容词和副词,加后缀-(e)r/-(e)st,变成比较级和最高级形式。

序号	变化方式　　　　例词 等级		原　级	比较级	最高级
1	直接加-er,-est	*a.*	bright	brighter	brightest
		ad.	soon	sooner	sooner
2	以-e 结尾的只加-r,-st	*a.*	nice	nicer	nicest
		ad.	wide	wider	widest
3	结尾是重读闭音节并且是"辅音字母 + 元音字母 + 辅音字母",双写结尾字母再加-er,-est	*a.*	hot thin	hotter thinner	hottest thinnest
4	以"辅音字母 + y"结尾,变 y 为 i,再加-er,-est	*a.*	easy	easier	easiest
		ad.	early	earlier	earliest

2)许多双音节的和多音节的形容词/副词,在前面加 more,most 来构成比较级和最高级。

	原　级	比较级	最高级
形容词	important beautiful	more important more beautiful	the most important the most beautiful
副词	slowly quickly	more slowly more quickly	（the）most slowly （the）most quickly

3）少数以-er,-ow,-le,-y 结尾的双音节形容词/副词,可加-er/-est 来构成比较级和最高级。

原　级	比较级	最高级
clever narrow	cleverer narrower	the cleverest the narrowest

4）不规则变化

	原　级	比较级	最高级
形容词	good（好的）/well（健康的）	better	best
	bad（坏的）/ill（有病的）	worse	worst
	old（老的）	older/elder	oldest/eldest
	many/much（多的）	more	most
	little（少的）	less	least
	far（远的）	farther/further	farthest/furthest
副词	well（好）	better	best
	badly（坏）	worse	worst
	much（多）	more	most
	little（少）	less	least
	far（远）	farther（较远） further（进一步）	farthest（最远） furthest（最久的）
	late（迟）	later（较迟） latter（后者）	latest 最近（时间） last 最近（顺序）

2. 形容词/副词比较级和最高级用法归纳

1）原级的用法

句型:as + 形容词/副词 原级 + as...（肯定句）

表示两者之间某种性质程度相等

例:Tom is as honest as Jack. 汤姆与杰克一样诚实。

　　He runs as fast as I. 他和我跑得一样快。

This car is as expensive as that one. 这辆小汽车和那辆一样昂贵。

He got up as early as usual. 他和平常一样起得早。

句型:not so(as) + 形容词,副词 + as…(否定句)

表示前者某方面不如后者后与后者不一样。

例:He is not so(as) tall as she. 他不如她高。

He can't speak so(as) fast as you. 他说话不如你快。

There is not so(as) much water in this glass as in that glass.

这玻璃杯里的水不如那玻璃杯里的多。

She does not run so(as) fast as he. 她不如他跑得快。

2)比较级的用法

句型:形容词,副词比较级 + than…

表示前者某方面更胜于后者,than 是一个连词,它连接一个状语从句表示和什么相比,因此一般译为"比"。通常,为了避免重复,从句中有些成份可以省略。

例:You look younger than your elder brother. 你看起来比你哥哥年轻。

He did better than you. 他比你做得好。

Their work is more difficult than yours. 他们的工作比你们的更难做。

The old woman was received more warmly than she had expected.

老奶奶受到了比她想象中更热烈的欢迎。

3)最高级的用法

句型:形容词/副词 最高级 + 比较范围(of…/in…)

用于三者及其以上的范围进行比较。形容词最高级前要加定冠词 the,副词最高级前可加可不加。

例:Kent is the happiest of us all. 肯特是我们中最幸福的。

Spring is the best season of the year. 春天是一年中最好的季节。

George jumps(the)highest in his class. 乔治在班上跳得最高。

Who can run (the) fastest in your school? 你们学校谁跑得最快?

三、注意要点

1. 比较对象要清楚、正确、前后一致。

His English is as good as I. (误) His English is as good as mine. (正)

Our classroom is larger than they. (误) Our classroom is larger than theirs. (正)

2. 要避免比较结构方面的错误,如多词、少词或用词错误。

She works more harder than I. (误) She works harder than I. (正)

He runs fast as I(do). (误) He runs as fast as I(do). (正)

She dances as good as I. (误) She dances as well as I. (正)

3. 比较状语从句的行为动词或整个谓语常用 **do, does, did** 替代。若从句谓语中有"**be** 动词、助动词或情态动词",则用相应的"**be** 动词、助动词或情态动词"替代。

例：She speaks English as fluently as I(do). 她说英语和我一样流畅。

Try as hard as you can. 尽你最大努力。

4. 有时为避免重复,在从句中常用(the) one 或 that 代替前面出现过的单数可数名词,用 those 或(the) ones 代替可数名词复数,用 that 代替不可数名词。

1)泛指,表示"任一个/些……"

替换对象	替代词	例　句
可数名词单数	one	This picture is more beautiful than that one.
可数名词复数	ones	Small bananas are often better than bigger ones.

2)特指,表示"……的(那种/个/些)……"

替换对象	替代词	例　句
不可数名词	that	The air in the country is cleaner than that in the city.
可数名词单数	the one 或 that	The pen on the desk is more expensive than the one(that) in your hand.

5. 若在同一范围内比较时,必须把主体排除在被比较的对象之外。

例：He runs faster than any boy in his class. (误)

He runs faster than any other boy in his class. (正) 他比班上其他任何男同学都跑得快。

He runs fastest in his class. (正) 在班上他跑得最快。

注：any other 之后要用单数。

6. 有些词可用在形容词或副词的比较级之前,表程度：

a bit/ a little 有点儿,a lot/much/ a great deal 很,非常,even/still 更,far/by far 远远,rather 相当,slightly 稍微,twice, an inch, many, etc.

例：She's been to more places than I have. 他去过的地方比我去过的多。

You had made even more mistakes in your composition than Mr. Liu.

在写作中,你甚至比刘先生犯的错还多。

Japan is a little larger than Korea. 日本比韩国稍大一点儿。

7. 如果表比较的形容词是 senior,junior,superior,它们的后面跟"介词 to + 名词",不用 than。

例：She is two years senior to me. 她比我大两岁。

Tom is 3 years junior to me. 汤姆比我小三岁。

8. 使用最高级时要注意应有比较范围,比较范围可以由 in 或 of 引出。其中,"of + 复数"表示"在……之中的"、"在……中",如：of the three 在三个之中,of all (people)在所有(人)之中；"in + 范围、场所"表示"在……之中"、"在……之内",如：in the house 在家中,in our school 在我们学校。

例：Mary is the best student in her class. 玛丽是她班上最好的学生。

This school is the largest of the four. 这所学校是四所中最大的。

9. "one of the ＋ 最高级 ＋ 名词复数"，表示"是最……之一者"。

例：He is one of the most handsome boys in his school. 他是学校里最英俊的男同学之一。

10. 最高级前可用 by far, almost, about, much, nearly, not really, not quite, the second (third)等修饰。

例：It's the second longest river in the world. 这是世界上第二长的江河。

四、几种常见句型

1. the same ＋ 名词 ＋ as：与……一样

例：The road is the same length as that one. 这条路和那条路一样长。

The boy is the same height as his father. 那个男孩和他父亲一样高。

2. the ＋ 比较级 ＋ of the(两者)：两者中较……的

例：He is the braver of the two boys. 他是两个男孩中比较勇敢的一个。

This book is the more interesting of the two. 两本书中这本书比较有趣。

3. the ＋ 比较级 ＋ ……, the ＋ 比较级 ＋ ……：越……，就越……

例：The harder you work, the greater progress you'll make.

你工作越努力，就能取得越大的进步。

The busier he is, the happier he feels. 他越忙越快乐。

4. 比较级 ＋ and ＋ 比较级，more and more ＋ 原级(多音节)：越来越……

例：It is colder and colder. 天气越来越冷。

He is more and more active. 他越来越活跃。

5. 表示倍数的句型

1) times as ＋ 形容词原级 ＋ as：是……的几倍

例：This room is 3 times as large as that one. 这间屋子是那间的三倍。

2) times ＋ 形容词比较级 ＋ than：比……大/多几倍

例：This room is twice larger than that one. 这间屋子比那间大两倍。

3) "大多少岁"、"高几厘米"要用"表示数、量的词 ＋ 比较级"来表示。

例：I'm three years older than you. 我比你大三岁。

He is a head taller than I. 他比我高一头。

6. as...as possible：尽可能

例：I will come back as quickly as possible. 我会尽快回来。

He can give us help as much as possible. 他给了我们尽可能多的帮助。

Language Tips for Writing

1. 有关休闲活动方面的一些词汇：

休闲活动 leisure activities；劳逸结合 strike a proper balance between work and leisure；有独立支配的时间 have some time at one's own disposal；唱卡拉 sing songs in a karaoke bar；垂钓 go fishing；打保龄球 play bowling；打高尔夫球 play golf；打牌 play card-games；逛公园 visit a park；stroll around a park；逛街 stroll up / down the streets；睡懒觉 sleep in；lie in；踏青 go for walk in the country in spring（when the grass has just turned green）；去远足 go on an outing；买打折商品 buy goods at a discount；驾车兜风 go for a drive in one's car；泡吧 hang about in a bar；上网冲浪 surf the web；surf the Internet；充电 enrich oneself（through a refresher course, etc.）；learn the new developments ；bring up to date（in technology, etc.）；看电影 watch movies（see a film）；京剧 Peking Opera；恐怖片 thriller film；侦探片 detective film；管弦乐队 orchestra；杂耍 variety；动作片 action film；杂技 acrobatics。

2. 有关休闲活动方面的一些句型：

1）How do you usually spend your weekends/ holiday/ vacation?

你通常怎么度过周末/假期/ 假期？

2）I'm going to visit Hollywood.

我打算去参观好莱坞。

3）—What's on Channel Four at eight o'clock tonight？今晚八点第四频道上演什么？

—A fashion show. After that, a variety show/ an orchestra concert/ the Peking Opera.

有场时装表演,之后还有杂耍表演/管弦音乐会/京剧。

4）Do you like action films/ western films/ thriller films/ detective films?

你喜欢动作片/西部片/恐怖片/侦探片吗？

5）Do you know what film that cinema is showing right now?

你知道那家影院正上映什么吗？

6）I'd like to have two good seats for tonight's concert/ show/ play.

我要买两张今晚音乐会/表演/戏剧的好票。

7）I prefer classical music to rock music. 我喜欢听古典音乐而不喜欢摇滚乐。

I like pop music rather than sports. 我喜欢流行乐而不是运动会。

I prefer coffee to tea. 我更喜欢咖啡而不是茶。

I like playing bridge/the piano. 我喜欢打桥牌/弹钢琴。

I like going to a disco bar/a karaoke bar. 我喜欢参加迪斯科舞会/去卡拉 OK。

I like watching acrobatics. 我喜欢看杂技表演。

8）Which night club around here would you recommend to us?

您给我们推荐附近哪家夜总会?

9)—Who was performing just now? 刚才谁在演出?

　—The Joffrey Ballet. 乔弗雷芭蕾舞剧团。

10)During my spare time, I like playing bridge, going to a disco or going to a karaoke bar.

　业余时间我喜欢打桥牌、去迪斯科舞厅或去卡拉 OK 酒吧间。

3. 有关邀请他人的一些表达:

I'd like to invite you to (v. / sth.)

to have dinner/ dinner/ our party / my birthday party / the conference.

我打算邀请你(吃晚饭、参加我们的聚会、参加我的生日宴会、会议)……

Why don't you come and join us for disco? 为什么不来和我们一起跳迪斯科?

How would you like to join us? 加入到我们中来,怎么样?

How about / What about + v-ing (going to see a film this evening/ going shopping on this weekend.)?

……怎么样? (今晚去看电影、这周末去购物如何?)

Are you doing anything special on Friday, Mr. Smith?

史密斯先生,周五有什么特别安排吗?

Would it be alright if I …? 如果……好吗?

That would be fine / super. 那样挺好、非常好。

Yeah. Why not? 好的。为什么不呢?

I'll be delighted to go. 我很高兴去。

It's very kind of you to invite me. 邀请我,你真是太好了!

Thank you for your invitation / for inviting me. 谢谢你的邀请。

I'd like / love to, thank you. 我很愿意,谢谢!

How nice of you! Many thanks. 你真好! 多谢了!

That sounds fine, but I'm afraid I can't because… 听起来不错,但恐怕我不行,因为……

but I don't think I can manage it. 听起来不错,但我没法做到。

I'm sorry I can't, but thank you all the same. 对不起我不能,但仍然很谢谢你。

Could you make it another time, perhaps next Sunday.

你可以安排另一个时间吗? 或许下个周日。

Text B　How Do the British Spend Their Leisure Time?

Reading Strategies (7): Reading for Drawing a Conclusion

在阅读理解中,一部分结论在文章的结尾直接给予了读者,但更多的是靠读者通过理解文章直接陈述的观点或描述的事实的基础上,领悟作者的言外之意(implied meaning),得出符合作者意愿的结论,即根据作者暗示的内容,推断出合理的结论。

推断结论常见的题型有:

1. It can be inferred / concluded from the passage that _____.

2. What does the author probably mean by "…"?

3. What conclusion can be drawn from the passage?

4. Where would this passage most probably appear / be found?

5. The paragraph preceding / following this one would most probably discuss / state /deal with _____.

6. From the last paragraph, we infer/learn / conclude that _____.

7. By the first sentence of the passage, the author means that _____.

8. We can infer / conclude / draw from the passage that _____.

9. "…" are used in the text to refer to _____.

在解答推断结论性问题时,应清楚所要解答的问题是需要针对某个细节进行推断,还是针对主题思想、作者的意图进行推断。

针对细节的推断可运用 scanning 方法,迅速在阅读材料中确定推理依据的位置或范围,然后再进行推理判断。

针对主题思想作推断时,其解题的主要依据是文章的主题思想,然后再分析句子之间的逻辑关系,区分观点与例证(opinion and fact)、原因与结果(cause and effect)、主观点与次观点(main idea and supporting idea)。

以学生练习册阅读理解 passage 2 为例:文章介绍了比彻·斯托夫人的小说《汤姆叔叔的小屋》对美国历史的发展所起的重要作用。文中尽管没明确告诉我们文学艺术的重要性,但通过文中描述的句子,如:第一句话 The pen is more powerful than the sword. ,第二段最后一句 but the Northern Americans were wildly excited over it, and were so inspired by it that they were ready to go to war to set the slaves free. 以及文章最后一句 As Lincoln took her hand, he said, "So you are the little woman who started the big war." 能读出结论:文学艺术是多么重要呀!

Word Study

1. spend *v.*

1）花费

例：Don't spend without the thought of the next day. 花钱不要只顾眼前不想明天。

2）度过

例：How do you spend your leisure? 你是怎样消磨空闲时间的？

2. interview

n. 采访；接见，面试

例：Thank you very much indeed for this interview. 非常感谢你这次接见。

How was your interview? 面试怎么样？

v. 接见；会见；（记者的）访问；

例：He interviewed a number of candidates. 他对多名候选人进行面试。

3. base

v. 以……作基础，基于……（与 on, upon 连用）

例：This news report is based entirely on fact. 这篇新闻报导完全是根据实际情况写成的。

One should always base one's opinions on facts. 意见应以事实为根据。

n. 基础，根据地

例：That company has offices all over the world, but their base is in Paris.

这个公司的办事处遍布全世界，但本部在巴黎。

4. tired *a.*

1）疲劳的，累的，疲倦的

例：He was too tired to go any further. 他累得一步也挪不动了。

Tired as he was, Peter tried to finish all the homework that day.

尽管彼得很累了，他还是努力完成当天所有的家庭作业。

2）（感到）厌烦的，厌倦的（与 of 连用）

例：I'm tired of your conversation. 你的讲话我听腻了。

Everybody's tired of your everlasting complaints!

大家对你喋喋不休的抱怨感到厌倦了！

5. popular *a.* 流行的，受欢迎的

例：This dance is popular with young people. 这种舞很受青年人青睐。

He's a good politician but he isn't popular. 他是一位好的政治家，但不受大众欢迎。

a popular resort 受欢迎的旅游胜地

6. mention

v. 提及；说起

例：Did you mention this to my sister? 你对我姐姐说到这件事了吗？

On the telephone, he mentioned that he had been ill. 在电话里,他说自己病了。

Don't mention it. 不要客气/不用谢/没关系/不要紧/哪里哪里(作客套语)。

not to mention（= without mentioning）更不必说, 更谈不上

as mentioned above 如上所述

n. 提及；说起

例：There was no mention of the fundamental cause of the dispute between the two neighboring countries in the newspaper. 报上没提及这两个邻国间争端的根本原因。

7. party

n. 集会,聚会,宴会等

例：Could you please take part in his birthday party? 你可以参加他的生日宴会吗？

a cocktail party 鸡尾酒会

a. 1）政党的,党派的

例：It's an activity for party members. 这是党员活动。

　　2）适用于宴会的

　　例：The girls like this type of party dresses very much.

　　　　这些女孩非常喜欢这种类型的宴会服。

　　　　a party hat 礼帽

8. meet　*v.*

1)（赴约）和……会面,遇见

例：I met my teacher in the street today. 我今天在街上遇见了我的老师。

2）接合；相交；靠近

例：The two roads meet at the north of the city. 两条马路在城市的北面汇合。

3）引见；结识

例：I know Mrs Hill by sight, but have never met her.

　　我见面认得希尔夫人,但是从来没人给我们引见过。

meet with 偶遇；碰到

例：I met with a friend in the train yesterday. 昨天我在火车上遇到一位朋友。

His speech met with a cold acceptance. 他的演讲受到冷遇。

9. relative

n. 亲戚

例：They are talking about family and relative. 他们在谈论家庭和亲属。

a. 有关的,相关的

例：Please find out the facts relative to the problem. 请查处与此问题有关的事实。

All the details relative to the matter under discussion.

所有的细节与正在讨论的事情有关。

10. possibly *ad.*

1）可能,或者

例：You may possibly get a new job. 你也许能得到一个新工作。

2）（用于否定句和疑问句）无论如何,不管怎样

例：—Will they put your salary up? 他们会提高你的薪水吗?

　　—Possibly. 也许会。

　　We cannot possibly do it. 那件事我们无论如何也不能做。

11. paint

v. 1）给……上油漆

例：He painted the wall yellow. 他把墙漆成黄色。

　　She painted the window sills a bright color. 她把窗台漆上鲜艳的颜色。

2）（用颜料等）绘,画

例：I paint a lot of pictures. 我画了许多画。

n. 油漆,颜料

例：There's paint on your clothes. 你衣服上有油漆。

　　The paint on the wall is chipping off. 墙壁上的漆在剥落。

12. arrange *v.*

1）排列;整理

例：He arranged the books on the shelf. 他把书架上的书整理了一下。

2）安排;准备

例：We have arranged a party. 我们准备了一个晚会。

13. right

n. 1）权利

例：We must work for equal rights for everyone. 我们必须为每个人争取同等的权利。

　　right to vote   投票权

　　in one's own right   依照自己的权利

2）右边

例：The school is on the left of the road, and his house is on the right.

　　学校在马路的左边,他家在(马路的)右边。

　　Keep to the right!   靠右!

a. 1）正当的,正确的

例：a right answer   正确的答案

2）右边的;右方的

例：right bank   右岸(顺流而下时的右岸)

14. abroad *ad.* 在国外,到海外

例：My brother has never been abroad before, so he is finding this trip very exciting.

我弟弟以前从未出过国,所以他觉得这次旅行十分令人兴奋。

get abroad ╱ go ╱ travel abroad 到国外去

live abroad 住在国外

at home and abroad 在国内外

15. trip   *n.* （短途）旅行

例：One way trip or round trip？单程还是来回？

Have a good trip. 祝你旅途愉快。

Have a nice trip! 祝你一路顺风!

a trip to a place   到某个地方的旅行

16. country   *n.*

1）国家；国土

例：France and Switzerland are European countries. 法国和瑞士是欧洲国家。

2）国民；选民

例：The country is opposed to war. 这个国家是反战争的。

3）乡下,农村

例：to live in the country 在农村生活

Key to Exercises

Text A

Getting the Message

Ⅱ. A

Vocabulary and Structure

Ⅰ. 1— b   2—d   3—e   4—c   5—g

6—j   7— i   8—h   9—f   10—a

Ⅱ. 1. particularly   2. go   3. earn his living   4. retire   5. worthwhile   6. contributes to

Ⅲ. 1. The teacher is so wonderful that he is quite popular with all his students.

2. The weather was so hot that all the children went swimming the whole afternoon.

3. The little boy saved every coin so that he could buy his mother a present on Mother's day.

4. Please speak loudly so that your classmates can hear you clearly.

Ⅳ. 1. 而对病人、老人和已经退休的人来说,这更是一个特别棘手的问题。

2. 我们工作不是为了得到闲暇时间或是获得闲暇时光所带来的快乐,而是通过明智地使用空闲时间使得工作本身变得更有意义和愉快。

3. 当一个人讲自己善于利用空闲时,就是指他选择有助于促进健康、成长和精神的休闲活动。

Ⅴ. 1. What is the average rainfall for August in your country?

2. It is worthwhile seeing ╱ to see the film.

3. His family depends on him.

4. Beer and cheese go well together.

5. We must make good use of our time.

Speaking

Ⅱ.1.1) Peter and Man Lin went fishing together. They chatted with each other.

Peter：How many fish have you caught, Man Lin?

Man Lin：Five. What <u>about</u> you?

Peter：I have <u>more</u> fish. I've caught eight.

Man Lin：<u>What time</u> is it now?

Peter：It's half <u>past</u> five.

Man Lin：Oh, it's time <u>for</u> supper. Let's go home.

Peter：OK. Let's <u>go</u>.

2) Grace：Li Jian, <u>what day</u> is it today?

Li Jian：<u>It's</u> Wednesday.

Grace：And what's the <u>date</u> today?

Li Jian：Er…it's March 11.

Grace：Oh, it's Tree Planting Day tomorrow.

Li Jian：Yes. <u>Shall</u> we go and plant some trees?

Grace：That's a good idea.

Listening

1. B　　2. B　　3. D　　4. C　　5. B　　6. B　　7. C　　8. A

Sounds and Spelling

Ⅲ. 1. His tails.　　2. A hot dog　　3. Heat. Because you can catch a cold.

Grammar

Ⅰ.1. the biggest　　2. more beautiful　　3. the cheapest　　4. the strongest

5. more carefully　　6. happy　　7. harder, greater　　8. exciting, tired

9. hotter, hotter　　10. quickly

Ⅱ. 1. B　　2. D　　3. D　　4. D　　5. B　　6. A　　7. D　　8. C　　9. C　　10. B

Text B

1. F　　2. T　　3. T　　4. F　　5. T

Translation of the Texts

Text A

休闲问题

休闲是一个新的问题。一直到最近，人们每天都工作至精疲力竭。当然极少数有特权的人可享有空闲，但是大多数人都每天工作 12、14 甚至是 16 个小时，一周 6 天。直至 1840 年，工厂工人平均每周工作时间仍为 72 小时。农民每天都是日出而作，日落而归，可以说从早到晚从不间断。

现在，人们一周工作不到 40 小时，享有的闲暇时间更多了。因此，对每个人来说，无论是年轻人还是老年人，如何明智地利用闲暇时间已经成为一个很重要的问题。而对病人、老人和已经退休的人来说，这更是一个特别棘手的问题。这些人有太多的空闲时间，对他们来说，很难找到既有趣又有意义的方式来利用这些时间。

　　无论工作时间缩到多短,工作仍然是生活最重要的一部分。我们工作不是为了得到闲暇时间或是获得闲暇时光所带来的快乐,而是通过明智地使用空闲时间使得工作本身变得更有意义和愉快。做日常工作所获得的成就感,无论是干一份工作、操持家务、还是上学,在很大程度上取决于每天是否充满新的活力和保持积极的兴趣。

　　休闲和娱乐总是联系在一起,虽然它们不一定是同一件事情。"娱乐"含有一种明显的意义:它是一种闲暇活动,这种活动可以带来力量和精神的"再创造"。当一个人讲自己善于利用空闲时,就是指他擅长于选择有助于促进健康、成长和精神的休闲活动。

Text B

英国人如何度过闲暇时间?

　　根据我们的访谈,在利兹市中心,英国最常见的休闲活动是家庭或社交活动,但在不同的时段休闲活动又是不同的。

　　1. 平日下班后:平日下班后的时间不是很长,很多人都觉得下班后很累,他们觉得他们真正所需要的是有时间可以休息。我们所采访的大多数英国人都喜欢待在家里看电视和录像、听收音机、作运动、上网、玩电子游戏、或是阅读一些书籍。所以,这些活动是目前最流行的休闲消遣活动。

　　当然,除上述外还有更多的活动。一些年轻人下班后喜欢去酒吧、戏剧院、电影院、舞会、咖啡厅和俱乐部。

　　2. 周末:"周末是我所期待的日子。"琳达说,"我可以购物,特别是可以挑选漂亮的衣服,可以和朋友约会,也可以一起去酒吧、剧院、电影院、舞会、咖啡厅、俱乐部等。我也可以看望父母或亲戚。如果天气好的话,还可以和家人出去走走。"这可能就是我们在采访中所听到的。一些男人说他们可以整理自己的花园,也自己制作一些东西,如刷墙、做凳子或是在花园里修建一些东西。他们把这些活动叫做 DIY(Do It Yourself)。

　　3. 假期:假期是安排休闲活动的最好时机,因为在英国每年有五周的带薪假期。(工人在 1981 年获得此权利。)"如果假期长,我愿意在国外度过。"利兹都市大学的一位老师说道,"如果不是很长,我喜欢前往附近的一些地方旅行。我喜欢大自然,我也喜欢看不同的国家。"当然还有很多其他的回答:一些人喜欢呆在家里看电视;一些人喜欢去拜访亲戚。

Scripts for Listening

Conversation 1　　Alice：What's the date today, Wang Yan?

　　　　　　　　Wang Yan：I've no idea. Let me have a look at the calendar. Oh, it's Friday, December 20th.

　　　　　　　　Alice：Then Christmas Day is in 5 days' time.

　　　　　　　　Wang Yan：Right. Come to our party then.

　　　　　　　　Alice：Sure. Thanks a lot.

　　　　　　　　Question 1：What's the date today?

　　　　　　　　Question 2：What's the name of the second speaker?

Conversation 2　　Peter：Hi, Kate, do you know how long will Mr. Smith stay in the hotel?

　　　　　　　　Kate：He will stay in the hotel from Monday, October 1st to Saturday, October 6th.

　　　　　　　　Question 3：When will Mr. Smith begin to stay in the hotel?

Question 4: When will Mr. Smith leave the hotel?

Conversation 3   Wang Hai: What's the time, John? My watch has stopped. I forgot to wind it last night.

John: Sorry, I don't have my watch with me. I left it at home.

Wang Hai: That's OK. I'll ask that man…Excuse me, sir. Could you tell me the time, please?

Stranger: Sure. It's one o'clock sharp.

Wang Hai: Thank you, sir.

Stranger: You're welcome.

Wang Hai: Hurry up, John. It's one o'clock now.

John: OK, let's go, or we'll miss the train.

Question 5: From whom did Wang Hai ask the time?

Conversation 4   Peter: What time do you usually leave for school, Carol?

Carol: A quarter past seven.

Peter: Do you take the bus or ride a bicycle?

Carol: I usually catch the 7:30 bus.

Peter: Oh, school starts at 8:30?

Carol: Right.

Peter: What time will you be at lunch?

Carol: Between 12:00 and 1:00.

Peter: What time do you finish school?

Carol: At 5:30.

Peter: Can you join me for dinner after school?

Carol: Er… Ok. Thank you. I'll be at the front school gate. Is that OK?

Peter: No problem. I will pick you up at about 5:45. Let's enjoy some Chinese food tonight.

Carol: That's great.

Question 6: What time does Carol take the bus?

Question 7: When will Peter pick Carol up then?

Question 8: What can you infer from this dialogue?

Unit Eight Internet

Text A   The Internet

Background Knowledge of the Text

What is the Internet was written by Robert E. Kahn and Vinton G. . Cerf. Vinton G. Cerf, widely known as a "Father of the Internet", is the vice president and Chief Internet Evangelist of Google. He co-designed with Robert Kahn the Transmission Control Protocol/Internet Protocol (shortened as TCP/IP) — the basic communication language or protocol of the Internet, and basic architecture of the Internet.

The paper *What is the Internet* was prepared by the authors at the request of the Internet Policy Institute (IPI), a non-profit organization based in Washington D. C. , for inclusion in the upcoming series of Internet related papers. After reading the papers, readers could get a basic idea of the Internet, how it came to be, and perhaps even how to begin thinking about it from an architectural perspective. But text A is just the introduction of the related papers: *The Evolution of the Internet*; *The Internet Architecture*; *Government's Historical Role*; *A Definition for the Internet*; *Who Runs the Internet and Where Do We Go from Here*. If you want to get more information of the Internet, you can search on the Internet.

Warming-up Questions

1. We all know that the Internet is playing an important role in our life. Sometimes we even can't work without the Internet, but do you know the history of the Internet?
2. Today many students at college have their own computers. They like to search information and chat on the Internet. The Internet is more and more common in their life. Can you imagine how many Internet users are there in the world today?

Sentence Analysis

1. As we approach a new millennium, the Internet is revolutionizing our society, our economy

and our technological systems.

此句中 as 引导时间状语从句,译为"随着……"

例:As it becomes colder, some animals seldom come out.

随着天气变冷,一些动物极少外出。

时间状语从句还可以由 when, while, until, before, as soon as, since 等词引起。

例:When we arrive there, they were having supper. 我们到那儿的时候,他们正在吃晚饭。

I'll come back as soon as possible. 我会尽快回来。

2. Over the past century and a half, important technological developments have created a global environment that is drawing the people of the world closer and closer.

此句中的 that 作为关系代词引导了一个定语从句。定语从句是由关系代词或关系副词引起的。关系代词有 which, that, who, whom, whose。关系副词有 when, where, why。选用何种关系词,取决于此关系词前面的先行词。

例:The problems which we are facing need to be solved quickly.

我们所面临的问题需要马上得到解决。

Have you heard of the man who won the first prize?

你听说过那个得了一等奖的人吗?

The girl, whose mother is very rich, is always wearing new clothes.

那个女孩的母亲很有钱,她总有新衣服穿。

当先行词是表地点、原因或时间的名词时,关系词用 where, why, when。

例:This is the school where I study in. 这就是我学习的学校。

This is the reason why I don't like him. 这就是我不喜欢他的原因。

试让学生比较:I can't forget the days when I stayed in Chengdu.

我不会忘记呆在成都的日子。

I can't forget the days which I spent with my old friends.

我不会忘记和老朋友一起度过的日子。

3. … by putting the power of computation wherever we need it…

此句中 wherever 引导一个地点状语从句。地点状语从句还可以由 where 引导。

例:Wherever we go, we won't forget our hometown.

无论我们走到哪里,都不会忘记我们的家乡。

Their company stands where RenMing Road and HongXing Road meet.

他们的公司坐落在人民路和红星路汇合处。

4. The Internet, as an integrating force, has melded…

as an integrating force 是前面 Internet 的同位语,对 Internet 作补充说明。

一个名词或代词后面有时可跟一个名词、代词、数词和形容词(或起类似作用的其他形式),对前者作进一步解释,说明它指的是谁,是什么等,叫作同位语。同位语可以分为限制性和非限制性的。以上这句话中的同位语就是非限制性的。

非限制性的同位语和前面的名词关系比较松散,中间以逗号分开,语调上属于不同意群,中间有停顿。同位语去掉后句子还能成立。

例:This book was written by LuXun, a famous writer. 这本书是著名作家鲁迅写的。

Li Lei, our monitor, always studies very hard. 我们班长李磊总是学习非常努力。

限制性同位语和它前面的名词关系比较紧密,形成一个整体,两者不用逗号分开,语调上属于同一意群,中间不停顿。同位语去掉后句子意思会受影响。

例:This book was written by the famous writer Lu Xun. 这本书是著名作家鲁迅写的。

We young people should try to get more knowledge. 我们年轻人应当多学知识。

另外在某些词(如 idea, fact, news, hope, thought 等)后我们有时还可以用 that 或连接代(副)词引起的从句作同位语,称为同位语从句。

例:I had no idea that you would come. 我不知道你会来。

The news that our class won the football game made us very happy. 我们班在足球比赛中获胜的消息令大家非常高兴。

5. It is estimated that about 60 million host computers on the Internet today…

estimate 估计,估算,估价

It is estimated (that)… 据估计……

类似的搭配还有:It is reported (that)… 据报道……

　　　　　　　　 It is said (that)… 据说……

例:It is said that a shopping mall will be built here next year.

据说明年这里会有一个购物中心。

6. The telephone service, in comparison, grows an average of about 5% -10% per year.

此句中 in comparison 是一个介词短语作插入语,对整句话进行解释。还有这些介词短语可作插入语 in my opinion, in other words, by the way, in conclusion 等。

例:By the way, where is the meeting room? 顺便问一下,会议室在哪里?

常用来作插入语的结构有:I think, I hope, I guess, I'm afraid, I suppose, you see, you know 等,这些结构可以插在句子中间,也可以放在句子末尾。

例:That girl, you know, is very active in class.

你是知道的,那个女孩在课堂上是非常积极的。

You should take her advice, I think. 我认为你应当听取她的建议。

此外,插入语还可以由不定式、现在分词、形容词引起的词组、副词等充当。

例:To be frank, I can't agree with you. 坦白地说,我不同意你的观点。

Generally speaking, this is a good idea. 总的来说,这是一个好主意。

 Word Study

1. underestimate *v.* 低估;轻视

例:Do not underestimate that little girl. She is very brave.

别低估了那个小女孩。她非常勇敢。

2. global　*a.* 全球的；全世界的

　　例：Scientists have found out the reasons for global warming.

　　　　科学家们已经找到了全球变暖的原因。

3. magnify　*v.* 增强；放大

　　例：The light is magnified by the special device. 这个特殊的装置使灯更亮了。

4. information　*n.*

　　1）信息；消息

　　例：Newspaper provided a piece of information that the murder who killed two children was arrested yesterday. 报纸上有一则消息，讲那个杀了两个小孩的凶犯昨天被抓住了。

　　2）情报

　　例：Police got the information that the little girl was taken by a stranger.

　　　　警察得到的情报是那个小女孩被一个陌生人带走了。

5. integrate　*v.*

　　1）成为一体；（使）合并　　~ A into/with B

　　例：Class Three will be integrated with Class Four next term. 下学期三班会和四班合并。

　　2）（使）加入；融入群体　　~ sb. into/with sth.

　　例：You should try to integrate with this big family. 你应当设法融入这个大家庭。

6. technology　*n.* 科技；工艺；技术

　　例：This new technology will be used in the factory next year.

　　　　明年这种新的技术会在这个工厂投入使用。

　　technological　*a.* 科技的

7. instant

　　a. 1）立即的；立刻的

　　　　例：I will give you an instant reply after work. 下班后我会立即给你回复。

　　　　2）速溶的；方便的

　　　　例：I don't like to drink instant coffee. 我不喜欢喝速溶咖啡。

　　n. 瞬间；片刻

　　　　例：Just stay where you are. I'll be there in an instant. 呆在原地别动，我马上回来。

8. private　*a.*

　　1）私人的；个人的

　　例：Those are my private letters. 那些是我的私人信件。

　　2）隐秘的；私下的

　　例：She doesn't want to share her private thoughts with others.

　　　　她不想和别人分享她私下的想法。

　　in private 私下；悄悄的

9. colleague　*n.* 同事;同僚

例:She is my colleague and friend. 她既是我的同事又是朋友。

10. respective　*a.* 各自的;分别的

例:They are very famous in their respective fields. 他们在各自的领域都很出名。

11. discipline

n. 1)知识领域

例:They are experts in this discipline. 在这个知识领域他们是专家。

2)训练方法;行为准则

例:As a student, you should obey the disciplines at school.

作为学生,你应当遵守学校的行为准则。

v. 1)自我控制;严格要求

例:She disciplined herself to write an essay every week. 她要求自己每周写一篇文章。

2)惩罚;处罚

例:The naughty boy was disciplined for breaking the windows.

这个淘气的小男孩因打坏玻璃受到处罚。

12. decade　*n.* 十年期(尤指一个年代);十年

例:Over the past few decades, the small town has changed a lot.

在过去的几十年里,这个小镇发生了巨大的变化。

13. estimate

v. 估计;估算

例:It is estimated that the work will be finished in 4 days.

据估计,这个工作会在 4 天内完成。

n. 估计;估价

例:I can give you a rough estimate of the apartment.

我可以帮你粗略估计一下这套公寓的价格。

14. territory　*n.* 地区;领土

例:Our branches cover a very large territory. 我们的分支机构遍布各地区。

15. serve　*v.*

1)能满足……的需要;对……有用

例:How can the government best serve the needs of the people?

政府怎样做最能满足人民的需要?

2)(给……)提供;端上　　~ sth. (with sth.); ~ sth. (to sb.); ~ sb. /sth.

例:They served a delicious supper to the hungry children.

他们给饥饿的孩子们提供了美味的晚餐。

Phrases and Expressions

1. interact with

1）交流；沟通   ~（with sb.）

例：Work will be easier for us if we often interact with others.

如果我们经常和别人交流，工作就会变得更容易。

2）相互影响；相互作用

例：Lime interacts with the water. 石灰和水相互作用。

2. It is estimated that… 据估计

例：It is estimated that 300 students will join in the sports meeting. 据估计有300个学生会参加运动会。

3. at least 至少

例：This coat may cost at least 500 yuan. 这件衣服可能至少要花500元。

4. In comparison with…（与……相比较）

例：This football game is wonderful in comparison with that one.

与那场球赛相比，这场更精彩。

Differentiations and Analysis of Words and Expressions

1. economy, economical, economics, economic

这四个词词形相近，意思也相近，非常容易混淆。

1）economy   *n.* 经济；经济情况；节约；节省

例：a market economy 市场经济；a economy pack 实惠装

2）economical   *a.* 经济的；实惠的；节约的

例：It will be more economical for you to buy the bigger size.

对你来讲，买尺寸大点的更实惠。

He is economical in his life. 他在生活中非常节约。

3）economics   *n.* 经济学

例：He studies economics at Sichuan University. 他在四川大学学习经济学。

4）economic *a.* 经济的；经济学的。这里的"经济的"和 economical 中的"经济的"意思完全不一样。

试比较：the governments' economic policy 政府的经济政策

economical car 经济型汽车

2. instant；constant

这两个词虽然意思相差甚远,但词形相近,也容易混淆。

1)instant   *a.* 立即的;立刻的;速食的   *n.* 瞬间;片刻

例:instant reply 立刻回复

  instant noodles 方便面

  in an instant 立刻,马上

2)constant   *a.*

(1)不断的,重复的

例:constant interruptions   无休止的打扰

(2)不变的,固定的

例:This car is traveling at a constant speed of 60 miles per hour.

  这辆车以每小时 60 英里的恒定速度行驶。

n. 常数,常量(数学和生物学科用语)

3. ago，before

1)"时间段 + ago"表示从说话时刻算起的若干时间以前,常用于一般过去时。ago 不能单独使用。

例:I met that girl in Chengdu 3 days ago. 我是三天前在成都认识那个女孩的。

  a short/long time ago 不久/很久以前

  I bought this sweater a long time ago. 我是很久以前买的这件毛衣了。

2)"时间段 + before"表示从过去某时起若干时间以前,常与过去完成时连用。before 还可以单独使用,用于过去完成时或现在完成时,表示不明确的以前。

例:When we got talking, I found out that we had been at the same school 10 years before.

  我们聊起天来,我发现从当时算,十年前我们在同一所学校上学。

  Have you been to Sichuan before?   你以前去过四川吗?

  I realized that I had seen him before. 我意识到以前就见过他。

Word Building

在本课中出现较多的前缀、后缀有:

1. 前缀:inter-

方位前缀 inter-表示"相互"、"之间的"。

act→interact（相互作用）   change→interchange（互换、交换）

national→international   dependent→interdependent（相互依存的）

2. 动词后缀:-ize

后缀-ize 加在形容词后,构成动词,表示"使……化","使……成为……"。

real→realize   modern→modernize（现代化）

popular→popularize(使通俗化)　　　normal→normalize(使正常化、使标准化)

3. 名词后缀: -ion, -tion, -ation

名词后缀-ion, -tion, -ation 加在动词后边,使动词变成名词,但不改变词义。

observe→observation(观察)　　　　compute(计算)→computation

decide →decision　　　　　　　　　compose(创作)→composition

4. 形容词后缀:-ical, -ic

形容词后缀-ical, -ic 加在名词后,构成形容词。

atom→atomic(原子的)　　　　　　　biology→biological(生物学的)

economy →economic(经济学的)　　　class→classical(古典的)

　　　　→economical (节约的)　　　　　→ classic(经典的)

Grammar Focus

一、助动词的特点及种类

　　在英语中,动词可以根据在句子中的功能和用法又细分为五大类:及物动词(Transitive Verbs)、不及物动词(Intransitive Verbs)、系动词(Link-verbs)、情态动词(Modal Verbs)、助动词(Auxiliary Verbs)。各类动词在使用中既有动词的普遍特征又有其各自的特点。在这里,我们着重对助动词的特点进行讲解。

1. 助动词的特点:助动词一般没有具体的词义,主要协助主动词构成谓语,用来表示时态、语态、语气等,或构成疑问及否定形式。

2. 英语中的助动词

　　1)be 类助动词:be, been, being, am, is, are, was, were

　　2)have 类助动词:have, has, had, having

　　3)do 类助动词:do, does, did

　　4)shall, will, should, would 类助动词

二、各类助动词的主要功能

1. be 类助动词的主要功能

　　1)构成进行时态:

　　例:I am watching an interesting football game now.

　　　　我正在观看一场有趣的足球比赛。

　　2)构成被动语态:

　　例:My wallet has been stolen by someone. 我的钱夹被人偷走了。

　　3)与动词不定式构成谓语,表示按计划安排要发生的事或打算做的事:

　　例:A new school is to be built here. 这里将建一所新的学校。

2. have 类助动词的主要功能

　　1)构成完成时态和完成进行时态:

例：The book has been translated into English. 这本书已经被译成了英语。

　　I had been writing the letter for two hours. 我写这封信已经写了两个小时了。

2）与动词不定式构成谓语,表示因客观环境促使不得不做的事情：

例：We had to make a decision at that time. 那时候我们不得不做出个决定。

3. do 类助动词的主要功能

1）构成疑问和否定形式：

例：When did you begin to study English? 你什么时候开始学习英语的?

　　I don't want to cheat you. 我不想欺骗你。

2）加强语气：

例：I do think Tom is right. 我确实认为汤姆是对的。

3）替代前面刚出现的动词来避免重复：

例：He works harder than he did before. 他比以前工作还要努力。

4. shall, will, should, would 类助动词的主要功能

这类助动词的用法相对比较复杂,因为它们有时有一定的词义,作用接近情态动词。因此,我们在这里主要列举几种助动词功能的用法。

1）构成将来时态和过去将来时态：

例：I shall leave for Guangzhou tomorrow. 我明天将启程去广州。

　　They will give us a surprise at the party this evening.

　　他们将在今晚的晚会上给我们一个惊喜。

　　Did you expect that I should come to your wedding ceremony?

　　你想没想到我会来参加你的婚礼?

　　I told him you would wait for him at the airport. 我告诉过他你将在机场等他。

2）should, would 可用于构成虚拟语气(The Subjunctive Mood)：

例：He suggests that I should accept the job offer. 他建议我接受这份工作。

　　If I were you, I would stand with him. 如果我是你,我就会支持他。

3）would 可用来委婉地提出请求、建议或看法：

例：I'm afraid the house would be too expensive for us.

　　恐怕这房子对我们而言太贵了。

4）will 可用来表示某种倾向或习惯性的动作：

例：Fish will die without water. 鱼没有水会死。

5）will 可用于疑问句,表示请求、邀请：

例：Will you send the letter for me, please? 请你帮我寄一下这封信好吗?

　　Won't you have a drink? 喝一杯好吗?

6）shall 在问句中可表示征求对方的意见和指示,这时可用于第一人称和第三人称：

例：Shall I turn down the radio? 我能把收音机关小声点吗?

　　Shall these pictures be sent to your office now?

这些图片现在送到你的办公室吗?

Language Tips for Writing

在我们的生活中,电脑和网络扮演着越来越重要的角色。然而无论是我们在使用电脑或是在网上冲浪时,常常都会遇到一些用英语标示的名称或提示。因此,我们简单地给大家总结了一些常见的与电脑和网络相关的词汇。

1. 电脑相关词汇:

hardware 硬件;software 软件;display 显示器;keyboard 键盘;mouse 鼠标;CD driver 光驱;word processor 文字处理器;CPU (Central Processing Unit) 中央处理器;flash disk USB device U盘;Intel Pentium processor 英特尔奔腾处理器;operating system 操作系统;backup file 备份文件;PC (personal computer) 个人电脑;laptop 便携式电脑;MPC (multimedia personal computer) 多媒体个人电脑

2. 网络相关词汇:

network 网络;download 下载;IE 互联网浏览器;website 网站;URL (Uniform Resource Locator) 网址;home page 主页;gateway 网关;administer 网管;BBS (bulletin board system) 电子公告板;blog 博客;link 链接;WWW(World Wide Web) 万维网;e-mail box 电子邮箱;remote login 远程登录;HTTP (Hyper Text Transmission Protocol) 超文本传输协议;DN (domain name) 域名;hypertext 超文本;hyperlink 超链接;firewall 防火墙;cyberia 电脑咖啡店

3. 网上购物相关词汇和句型:

online shop 网店;e-bookshop 电子书店;registered name 登陆名;password 密码;online account 网上账户;order no. 订单号;payment 支付方式;delivery receipt 送货回单;on cash 现金支付;by credit card 信用卡支付;COD (cash on delivery) 货到付款;sales return 退货;offer 报价;OSS(out of stock) 缺货;discount 折扣

I'm writing to ask the offer for…	我想询问……的报价。
I'd like to confirm my order for…	我想确认我的……(商品)的订单。
A receipt is necessary for my order.	所订商品需随附发票。

Text B   The History of the Internet

Reading Strategies (8):
Scanning for Wanted Information

在日常生活中,尤其是如今的信息时代,我们每天都需要阅读大量的信息。如果对所有的材料都进行精读和细读,我们便无法适应快速发展的社会。因此,我们还需要养成"扫读" (scan)的习惯。所谓扫读,就是用眼扫视,是以最快的速度从一篇文章中披沙拣金,很快地寻找你所期望得到的某项细节。要做到这一点,读者首先要了解扫读的对象是什么及需要的信息(wanted information)是什么。

其次,读者要逐渐养成快速"扫读"(scan)的能力,即:不能像精读那样逐词阅读,要囫囵吞枣,多词、多意群(sense groups)甚至多行阅读,迅速找到与需要信息相关的段落和意群,然后通过快速的阅读最终找到所需要的信息。

以 text B 为例,请大家在扫读 text B 前先阅读以下两个问题,明确扫读的对象:1)Who project to create ARPAnet? 2)In late 1996, how many Internet users were there in the U. S.?

阅读完以上问题后,我们就很清楚扫读的对象是:1)阿帕网的创始者是谁? 2)1996 年年末,美国有多少因特网的使用者? 并且我们可以从问题中提炼出帮助扫读的关键词或词组如:ARPAnet 和 1996。我们对文章进行快速扫读后,发现全文中只有第一段的第二句话提到 APARnet,而文章的第五和六段中都出现了 1996。通过对第一段的第二句快读后我们不难从非限定性定语从句中得出 the U. S. Department of Defense 就是我们需要的信息。针对第二个问题,我们读完第五段后便可发现第五段中是"in 1996"而不是"In late 1996",所以我们读完第六段后,不难找到所需的信息是 47 million。

Word Study

1. essence　*n.* 实质;精髓

例:The essence of our problem is what we shall do next.
　　我们问题的实质是下一步该做什么。

2. project

v. 规划;计划

例:Our school projects to build a new library next year.
　　我们学校计划明年建造一座新的图书馆。

n. 方案;项目

例:Our government has set up an urgent project to help those victims of snowstorm. 我们政府已经制定了紧急方案来帮助那些暴风雪的受灾者们。

3. portion　*n.*

1)部分

例:The central portion of the building was destroyed in the war.
　　这栋建筑的中部毁于战争。

2)一份

例:The girl cut the pizza into five small portions. 这女孩把比萨饼切成了五小份。

4. nuclear　*n.* 核武器的;原子能的

例:The nuclear weapons are banned internationally. 国际上禁止使用核武器。

5. appeal

  n. 1)魅力;吸引力

   例:The prospect of studying abroad has little appeal for me.

    出国学习对我没有什么吸引力。

   2)上诉

   例:I'll file an appeal against the ruling. 我将对判决提出上诉。

  v. 1)上诉;申诉

   例:The defendant has decided to appeal to the High Court.

    被告决定向最高法院上诉。

   2)有吸引力;引起兴趣

    例:A bestselling book has to appeal to all ages. 一本畅销书必须老少皆宜。

6. via *prep.* 通过;经由

  例:Now we can chat with each other via Internet. 现在我们可以通过因特网聊天。

7. commercial

  a. 商业性的;商业化的

  例:The International Channel is not a commercial TV channel.

   国际频道不是商业电视频道。

  n. 广告

  例:Usually there are three commercial breaks during the time of soap opera.

   通常在肥皂剧时段会插播三次广告。

  commerce   *n.* 商务;贸易

8. mark

  v. 1)成为······的征兆;表明

   例:Yaoming's playing abroad may mark a great change in Chinese basketball history.

    姚明到国外打球标志着中国篮球史上的一次重大变化。

   2)做记号

   例:Sentences marked with tick are all correct. 标有钩号的句子都是正确的。

  n. 符号;标志

   例:He put a kind of special mark on the trees to show me the way to the castle.

    他在树上做了特殊的符号来告诉我通向城堡的路。

9. expansion   *n.* 膨胀;扩展

  例:The past two decades is a period of rapid economic expansion for our country.

   过去的二十年对我国而言是经济迅猛发展的时期。

10. survey

  n. 1)民意调查;民意测验

   例:According to a recent survey, in Chengdu alone there were 1. 2 million couples who would like to have a baby in the year of pig.

根据最近的民意测验,仅成都就有一百二十万对夫妇愿意在猪年生小孩。

2)勘测;测量

例:Scientists have made a geological survey of the mountain.

科学家们已经对这座山进行了地质勘察。

v. 1) 对……作民意测验

例:We surveyed 1,000 students and found that over three quarters spent about 4 hours on the Internet per day.

我们对一千名学生作民意测验发现超过四分之三的学生每天花大约4小时上网。

2)查看;审视

例:These days Mr. President surveyed the damage caused by the heavy snow.

这些日子总统先生查看了大雪造成的灾害情况。

11. conduct

v. 组织;安排

例:The government conducted the survey of population.

政府组织了这次的人口调查。

n. 行为;举止

例:As an adult, our conduct should agree with our words.

作为成年人,我们应该言行一致。

12. statistic　*n.*

1)(*pl.*)统计数字;统计资料

例:The statistics show that smoking killed over 5 million people every year.

这些统计数字显示每年吸烟会导致500万人死亡。

2)(statistics)统计学

例:I have a compulsory course in statistics this term.

我这学期有一门统计学的必修课。

13. traffic　*n.* 交通

例:We met the traffic jam and missed our flight. 我们遇到了交通堵塞,没有赶上飞机。

rush-hour traffic　高峰时刻的交通

traffic police　交通警察

14. graphical　*a.*

1)形象的;生动的

例:The metaphor is very graphical. 这比喻很形象。

2)绘画的

例:She created a form of graphical symbol used to convey the information of language independently. 她创造了一种图形符号,用以独立地传达语言信息。

15. operate　*v.*

　　1）操作；控制

　　例：Do you know how to operate the machine? 你知道怎么操作这个机器吗?

　　2）经营；管理

　　例：He operates a bakery in the downtown. 他在城里经营一间面包店。

　　3）动手术

　　例：Doctors decided to operate on his eyes. 医生们决定给他的眼睛做手术。

　　operation　*n.* 操作；经营；手术

16. convert

　　n. 改变观点（或信仰）的人

　　例：John is a convert to Buddhism. 约翰是一个改信佛教的人。

　　v. 转换；转变

　　例：The school was converted from a temple. 这所学校是一座寺庙改建的。

　　convert into　改变；兑换

　　convert to　转变成；使……改变

17. exploit　*v.*

　　1）开发；利用

　　例：The mankind learned to exploit the oil under the sea. 人类学会了开采海底石油。

　　2）剥削

　　例：Marx said capitalists became rich by exploiting workers.

　　　　马克思说资本家是靠剥削工人致富的。

18. wealth　*n.*

　　1）丰富；大量

　　例：He proved his innocence with a wealth of evidences.

　　　　他用大量的证据证明了他的清白。

　　2）财富；钱财

　　例：He got his family's wealth from his grandfather.

　　　　他从他的祖父那里继承了一笔家产。

Phrases and Expressions

1. in fact 确切地说；事实上

　　例：I used to live in China, in fact, in Chengdu city.

　　　　我曾在中国住过,确切地说,是成都市。

　　　　I thought the movie would be interesting. In fact, it is so boring.

　　　　我原以为这部电影很有趣。事实上却很枯燥。

2. as well as　也;还

例:The restaurant sells Chinese food as well as western food.

这家餐馆既卖中餐又卖西餐。

My father as well as my mother is a teacher. 我的父亲和母亲都是教师。

3. pull out of　退出;脱离

例:Our products are banned in China. We have to pull out of the market.

我们的产品在中国被禁售。我们不得不退出这个市场。

Key to Exercises

Text A

Getting the Message

Ⅱ. B

Vocabulary and Structure

Ⅰ. 1—e　　　2—g　　　3—f　　　4—h　　　5—a

　　6—d　　　7—i　　　8—b　　　9—j　　　10—c

Ⅱ. 1. cconomics　2. developing　3. provides　4. instant　5. approach　6. information

Ⅲ. 1. The weather is good in comparison with that in Beijing.

2. The tallest boy in our class is short in comparison with Tom.

3. It is estimated that the increasing of the population will be slower and slower.

4. It is estimated that computers will be cheaper in the future.

Ⅳ. 1. 伴随着一个新的世纪的到来,因特网正变革着我们的社会、经济和科技体系。

2. 在工业革命时期,我们学会了使用发动机,使人类和动物的肌肉力量更强大。

3. 十年前,世界上大多数人都对因特网知之甚少,或者根本一无所知。

Ⅴ. 1. Parents should spend more time interacting with their children.

2. By the end of last term, we had learned 5,000 words.

3. This film is more interesting in comparison with that one.

4. It's impolite to ask others' private affairs.

Speaking

Ⅱ. 1. 1)Kerry and Shelley are spending their holidays in Sanya.

　　Kerry:How nice it is here.

　　Shelley:It certainly is. The sun is shinning but there's a pleasant breeze. It's lovely.

　　Kerry:I've heard the weather here is ideal, just like spring most of the year.

　　Shelley:That's just like Dali, my hometown. We have four seasons of spring.

　　Kerry:It never rains or drizzles all the year, does it?

　　Shelley:Yes, it does rain, but it doesn't last long.

　　Kerry:It must be easy to see the rainbow after the rain?

　　Shelley:It's as plain as the nose on our face.

2）The woman and the man are talking about the weather.

Woman：What a cold <u>day</u> today！

Man：Yes, it <u>is</u>. It is snowing now.

Woman：Really？

Man：Yes, it is the first snow this year. <u>Let's</u> make a snowman together.

Woman：<u>Good idea</u>！Let's go.

Listening

1. B   2. C   3. A   4. B   5. C   6. A   7. C   8. B

Grammar

Ⅰ. 1. is   2. am   3. was   4. Have, haven't   5. will

6. be   7. Don't   8. doesn't   9. didn't   10. Had

Ⅱ. 1. B   2. A   3. C   4. A   5. C   6. C   7. D   8. B   9. B   10. C

Text B

1. F   2. F   3. T   4. T   5. F

Translation of the Texts

Text A

因特网

随着新世纪的到来,因特网正变革着我们的社会、经济和科技体系。没人确切地知道因特网会发展到什么程度,或者会朝什么方向发展。但是谁也不应当低估它的重要性。

在过去的一个半世纪中,重大科技的发展创造了一个全球性的环境,使全人类越来越紧密地联系在一起。在工业革命时期,我们学会了使用发动机,使人类和动物的体能得到放大。在新的信息时代,我们学会了让计算机在任何需要它的地方发挥作用,并且在全球范围提供信息服务,通过这种方式使人类的职能得到放大。因特网作为一种整合的力量,融合了通信和计算技术,以非常低的成本为其用户提供快速连接和全球的信息服务。

十年前,世界上大多数人都对因特网知之甚少,或者根本一无所知。因特网是计算机科学家和研究者专有的领地,他们用因特网在各自的领域和同事进行交流。今天,因特网的规模是十年前的数千倍。据估计,因特网上大约有6千万台主机正为超过200个国家和地区的约2亿用户提供服务。现在的电话系统还是比网络系统庞大的多:全球约30亿的人在使用9亿5千万的电话线路进行通信(其中约有2亿5千万使用的是无线手机)。但是人们估计,到2000年年底,至少会有3亿的因特网用户。而且,自1988年以来,计算机主机和用户的人数正以每半年约33%或每年80%的速度在增长。相比较而言,电话通信系统增长的速度约为每年5%～10%。

Text B

因特网的历史

许多人认为互联网是一项新近的创新,而事实上,因特网在约四分之一个多世纪前已经出现。因特网起源于阿帕网。阿帕网是美国国防部规划实施的一项计划,目的是构建一个全国性的计算机网络,这个网络即使在其大部分被核战争或自然灾害破坏的情况下,也能继续发挥作用。

在这之后的20年里,由此发展起来的网络主要被一些学术机构、科学家们以及政府用于研究和交流。

由于因特网使不同的机构的计算系统和数据库得以相互连接,还可以通过电子邮件共享数据,因此它对这些机构及团体的魅力是显而易见的。

因特网的性质发生突变是在 1992 年。从这年开始,美国政府逐渐退出网络的管理,商业性的实体公司第一次向普通公民提供了因特网的接入通道。这一重心的变化标志着因特网惊人扩张的开始。

CommerceNet 和尼尔森媒体研究早在 1997 年初的调查报告显示,大约每 4 个 16 岁以上的美国人中就有 1 人是因特网的使用者。全世界的因特网使用者已是成千上万。其他的统计数字同样地令人震惊:

一份有线电视新闻网的报告中提到因特网 1996 年的流量是两年前的 25 倍。

市场调查机构 InteliQuest 指出 1996 年末美国的因特网用户已达到四千七百万。

科技研究公司美国国际数据集团预计到 20 世纪末全世界有 10 亿人使用个人电脑,该数字与 1996 年相比已翻了一番多。

因特网随着功能日趋强大、价格合理且具有简单易用的图形操作系统的个人电脑的出现而快速膨胀。这就促使近来计算机向网络化转变,并且为开发丰富的多媒体功能提供了新的机会。

Scripts for Listening

Conversation 1　Son：Hey, Dad. Look out of the window. What's that?

Dad：Oh, my God! It's snowing outside.

Son：Do you mean those little white spots are snowflakes?

Dad：Absolutely right.

Son：Dad, do you remember that you have promised to help me make a snowman?

Dad：Yes, I do. But I have to go upstairs and make a phone call to your mother in Kunming. You'd better put on your overcoat and gloves before I come down.

Son：Yes, sir! I promise. By the way, tell Mum I miss her.

Question 1：*What's the weather like today?*

Question 2：*What do they plan to do together?*

Conversation 2　M：Hi, it is not good weather for the party, is it?

W：No, it isn't. Does it always rain in the fall here?

M：Yes, it usually lasts for a whole month. Are you new here?

W：Yes, I came to Chengdu for study. Which season do you think is the best one here?

M：Um… it must be spring. The city is all covered with green trees and colorful flowers.

W：Really? Then we'd better hold a party in spring again.

M：That's a good idea!

Question 3：*Where did the conversation most probably take place?*

Question 4：*What's the weather like in the fall here?*

Conversation 3　W：Oh, it seems to be raining outside. I have made a good preparation for tomorrow's excursion.

M：Don't worry. The weather is changeable here.

W：I'm afraid that we have to cancel our plan.

M：Why don't we listen to the weather forecast, and then make a decision.

W：Go ahead!

Weather Reporter: Hi, I'm Jack. Let's take a look at the weather in Sichuan province for the next 24 hours. Chengdu should be sunny at the time with the temperature from fifteen to twenty. A strong wind should reach Yibin, which could cause much rain, the temperature should be twelve to sixteen ...

M: Now, we don't have to cancel our excursion.

W: Yes, I'll make some more cookies for tomorrow.

Question 5: What's the weather like in Chengdu tomorrow?

Question 6: What would the temperature be tomorrow in Yibin?

Conversation 4   M: I think we should leave the door open. It's boiling in the classroom.

W: I agree. It's said that the high temperatures will last for at least two weeks.

M: If that's the case, the only thing I love will be water.

W: Water? Then we'd better send you to Heilongjiang.

M: Why?

W: Because the heavy rain has caused the floods there.

Question 7: What does the man mean by saying "It's boiling in the classroom"?

Question 8: What has happened in Heilongjiang?

教师信息反馈表

为了更好地为教师服务,提高教学质量,我社将为您的教学提供电子和网络支持。请您填好以下表格并经系主任签字盖章后寄回,我社将免费向您提供相关的电子教案、网络交流平台或网络化课程资源。

书名:		版次	
书号:			
所需要的教学资料:			
您的姓名:			
您所在的校(院)、系:	校(院)		系
您所讲授的课程名称:			
学生人数:	_____人 _____年级	学时:	
您的联系地址:			
邮政编码:	联系电话		(家)
			(手机)
E-mail:(必填)			
您对本书的建议:	系主任签字 盖章		

请寄:**重庆市沙坪坝正街 174 号重庆大学(A 区)**
重庆大学出版社市场部

邮编:400030
电话:023-65111124
传真:023-65103686
网址:http://www.cqup.com.cn
E-mail:fxk@cqup.com.cn

请按此裁下寄回我社或在网上下载此表格填好后E-mail发回